Henry County Library
172 Eminence Terrace
Eminence, KY 40019

INTO THE SUNSET

Center Point
Large Print

Also by Jackson Gregory and available from
Center Point Large Print:

The Far Call

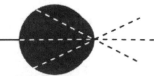

**This Large Print Book carries the
Seal of Approval of N.A.V.H.**

INTO THE SUNSET

Jackson Gregory

CENTER POINT LARGE PRINT
THORNDIKE, MAINE

This Center Point Large Print edition is published
in the year 2017 by arrangement with
Golden West Literary Agency.

First US edition: Dodd, Mead & Company.
First UK edition: Hodder & Stoughton.

The text of this Large Print edition is unabridged.
In other aspects, this book may vary
from the original edition.
Printed in the United States of America
on permanent paper.
Set in 16-point Times New Roman type.

ISBN: 978-1-68324-253-6 (hardcover)
ISBN: 978-1-68324-256-7 (paperback)

Library of Congress Cataloging-in-Publication Data

Names: Gregory, Jackson, 1882–1943, author.
Title: Into the sunset / Jackson Gregory.
Description: Center Point Large Print edition. | Thorndike, Maine :
Center Point Large Print, 2017.
Identifiers: LCCN 2016045621| ISBN 9781683242536 (hardcover :
alk. paper) | ISBN 9781683242567 (pbk. : alk. paper)
Subjects: LCSH: Large type books. | GSAFD: Western stories.
Classification: LCC PS3513.R562 I58 2017 | DDC 813/.52—dc23
LC record available at https://lccn.loc.gov/2016045621

INTO THE
SUNSET

I

The Haverils, a widely scattered clan across hundreds of southwestern wilderness miles, were reputed a folk it was just as well not to antagonize. There were the Texas Haverils, big lean men with blue-black beards and challenging eyes, their women folk as hardy as the males, or they did not last—and many of them beautiful too, for the Haveril men had been taught in their cradles that the best was none too good for any of them. There were the Panhandle Haverils still farther westward, another branch of the same family and perhaps even a hardier lot, the sort to forge on ahead of all others, to breathe more freely in more spacious solitudes. Then, still farther west were the New Mexico Haverils, the Sundown Haverils as they came to be known, since it was said of them that waking or sleeping these men had the trick of a back to the place of sunrise, a face turned toward the West.

Of the Sundown Haverils there was one called Barry who in many ways could have been looked on as the embodiment of the outstanding qualities of the whole family. In his latter teens he took up his rifle and knife and belt ax, and departed from the hearth of his mother, father, sister and two brothers, and crossed Lonely

Ridge, Blue Valley and the shaggy spur of Indian Mountain to build him his own log cabin.

His father, Ben Haveril, one of the blue-black bearded Haverils, was still a young man, lusty and rugged and violent, generous and kindly enough with his small flock at most times, little short of a devil when in drink. His mother, Lucinda, was one of the Oakwoods of Virginia who still clung tenaciously to their own family traditions and pride. She had a small trunk with iron straps about its solid oak, and in it carried from one place to another things which she called heirlooms, and with them some books and sheet music. She taught her small children to read and write, even when big blue-black bearded Ben scoffed. Once, drinking, he had made a move to toss the whole outfit into the fire; Barry's mother, her face as white as death, had snatched the rifle up from the chimney corner. Big Ben had only laughed. But, drunk or sober, he never lifted a hand toward her "jim-cracks" after that.

It was she who had given her youngest his name, which wasn't Barry at all but Baron. She said proudly that there had been a Baron Oakwood long ago, which meant nothing to little Barry himself. What a baron might be he didn't know and wouldn't have cared. In fact when the schoolmaster, a hulking young brute of a fellow who had started out as a blacksmith and some day would be a lawyer, had said to him one day, "So

8

you're Baron, are you? How'd you get a name like that, Buddy?" Young Barry had groped and shrugged and had guessed at the answer in this fashion: "Dunno, Mist' Blount; reckon it's ca'se we was livin' on purty dam' barren lands when I was borned." Whereupon Zack Blount laughed uproariously and was joined by Ben Haveril; and Barry's mamma turned red with shame, and young Barry flung out of the house and went off with his dog and gun, and did not return for three days.

When he came home his mother explained to him; she showed him faded old daguerreotypes and told him faded old legends; also she begged him to get back to his studies, so sadly neglected of late. Zack Blount was starting a school in Cloudy Valley and after a while Barry trudged the seven miles and hid in the buck brush and spied through door and window, listening to what he could hear—the subdued, half-frightened voices, the roar of the master, the thwack of the leather strap.

"I'll make a dicker with yuh, Mist' Blount," said young Barry that afternoon when school was over. "I'll come to yore school an' Pap will pay yuh or else I'll git yuh all yuh kin eat in venison an' fish an' bear meat, on'y eff'n yuh try to lay leather on me I'll swear to cut your heart out."

Blount clapped so heavy a hand on his back that Barry buckled at the knees.

"We've made a bargain, Baron," he said when he got through laughing. After that he always called the boy Baron, and sometimes, in his roughly merry way, calling on Barry in school for something, he'd say, with a wink to the rest of his flock, "Listen good now, you whelps; you're goin' to hear from Baron Oakwood Haveril, esquire."

"I don't know why I go to your damn school, Blount," Barry growled at him one time a full two years after, a two years during which he, like the other boys, had been absent hunting and fishing and just loafing ten days to one in school. "Unless it's just that it don't set good on my stomach to have a man like you better'n me in anything, even if it's only book-learnin'."

"Some day," said Blount, "I'm goin' to be a right big lawyer. By that time you'll be a horse thief and I'll be the one that gets you hung."

Four years later Zachary Blount got himself a long-tailed black coat, a high hat and shiny boots, and announced that now he was a lawyer ready to take any and all cases. Just how he had acquired his new estate no one knew; perhaps it came along with the new city clothes. Blount moved on, westward of course, into the rip-roaring little cow town of Tylersville. He stopped in passing at the Haveril place, was impressed by Barry's seventeen-year-old sister in a pretty new pink dress, and remained to make sheep's eyes at her. Little Lucy, when she understood what it was all about, was both elated and frightened, and did what Barry accounted a right smart amount of girl-gigglin'. Blount, enamored, decided to post-pone establishing himself in the forty-mile-distant Tylersville, and remained to do his courting in earnest. "Not only I'm going to be a lawyer down to Tylersville, Miss Lucy," he said, with the family harkening as they sat in the twilight on the steps. "Some-day I'll be a judge, too, and after that a United States senator or a governor. And a man like that needs a wife to—to grace his home, sort of."

Barry glanced at his sister; she was looking at her mother, and her face was pinker than her dress. Ben Haveril was whittling and not looking at anyone.

Barry got up and went for his rifle. With that and his knife and belt ax, with a snug blanket roll in which were a few indispensable articles, he "struck out."

II

Barry didn't know why he went away. He didn't think about it. It was the forests pulling him, lifting him unresistingly out of his place as a cork is removed from a bottle neck by strong fingers. There was a round early moon and he walked nearly all night. He stopped a time or two to drink at some merry-mad stream frothing among the gray rocks; he ate bits of the dried venison from the buckskin pouch at his hip. The moon and the pines worked together at making black and tawny patterns under foot, and he moved across them like a swift lean shadow. To the night noises all about him he paid no attention.

Daybreak was not far off when he rolled up in his blanket and went to sleep in a dry grassy place under a cliff. Shortly after sunup he was on his way again, steering for a notch in the black pines against the sky on a distant ridge. He had no particular objective; that black gap was merely a gate, open in the West.

During the day he read signs. There were deer and bear and big cats; wild turkey and grouse and quail; in the pines the firm-bodied squirrels were swift gray graceful gleams. Of man-made signs there were few—black stones of an old camp fire, a cut willow stick whacked by a broad-bladed knife more than six months ago, the broken half of a horn button by a spring. These evidences of his own kind he came upon between daylight and high noon; he was glad, as he penetrated deeper this seemingly limitless forestland, moving higher upslope toward the gap, that there was nothing to tell him that any man had been here before him.

Already he was a tall rangy boy, long-legged and hard-muscled and all but tireless. Within forty-eight hours after starting out he put fifty or sixty miles behind him. His pack was light and didn't hamper him; when hungry he had but to knock a squirrel from a pine top or bring down a plump grouse or young turkey, the flesh of which he broiled in a jiffy over a quick small fire, dusted over with a little of his precious salt and bolted very much after the fashion of a hound dogdining on flung scraps. He took the long upslopes slantingly, he "breathed" on the crests, he went downhill at a trot; and the little open valleys or brown aisles through the timber were crossed with a long-paced swinging stride which devoured miles as he devoured a snack.

On the third day he started building his cabin. The world felt roomy hereabouts, a place of magnificent forest teeming with game and threaded by clear cold streams leaping with trout; towering mountains lifted bald crests high above timberline; he could look downward from his bench-land into a long, lovely, narrow valley, gay and bright with its flooring of uncropped grass, extending snakewise between timbered mountain flanks. There was a waterfall back of his cabin site, a deep cold pool for it to fall into, an overflow of bright water making a little creek that tumbled down into the valley to lend its aid in creating the willow-fringed valley creek.

"This looks like a pretty good place," said Barry.

His cabin when completed was as unobtrusive as a bird's nest in the crotch of a tree. Its low walls of unpeeled logs, its dry rock chimney, its thatch roof, part and parcel of the mountain, were not to be seen unless one knew just where to look and then looked twice. And he made no betraying trail to his place; going and coming he stepped softly, clearing no stone out of the way, breaking no dead limbs carelessly, never treading today where he had trod yesterday. It was not that he had any particular reason for hiding, nor had he any thought that another than himself was likely to come this way. It was only that one is apt to emulate those among whom he dwells, and here all Barry Haveril's neighbors were the wild things. He knew a lot more of them and their ways than he did of men; he liked being with them better.

During the six or eight weeks before he had any thought of turning back homeward he made many long exploratory trips toward both north and west through the mountains. Only twice in that time did he see human beings.

One day, a score of miles from his lair, he came upon the fresh tracks of two horses; as naturally as a needle swings to the magnet Barry Haveril turned to follow the tracks. Several hours later, with the sun sinking and purple shadows spreading through the cañons, he came within sight of the two men. He had stalked them as a man stalks his game; from a mountainside, screened himself by rocks and scrub timber, he watched them down in the bed of the ravine. They were stooping in a shallow stream, water half way to their boot tops; though dusk was gathering about them he made them out pretty clearly. They were much alike, slim, agile fellows with ragged black hair, and at first he took them for Indians. Wondering what they were doing down there, he made his way closer, crawling on his belly before he had done. He heard some of their talk and decided that they were such stock as the border breeds, mixtures of white and already badly mixed Mexican. And he discovered that they were washing gold.

They made their fire and cooked and ate and rode away in the early dark. He rolled into his blanket and slept on the ridge. Next morning he came down into the cañon to investigate. It was a long time before he discovered anything, not having the hang of it, but all the patience of a hunter was his and finally he made out that there were bright soft yellow flakes and tiny particles in the sand. Scooping out a little cuplike hollow he came by a handful of gravel in which were a couple of smooth gold pellets nearly the size of grains of wheat. He dropped them back where he had found them, had a long cold drink and returned to his pack.

Another day, again toward sundown, he sat on a rock in front of his cabin looking down into the long sinuous valley below, a sight he seldom tired brooding over. He had named it for himself Sun Creek Valley. The farther end of it was shut off by an encroaching timbered ridge but there was a notch in the sky line through which his eyes, traveling very far south, liked to run out across a vast plain that was always changing in drifting colors as the sun changed. This time something moving instantly focused his keen gaze.

Something flashing in the sunlight had winked at him; then he made out a blur of something vanishing in a shadow-filled copse of young timber. It was a couple of miles away, the light was none too good, the picture imprinted on his retina had been all but formless; it might have been anything, man or deer or bear. But he continued watching.

Then he heard rifle shots muffled with distance and an intervening neck of the woods. He had never heard so many shots so close together and wondered how many men there were and what they could be shooting at. He got his answer almost instantly. There were several men shooting at a single rider who had fled on ahead into the lower end of Barry's Sun Creek Valley, and that single fleeing rider was what Barry had seen.

He stood up slowly, his jaw dropping, his body very tense, his rifle gripped in both hands as he strained ears and eyes together. He saw the flash of reddish-yellow fire when the fugitive, fleeing no longer, fired at his pursuers whom Barry could not see. But he heard the rattle of their returned fusilade, and began muttering to himself.

"It ain't fair," said Barry. "I hope he gets away."

If it hadn't been so far he would have been drawn to go down and find out about things, perhaps to lend a hand to the one man being run down by five or six. But it was only common sense that the whole affair would be over before he could reach them. Also it was swiftly growing dark; it would be a moonless night and whatever was happening down there would be over in a few minutes or would have to await sunup.

But before sunup he was on his way to investigate. The dawn was brightening and he had traveled half the distance when a voice called to him from a brush thicket:

"Drop yore gun! Drop it quick or I'll kill yuh!"

The speaker was not ten steps away. Barry let his rifle slide out of his hands and felt a queer prickling chill along his blood as he jerked his head about to stare. At first he could see nothing but gray buck brush and gray rocks. Then he saw the muzzle of a rifle barrel resting on a flat-topped boulder.

"Step over this way," said the voice. He thought he had never heard a voice quite like it, so full of command, so somehow bleak and cold and arrogant.

"What do you want of me?" asked Barry.

"Step, kid, or I'll shoot yuh daid," said the voice.

Barry obeyed. He knew that the speaker would do as he promised. So, breathing hard and with his flesh crawling, he came slowly forward.

That was how he first met up with a sort of cousin of his, Jesse Conroy who had Haveril as a middle name. This Conroy, on the day Barry first saw him, was about twenty-three years old and, coiled as he was behind the rock, with his bright black eyes glittering and an ugly twist to his white-lipped mouth, he made Barry think of a rattlesnake, he seemed just that full of the menace of sudden death. He was a flashingly handsome young devil and none the less devilish for an almost girlishly fine-featured face. There was enough light for Barry to make out that he was pretty badly hurt.

Conroy was suspicious of him at first, afraid that he might be one of the crowd that had killed his horse under him and shot him down last night. Once that he learned otherwise his manner changed.

"I'm hurt right bad," he said, "but I'll make it yet. Especially if I can have help. Those fellers that rode me down, they'll be comin' back after a while. But they won't hurry; I knocked over anyhow two an' mebbe three, an' I'd of got 'em all if one o' their bullets hadn't of glanced off'n a rock an' drilled me."

"Why'd they want to drill you?" asked Barry.

"They're bandits, that's what," said Conroy. "Killers. Now yuh got to help me clean out afore they come sneakin' back."

"I'll go get me my rifle," said Barry.

"Shore," nodded Conroy. "Then come give me some help. I c'n hardly walk, but if I had both laigs shot off I'd somehow make it."

Barry had to carry not only his rifle but Conroy's carbine. It was a hard struggle back to Barry's hideout, since they traveled not the easiest, but a far harder way, hunting out rocky ground, careful to leave no tracks. Conroy had to lie down and rest more and more frequently. There was a buckskin bag slung to his belt; it was heavy and he gave that to Barry to carry too. The only bit of weight that he did not surrender was the long barreled Colt revolver banging at his hip; it had the most beautiful handle Barry had ever seen, made out of some sort of wood as red almost as blood, and Barry would have liked to carry it. The canvas bag Conroy explained just had shells in it. He pointed out that there were not many left in his cartridge belt; it came in handy to have extra ones, he said.

III

The two discovered their kinship only after they had been together several days. Until then there had been little talk. After they had done what they could do for Conroy's two wounds, one through his left arm, one through his left shoulder, he crawled into Barry's bunk and lay quiet. Barry thought surely the man would die, he had lost so much blood, he looked so sick and white. The bullet through Conroy's body, barely missing the lung, had remained just under the skin close to the shoulder blade; Barry, with his belt knife whetted razor-sharp, had cut it out, Conroy alternately gritting his teeth and cursing him for his awkwardness. Thereafter for a spell Barry looked white and sick himself.

But Jesse Conroy wasn't the easily dying kind. He was a Haveril, and Barry, after he knew, wondered that he hadn't known all along. Barry with his blackish hair with a glint of red in it, Conroy with the blue-black hair of the Texas Haverils, both of them seeming constructed of spring steel and whipcord, the two were as alike as a couple of young eagles.

When Conroy got out of bed to move restlessly about he began asking questions. He wanted to know how it was that Barry lived here all alone, where he had come from—and why.

Why *had* he come? Well, he didn't rightly know. He'd just left one place and gone another. Conroy watched him narrowly, plainly believing that he was being told a meager part of the truth. Then he asked, still eying Barry with bright suspicion as though watching for sign of another lie, what his name was.

"Barry. Me, I'm Barry Haveril."

Conroy started laughing.

"Say, that's funny," he said. "One o' the Texas Haverils, or the Panhan'le Haverils?"

"No," said Barry. "I don't know any of those folks. My ol' man is Ben Haveril, over th' other side Lonely Ridge."

"Shore," said Conroy. "Yuh're a Sundown Haveril. Well, I'm a Haveril, too, one o' the Texas Haverils; but my name's Jesse Conroy. Ever heard that name, Barry?"

"No," said Barry. "I never. But if you're a Haveril how's your name Conroy?"

"Shucks," said Jesse. "It's my ol' lady that's the Haveril, an' she married a man name of Conroy."

Barry pondered. "I'd reckon that makes you anyhow a half Haveril," he said.

That angered Jesse and he started on a tirade, but he was still too weak to enjoy a quarrel and besides was really interested in tracing relationship. In the end they agreed that they were some sort of cousins. Thereafter they called each other Cousin Jesse and Cousin Barry, until Jesse took to calling Barry just plain Sundown.

"I'd like to hear about the bandits that chased you up here, Cousin Jesse," said Barry one day.

There had been no reference to them after the day Barry had brought his cousin to his cabin. That afternoon Barry, sitting at his lookout point, watching the lower end of the valley, had seen the turkey buzzards gathering, coming from so far off that at first they were but tiny dots in the sky, then widely circling death-shadows sailing effortlessly and drifting down over the spot where Jesse Conroy had had a horse shot under him. After a while a whole crowd of the nauseous birds, hundreds of them Barry thought, flapped heavily up into the air above the pine tops, and Barry knew that something had come close enough to frighten them away. Half an hour passed and the buzzards began slanting earthward again, before he saw in the nearer distance two men on horses coming out from the pines. He thought, "They've missed our track; they're headed wrong." Presently the riders disappeared in the forest and he did not see them again. He had told Jesse.

And now Jesse said angrily, "I ain't finished with them hombres, Sundown. Shore, I'll tell you about 'em."

He told his tale forcefully and clearly, and

23

Barry Haveril, drinking it in, believed every word of it. There were six of them, said Jesse. They were Bud Walters, a cowboy; Bill and Tom Bedloe, ranchers near Tylersville; Sam Johnson, teamster and deputy sheriff and all around crook; Jeff Cody, the gambler; and Dan Hardy. Most folks didn't suspect them for what they were, they were that crafty. But Jesse Conroy knew! Hadn't he seen them when they held up the Cold Springs stage; they'd killed the driver and the guard and got away with the strong box. Then they had seen Jesse Conroy, who just happened to be cutting into the stage road from a side trail, and they knew it was all up with them unless they rubbed him out. That's why they had been after him like hell fire running up a dead tree.

"There were six; I guess now there's only five, mebbe only four of 'em," said Jesse. He pulled the heavy '45 out of its holster where it fitted so loosely and raised and lowered it as though making swift silent shots with it, and Barry's eager eyes left his cousin's face to watch a weapon which had already come close to being his first true love. "I'll get 'em some day, Cousin Barry," Jesse went on. "Yuh see if I don't. But for a while I better go slow."

"Yes," said Barry. "There's anyhow four to one."

"Where I got the aidge on 'em," said Jesse, "is

that they don't even know if I'm dead or alive. They know they hit me; that's all they know. An' I'm shore goin' to play daid for a spell."

Barry lifted his eyes in interrogation.

"Who's to tell anybody I'm alive?" asked Jesse softly. "Yuh won't, will yuh, Sundown? Yuh won't tell nobody yuh ever seen me, will yuh?"

"No," said Barry.

"That's a shore promise, ain't it?" Barry nodded. His eyes dropped to the '45. Jesse sat a long while playing with the weapon but keeping his gaze bent steadily on the boy's face. Presently a thin smile touched his lips as he said idly:

"What do yuh think o' this here six-gun o' mine, Sundown?"

"I never saw one like that," breathed Barry almost reverentially.

"Never shot with one, huh?"

"No, nor not even ever knew there was any like it."

"Try a shot with it," offered Jesse, "I'll show yuh."

Barry tingled; he held the weapon lovingly; he lowered it and raised it just as Conroy had been doing.

"I'll show yuh," said Conroy again.

With his old rifle Barry could bark a squirrel in the tallest pine; he shot the heads off his grouse and turkeys. But after the first shot with

Jesse's Colt he saw that the whole technique was different. He sat humbly listening as Jesse, leaning against the cabin wall, explained and demonstrated. Instantly he realized that his cousin was as deadly with the Colt as he himself was with his rifle.

Jesse said, "Here's some ca'tridges," and poured them into Barry's eager palm. And then he said laughing: "Yuh c'n have it, Sundown. I'm givin' it to yuh."

Barry just stood there, shells in one hand, gun in the other, and gawked at him. He knew that he had heard the words correctly; it must be that they meant something else.

Jesse laughed again, his handsome dark eyes flashing.

"Shore," he said. "I'm givin' yuh my gun, Cousin Barry. It's yore'n right this minute."

Barry looked at him with shining eyes. But that look was only a fleeting one since in a flash his eyes returned to the red-butted revolver and lingered there like a lover's gaze. Then his feet began shuffling in the dead pine needles. He couldn't think of anything to say.

That same day he went off by himself into the forest, for the first time in his life leaving his rifle behind. His eyes became predatory, flashing along the dim aisles between the tawny light-speckled boles of the trees. He kept practicing without really firing, saving his few precious cartridges. "I could get me a deer with this six-gun," he said under his breath, still awe-struck. "I could get me a bear even. This here is the way Cousin Jesse holds it—this is how he squeezes the shot off—" He smoothed the smooth barrel with his palm; he rubbed it softly against his cheek.

Jesse had given him only a couple rounds of ammunition; he wondered whether that was all he had. Barry wished he had a hundred! It was likely that there were more in that heavy little buckskin bag, though of course it might contain only shells for the carbine. Those which Jesse had given him he had shoved up out of his cartridge belt.

"I've got to get me some more," said Barry, diffident about asking his cousin.

As the days passed, young Conroy grew steady on his legs again and his wounds healed and the healthy tan came back into his face. Barry could see the restlessness surge up higher and higher in him every day.

"I'm goin' any day now, Sundown," he said. Then he fell to cursing, a habit of his to which Barry had grown used. "It's goin' to be fair hell to walk all them miles," he said in anger.

"Where you goin', Cousin Jesse?" Barry asked him.

Jesse for a split second glared at him, and the

glare said with all the violence of Jesse's words, "What the hell business is that o' yores?" What he said was: "No matter where I go, it's a long walk from here, ain't it? An' them damn' bandits kilt my hoss for me."

"The nearest place I know is home," said Barry. "It ain't so bad; you can make it in two days." He added: "I'm used to walkin' on foot. I like it best, too. On the plains I guess it's diff'rent, but in the woods a man on foot's got the best of it."

Jesse scoffed. "Me," he said, "I've traveled some in my time. Over to Laredo, then up all th' way to the Pecos an' acrost to Tylersville an' up here. A man needs a hoss when he travels like I do."

"I reckon," nodded Barry who had heard of Laredo and knew it was far away. He added, "I don't know where you're goin' to get you a ridin' animal aroun' here, Cousin Jesse."

One morning in a still dim bluish dawn Jesse Conroy slung his buckskin bag to his belt, shouldered his carbine and left.

"So long, Cousin Barry," he said.

"So long, Cousin Jesse," said Barry.

Barry watched him out of sight, only vaguely wondering where he was going. Then he returned to his cabin and sat on the step and unholstered his treasure. "I'm goin' to learn to shoot you, Mister, just as good as Cousin Jesse can. Just as good as anybody." For two or three days he did little beyond toy with the blood-red-gripped '45; he was never tired of cleaning and oiling it; within and without the speckless barrel gleamed. Next he began to grow restless; having Cousin Jesse with him so long, then having him gone, seemed to make things different. He began thinking of his folk, especially of his sister, little Lucy. He wondered too about Zachary Blount; had the teacher—lawyer now in long-tailed coat and high hat—carried her off?

He rolled his pack, closed his door, shouldered his rifle, and with the comfortable feel of a heavy long barrel bumping at his hip, turned back toward his father's place. He came within sight of the clearing and the rock-and-log cabin toward the end of the second day; the sun was below the tops of the pines so that already it was twilight all about the house, and he heard the call and saw the flickering wing-dip of a first night hawk. Otherwise all was very still. He experienced a queer, disturbing feeling, a swift consciousness of desertion. The track down to the lower meadow and the narrow crooked path to the spring house were weed-grown. The weeds told him, "There's been nobody here for a long time."

Within the house was that eerie, ghostly feeling which is experienced nowhere as in human habitations abandoned. Everything was gone, chairs and tables and beds. He went through the three small rooms, into the kitchen and to the back door, into the shed. There was a stillness, a hush, an emptiness which he had never known in the heart of the forest solitudes; it seemed to bear his spirit down.

Circling through the yard, he returned to the house, seeking "sign." Something ought to add to the tale told by the weeds in the paths; they had said nothing but "Gone a long time." They didn't say in what direction or why; and they didn't say, "They'll be coming back," or "They're gone for good."

Then he found his mother's letter. Over the fireplace, a wan square in the dimness, was a sheet of paper on a nail. Barry took it down and read it sitting on the stoop.

The first words were, "To Robert or Baron, whichever comes home first." Robert was Barry's brother, the oldest of the three sons. The rest of a hastily written letter answered all Barry's questions for him. First of all, Lucy *had* married Zachary Blount and the two were living in Tylersville; Zachary was practicing law and was associated with a great man, Judge Parker Blue. Through Zachary, Judge Blue had sent an offer to Barry's father to go into the cattle business with him; on shares it was. So all the family were moving down into the cow country, onto one of the Judge's several spreads. There was a postscript: "Whichever of you boys reads this first, let him leave it here for the other."

Barry, having read it twice, replaced it on the nail. Then again he sat outside, reflecting. He tried not to think of Lucy married to Zachary Blount. He did a lot of wondering about Robert, where he had gone, whether he had returned and read the letter? "No; if he'd read it he would have left a sign for me," he decided. He couldn't find a stub of pencil anywhere, but, with the leaden nose of a rifle bullet, he wrote at the bottom of his mother's letter: "I've read this. Barry."

Well, his mother and father and his brother Lute were on a cattle ranch now, and he guessed they'd like that and would be better off, and his mother would see more folks; times, she got lonesome up here. And Lucy was married and living in town. And Robert was somewhere or other. Barry guessed he'd go down into the low country to see them. But first there was something else. He'd start back to his own place, come daybreak.

But in the morning he decided to go out of his way a bit in making his return journey. That was because it dawned on Barry that he alone of his family might guess what Robert was up to.

"Anyhow I'll go past Tex Humphreys' place," Barry decided.

The Humphreys were the nearest neighbors,

back a piece in the mountains, and it would take him only a dozen miles or so out of his way to look in on them. Tex Humphreys, middle-aged now, had been a wild young cowboy on the run, with a posse after him, when he first dodged into these mountains. He hid out for a year, was unhurrying the next, and in the end gave up all thought of ever going back to his old stamping grounds. Instead he took up with a pretty Indian girl, carved himself out a ranch and found contentment. He lived as did most of the mountaineers, hunting, fishing, trapping, loafing largely. But also, a man born in the saddle and cradled there, he raised a few horses. And Robert, like Jesse Conroy in that, was a great hand for horses.

Further, Tex Humphreys had several children, among them a half grown girl with flashing black eyes and a glory of black hair and a skin like wild roses and a slim, quick figure to make a man think of a deer. Even Barry, at a time when he had no interest in girls as such, and wouldn't have swapped little bright Lucy for all the rest of them, had had to concede her points. And he alone happened to know that Robert was crazy about her. Barry had seen them one day in the forest; they had been riding, but were walking side by side, leading their horses; what first caught his eye was a sunflash on an unforgettable, silver-chased saddle that Tex had brought up with him from the south. Tex must have liked Robert a lot to let him use that favorite saddle: Barry got the idea that Tex was angling after a son-in-law.

So now, turning his back on the old log home, he headed toward the Humphreys' horse ranch. He meant just to drop in and say "Howdy," and ask casually, "Seen any o' my folks lately, Tex?" But there was to be no such casual talk that day. At the foot of Black Mountain in a peaceful and quiet little whispering glen shut in by quivering aspens, he came suddenly, all without warning, upon the stark horror of a thing which only a short time before, surely not more than a day before, had been Robert Haveril.

He knew it was Robert the instant he glimpsed the sprawling form, even before he looked for any face, and he knew too that he was dead. So it was a burning-eyed, blanched-faced, tragic boy who burst in upon the Humphreys, saying thickly as they stared at him:

"He's dead. Robert, he's dead. Somebody killed him. Who? I want to know who? You tell me, Tex Humphreys!"

Molly went back with him and Tex to where the body lay, a Molly who was all melting black eyes from which the tears streamed so unceasingly that even then Barry wondered dully that there could be room in her anywhere for tears like that. But when Tex stooped stiffly to draw back the blanket Barry had spread, she screamed and screamed, and then turned and fled, not homeward, but off into the forest, a wild thing into the mothering wilderness.

Tex sat a long while on his heels, then looked straight up into Barry's hardened face.

"He rode off this way late yestiddy," he said, speaking softly and drawlingly as so many Texans had the trick of doing, especially when deeply moved or profoundly thoughtful. "Somebody bushwhacked him. Stood right over yander, by that big tree. Shot him clean through the haid."

"Who?" demanded Barry. "And why?"

"Somebody that didn't like him mebbe," suggested Tex.

"Everybody liked Robert! Even me, I liked him, an' it didn't matter he was bigger an' used to lick me."

"Molly's growed up to be a right purty girl," meditated Tex. "Her an' Robert liked each other a heap. There was other young fellers that would liked to cou't her. One of them might 'a' got mad an' kilt him." He got up and moved about, looking for sign. "Here's where he stood, Barry. He was afoot; didn't have any hoss. An' Robert did; he was ridin' my Coaly. Damn! My bes' hoss, my Mex saddle an' bridle—all gone! Yuh see, Robert was jus' goin' to ride down to see yore folks, so I let him have the bes' I had, an'— Somebody might

34

mebbe thought he was wo'th killin' for that outfit; somebody afoot that wanted a hoss real bad; somebody mebbe the law was after."

"We c'n follow the tracks," said Barry. "We c'n see which way he rode off."

Tex agreed in all heartiness. He had brought pick and shovel along and they worked fast and in silence. With Robert buried in the little whispering glen and rocks piled above him, they hastened back to Humphreys' ranch for horses. They put in a dogged, determined day, and in the end turned back little wiser than when they started. The killer had known he could expect pursuit and had out-foxed them. All tracks were hopelessly lost when, twenty miles down in the hills, he had picked up a herd of range stock, had ridden with them and then scattered them on a barren strip that was all rock and shallow sand underfoot, sand which the prevailing whirlwinds sifted and heaped into new, rapidly shifting shapes.

That night Barry shook his head at Tex Humphreys' invitation to stay, and turned under the stars toward his own place.

IV

He walked half the night before he rolled exhausted into his blanket and slept. When he awoke he was so stiff and sore that he could scarcely stand; he had less use for a horse than ever before, and vowed he would never fork another. In a pink dawn with a chill mountain wind blowing he breakfasted and rolled his pack and went on.

The first thing he did when he entered his cabin was to stand over the bunk where Jesse Conroy had lain wounded and convalescent. He stared at it a long silent while, looking uncertain, vaguely distressed. Then he tore it down and made himself a new bunk in another corner and threw himself down on it to rest, to sleep and later to think.

It was almost a day's trip, north and west, to the spot where he had watched the two border cross-breeds engaged in their primitive gold-gleaning operations. He started in the morning with the first thinning of darkness, with the stars still bright, and arrived long before dark in the afternoon. But he had no thought of going down into the bed of the same creek the two men had worked in; there were other racing streams hereabouts, and, as Barry regarded it, this one

36

belonged to the border men and he would have his own. He mounted higher, crossed a ridge and came down into a wild and dusky ravine that smelled wet and fresh and clean, that was slashed by a cascading creek making white spray mists among the big boulders. At a spot where the lowering sun slipped through the ridge pines and even pierced the tender green of the aspens below and created a little rainbow in the spray, he began his quest. It seemed to him, having watched the border men, a very simple thing indeed to find gold.

He had never had any money; he had never wanted it. His father supplied his family amply with whatever they needed from stores; if Barry had clothes to wear, a gun and ammunition, there was nothing he wanted that he could not get for himself. Now however his ammunition was almost exhausted. And the Colt with its blood-red grip was empty. So he came here today in exactly the same frame of mind in which a man with a good bank account might go to his bank.

Down in the ravine he set his rifle aside, pulled off his worn boots, rolled up his overalls and went to work. He didn't have a pan as the others had, but he did have big strong capable hands. He found a sandy place between two big rocks, scooped up a lot of the wet sand and smeared it out thin and smooth on top of the flatter boulder. Then he began picking through it, disturbing particles with a horny fingernail, seeking the soft reddish pellets.

It struck him as rather odd that he didn't find a show of color that day. He made his supper on jerked venison and water and went early to sleep. Next morning he tried higher upstream. For hours he mounted, trying in all sorts of places. Before noon he found a pothole under water at the lower end of a pool. He spent about two hours at that hole, thinking that he might as well clean it out while he was at it; he could find another next time. Then figuring that he must have about all the gold he would need for the things he wanted in town, he started back cabinward. Hardly started, he stopped and looked back, undecided. He'd want to get a lot of shells for his new six-gun, a terrible lot of 'em; he wondered whether he had gold enough.

The next morning he set out, going down into his Sun Creek Valley for the first time, since he had only skirted its flanks when he had gone to a meeting with Cousin Jesse. It was a long walk to Tylersville; Jesse had told him it must be thirty-forty mile. Before he had come to journey's end he accounted it longer, but the walking was good down in the valley and afterward on gentle slopes and through other small narrow valleys and among rolling foot-hills, and a dozen hours or so of his swinging long strides brought him to his first glimpse of what to Barry Haveril looked like a splendid city.

Tylersville, a ragged and crooked cow town, sprawled in what had been once known as Cottonwood Flats, with an undulating grassy plain to the east, a region of broken, sparsely wooded hills to the south, and several rocky, pine-clad spurs of the mountains coming down upon the west. It was upon one of these slopes, a mile or more removed from the village, that Barry saw the first house; at first glimpse he thought it the biggest and finest house in the world, and the nearer he came the more did he marvel at it. It was two stories high with balconies on three sides; it was a glistening white, with the doors and window frames and balcony posts all a bright bluebird blue; all about it was as green as any green meadow, with shade trees and a mountain stream flashing through the yard so that there had to be a bridge over it. There was a paling fence, too, painted blue, and a winding white road through a gate. It was the sort of place, Barry thought, that a king might live in. And he wasn't far wrong.

But all this spick and span brightness on the upland found no reflection in the town below. Barry swung into a long narrow road which Tylersville called Main Street, passing between rows of flimsy board shacks, most of them with those false fronts which were so obviously false as to be quite honest about it, really meaning no deceit, and with their shed roofs overhanging the wooden sidewalks. He saw more men at one sweep of the eye than he was accustomed to seeing in many months, and more teams of various sorts, and saddle horses.

When a buckboard came dashing around a far corner in an enormous cloud of dust, he drew back against a wall as though afraid of being run down, even on a sidewalk. Speed, was what that outfit spelled to him. Then, seeing it close as it shot on by, he was impressed by its elegance. Two sleek, beautiful, matched bays with floating silver manes drew it; an imposing figure of a man drove it, a handsome big blond man in a broad dove-gray hat that looked brand new, in a blue frock coat, in glistening high black boots into the tops of which, almost at his knees, his striped gray trousers were stuffed. At his side was a little girl; she looked very little indeed beside the man's imposing bulk, and about all that Barry could make of her as she went past was that she too wore blue and that she had a big white hat from which blue ribbons streamed, and that she was laughing. More than all this, perhaps the crowning touch of extravagance to spell elegance to the forest boy as to many others, was the big, ebon-black Negro standing in the buckboard, holding on to the back of the seat, flashing a mouthful of white teeth and the whites of his eyes.

"I bet they live up there," thought Barry, and again was right.

Men clumped along the sidewalk, most of them dusty and in high-heeled boots with dragging spurs, with big hats, the brims pushed back, and with flapping, open vests worn mostly for the sake of their four outside pockets, in which a man carried his tobacco and papers and matches, and the one inside pocket in which maybe he had a letter or a cached bank note or the picture of his best girl. Among these, stepping this way and that, Barry moved more and more slowly, walking softly, Indian fashion.

His expression, too, was worn Indian style, as blank as an unwritten sheet of paper. But within him was a small tumult that was almost excitement, that was tinged with uneasiness, that was at once pleasurable and a bit disturbing. He saw everything, the cracks between the boards under foot, the dust in the road, the faces and costumes passing by, the things in the store windows. He smelled everything, the dust and the sweat of horses and men, the odor of fresh paint and of meat cooking and of fresh baking. And about the first thing he realized acutely was that he was as hungry as a bear.

He stopped fascinated before a window full of things to make his mouth water; some of them looked almost too pretty to eat. There was an enormous chocolate cake with a wedge cut out of it to show you its insides, rich layer on top of layer; and cheek by jowl with it a big white cake with glistening white "scum" all over it and with a wedge out, like the other, but showing fat inner layers as yellow as the yolk of an egg. There was an apple pie, a lemon pie, some sort of a pie oozing thick red juice—

Barry went in. At one side was a counter, at the other a series of small tables with low partitions jutting out from the wall to separate them. He sat down and when a waiter came said, after drawing a long breath:

"I want a hunk of choc'late cake and a hunk of the white cake that's yellow inside and some sody water."

What he asked for he received. He squared around in his chair, drew another deep breath, and stacked in. It was a meal he would never forget.

He had disposed of perhaps half of the chocolate cake and two-thirds of the white one, when he saw the big blond man and the little girl come in; they went to a table next to his but were hidden, when they sat down, by the partition. The waiter almost ran to serve them.

"Did your ice come through all right this morning, Benny?" asked the big man in a voice which rang out sonorously, round and full.

"It shore did, Judge," said Benny, all grins. "I know what Miss Lucy's achin' for! Ice cream, ain't it, Miss Lucy?"

"Please," said the sweetest voice Barry had ever heard, as liquidly musical as any forest bird's.

So her name was Lucy too. That started Barry thinking of his sister.

Barry wolfed down the rest of his cake and caught the waiter's eye.

"I didn't bring any real money along," he said, keeping his voice down. "You can take the price out of this."

He held a little pile of dust and fine grains of gold in his palm. Instinctively he refrained from showing all he had; it was not only that he had heard tales of what happened to men who flashed their rolls; it was just a part of his nature not to tell all he knew, not to invite questions.

The waiter looked startled. "Wait a shake," he said, and departed. Barry, leaning out from his cubbyhole, saw him go out on the sidewalk and disappear; he was seeking the proprietor who now, as most of the time, was to be found in the saloon next door.

Presently a stocky, sandy haired man with slate-blue eyes and a constant blink, came and stood over Barry and peered at what was in his hand.

"Two pieces o' fancy cake an' sody?" he said. He scooped the contents of Barry's hand into his own. "All right, buddy; we'll call it square this time," he said.

And then Barry was conscious of the big blond man, the Judge, standing up, towering over the partition. Barry looked straight into a pair of bold, very dark brown eyes which somehow conveyed to him the impression of boring into that part of his brain where he kept all his most secret thoughts.

"What is it, Al?" the Judge asked the proprietor. He spoke more softly than Barry had heard him before; actually almost as softly as even Miss Lucy could speak. "Doesn't happen to be gold, now, does it?"

Al whirled about. "Hello, Judge," he said. "I didn't see you."

"I reckon not." The Judge smiled after a fashion to warm a man. At least, so Barry thought. Al said hurriedly:

"I was jus' goin' to step out an' get it weighed so's I could give this young feller his change."

"Sure," smiled the Judge. "Sure."

He extended his hand and Al said, "Shore, Judge," and gave him the gold. Scarcely glancing at it, the Judge returned it to Barry.

"Step right next door into the General Hardware Store," he said. "You can get it weighed there and you'll get honest weight. I'll pay for your lunch here."

"I'm obliged, Judge," said Barry, "but I like to pay my own way."

44

The Judge laughed; Barry saw Miss Lucy's bright eyes peeking out at him from behind the big man.

"It won't amount to much, I reckon," the Judge said, "and you can pay me back. Go ahead into the store; I'm dropping in there myself in a minute."

So Barry thanked him again and took his hat and rifle and went out, conscious all the while of those lively bright eyes of Miss Lucy's.

"She is real pretty," he thought. "Something like Sister Lucy, too."

It was but a few steps to the store; in its windows were rifles and shotguns and revolvers, clasp knives and bowie knives, picks and shovels and frying pans, all sorts of intriguing things. As Barry stepped in he thought: "Judge, huh? Why, he's Judge Blue! Sure to be. And he can tell me about Lucy and all my folks!" To the man behind the counter he said, "I want to buy some things. The Judge told me you could weigh my gold for me."

"I shore can if you ain't got so much as to break my scales down," the storekeeper admitted. "What do you want to buy?"

"Some shells for my six-gun," said Barry. "This one." He unholstered it and put it on the counter. "Forty-fives," he said.

The storekeeper reached for the gun; he turned it over slowly in his hand, seeming to study it.

"Where'd you get this gun?" he asked.

"It's mine," said Barry. "Got any shells for it?"

"Seems like I've heard of a gun like this before," said the other, still turning it over. "Don't know what kind of wood this is; manzanita maybe, but it's so bloody-red a man sort of remembers it. Where'd you say you got it?"

"Didn't say," answered Barry. "Got any shells for it?"

"That gun belonged once to a killer, kid."

"What's his name?"

"They call him the Laredo Kid."

"His name, though?"

"Hell, them killers don't have names. Or if they do they have so many, changin' 'em like a man changes his socks, they don't count."

"What's he look like?" asked Barry.

"Never saw him, an' glad of it. You ain't him, are you?"

"No. And I guess there's other guns like this. Let's see your shells."

He holstered the six-gun; he meant to holster further discussion along with it. The storekeeper, however, hadn't finished with the theme. He put his elbows on the counter, his bristly chin in his hands and regarded his customer thoughtfully.

"There's some talk about him bein' around Tyler now," he said. When Barry said nothing but looked at him, he added: "There was two men killed night before last. They was men that

46

knew the Laredo Kid would kill 'em if ever he got a show."

"What men?" asked Barry.

"They was Bill an' Tom Bedloe, brothers, ranchers a little piece out." He saw Barry's eyes narrow slightly. "Know the Bedloes?" he asked.

"No," said Barry. But their names he did know. He, like most forest men, had a memory which seldom let anything go once taken stock of. Bill and Tom Bedloe were two of those men who Jesse Conroy said had chased him into Sun Creek Valley. Men, Cousin Jesse had said, who pretended to be square by day but were crooks in the dark o' the moon.

Just then the Judge came in.

"Hello, Digby," he said. "I told this young man you could handle his gold for him. Fix him up all right?"

"Evenin', Judge," said Digby. "Let the Judge see your gun, kid."

"He says one like this belonged to the Laredo Kid," said Barry, and held it out for the Judge to look at.

The Judge seemed interested; he handled the heavy weapon just as the storekeeper had done, then handed it back without saying anything.

"I asked him where he got it at," said Digby.

The Judge's lips twitched into a smile. "What did he say?" he asked of Digby though he was looking straight at Barry.

"He didn't say," snorted Digby, and the Judge laughed softly. "All right, all right," muttered Digby. "Pour out your dust, young feller, an' I'll tell you how much."

This time Barry emptied his pouch on a piece of wrapping paper, making a small neat gold hill. It did look just like a miniature mountain, with the larger pellets and a couple of nuggets sticking out like rocks. Digby jerked up his brows but said nothing; he did look sharply at the Judge. This time it was the Judge who spoke, and briskly. "Look here young fellow, I don't know where you got that—"

"It's mine all right," said Barry. To Digby he said, "Are you goin' to weigh it?"

"But I am going to tell you something." The Judge's voice was compelling and Barry looked into that pair of bold, leaf-brown eyes which gave him again the impression of being penetrated. "You went the right place when you showed your gold in the restaurant if you want word of it all over town inside half an hour. Well, it's your business and you look dry behind the ears." He turned and went out, merely saying curtly over his shoulder from the door: "If you get in trouble it's your doing, not mine. But let me know. Just tell anybody you're a friend of mine. It might help."

"Who's he?" asked Barry of the storekeeper. The other stared.

"Hell, don't you know him? He's Judge Parker Blue."

"Thought so," nodded Barry. "How much in money does it weigh?"

"Four hundred fifty dollars," snorted the store-keeper. "Want to take it all out in ca'tridges, huh?"

"Give me the money," Barry told him. "Then I'll do some buyin'."

He bought as much ammunition for his six-gun as he thought he could carry handily, then a plain cartridge belt which he filled and buckled around him, and then turned to a gun rack that had caught his eye. He took down one after another of half a dozen carbines, fitting them to his shoulder, pondering the heft of them. The one he finally selected went out with him; so too did a second cartridge belt filled with shells for it. The two were heavy over his lean hips but it was a comfortable weight. He was very careful not to swagger when he went out, and very conscious of the glory of the crossed belts.

On the sidewalk he looked up and down for the Judge. There were two things—the Judge could tell him where his folks were to be found, and there was still the matter of paying for lunch.

Failing to see the buckboard he wandered down the street as far as the corner, looking in at all doors for the Judge and Lucy. He could see the white road winding up the slope to the white palace trimmed in blue; it was empty. He turned and walked up the street again.

He crossed over, to look in through other doors; when he came to a point opposite the hardware store, he noted that a crowd of men had gathered there, some inside, others jamming the sidewalk. A big man, powerfully shouldered and with the keenest blue eyes Barry had ever seen and with a holstered gun at each hip, elbowed through the press, came to the edge of the sidewalk looking up and down, saw Barry, and made a purposeful bee line to him. His two big thumbs were hooked into his belt.

"Where do yuh think yuh're goin'?" he asked bluntly.

Barry looked at him. "Who're you that's askin'?" he wanted to know.

"I'm Ed Brawley, an' I'm sheriff here, an' I'm askin' where yuh got that gun!"

"It's mine," said Barry.

"Yeah?" said Brawley good-humoredly. "Well, s'pose yuh come along with me; we'll squat an' chin about things. Come ahead."

Barry nodded and swung into step with him; with the crowd eying them they were just turning into a narrow frame building with the sign, Sheriff's Office, painted over it, when Barry saw the buckboard with the two gleaming bays swing around a corner and come speeding down the street.

"Just a minute, Sheriff!" he said. "I've got some business with the Judge."

50

The Judge saw him and pulled up in such fashion as almost to set his two bays on their haunches. Barry stepped into the road and with one hand on a wheel looked up into the Judge's steady leaf-brown eyes.

"I forgot to pay you for my lunch today, Judge," he said. "How much?"

The Judge laughed and said, "Shucks," and then, seeing the look in Barry's dark eyes, no less steady than his own, said, "I gave the man a dollar."

Barry, fishing among coins in his pocket, brought forth a silver dollar and proffered it; the Judge, whip and reins in one hand, extended the other and accepted the money.

"There's one more thing," Barry added. "I guess you can tell me where I can find my folks." All the while he kept his gaze on the Judge, yet none the less was keenly aware of the presence of Miss Lucy of the gay bright eyes and windblown curls and blue ribbons, as also of the Negro standing behind her. He went on, "My father's Ben Haveril, and my sister Lucy married Zachary Blount and—"

"Well, well!" exclaimed Judge Blue. He turned toward the sheriff. "Haven't got my young friend here in tow, have you, Ed?" he asked blandly.

"Sort of," said Brawley, very blunt. "There's some questions—"

"About that gun of his maybe?" suggested the

Judge. Brawley nodded. "Well then!" said the Judge. "There's more guns than one with a fancy butt, Ed. How about turning this young man over to me? I know all about his people. His father and brother are running my new place for me; his sister Lucy is married to my assistant Zach Blount, and she and my Lucy are like two sisters. I'll be responsible for him, Ed. If you like, you can ramble up to my place and talk things over with him. Say, come up for supper!"

The sheriff looked doubtful. "If it was anybody but you, Judge—"

The Judge laughed. "But it happens to be me, Ed." To Barry he called cheerily: "Hop up, Haveril. There's room here for the three of us."

"Thank you a heap, Judge," returned Barry, "but I was counting on seeing my folks, and—"

"Hop up then, and don't keep my team pawing dirt all over town." Barry saw Lucy shift over on the seat closer the Judge, making room. "I'm going out to the lower ranch later, where your folks are; I'll take you with me. And my Lucy can have your sister Lucy over to supper. Climb aboard, Haveril."

Barry looked at the sheriff; Brawley drew back to the sidewalk.

"Go 'head," he said brusquely; and to the Judge: "I'll take yuh up on thet supper invite, Judge. Got the same cook?"

Barry climbed up, sitting with his left thigh

hard pressed against the iron guard rail about the seat lest his rough clothes besmirch the bright blue daintiness that encased Miss Lucy; the Judge slackened his reins and snapped his whip and they were off with a suddenness to catch the unwary in the small of the back.

Out of the corner of his eye, Barry saw how the crowd in front of the hardware store had doubled in numbers, and how all heads turned in the same direction, watching the buckboard out of town. After that, with his new carbine between his knees, he kept his eyes straight ahead. He felt a little spot burning on his suntanned cheek, the one nearer Miss Lucy; but he didn't once look her way. The Judge swung a corner on two wheels, snapped his whip again and they took the uphill road at a run. Never in his life had Barry traveled with such breath-taking speed; he began to think that horses were all right after all. They came to the wide open gate and for one stark second he was sure that a wheel was going to crash into a gate post; it didn't miss two inches. Then the big bright house loomed above them; the horses kept on around to the right and were pulled up again in front of a stable that might have been a hotel.

The Negro sprang down and ran to the horses' heads; a man just inside the stable door looked out from the harness room as he heard the lively clatter of hoofs; in his hands was a richly ornate

Mexican saddle, the silver chasings of which he was polishing. He hastened to set the saddle aside, and came to lend a hand with the fidgety bays.

The Judge threw his reins and sprang down nimbly, arms outstretched to Miss Lucy. She jumped into them with that gay little laugh of hers that was all tinkly music.

But Barry did not hear it. He sat rigid where he was, making no move to get down.

"Well, young Haveril," called the Judge. "Light down and make yourself at home." Still Barry sat, as in a daze. The Judge looked at him in perplexed fashion as did Lucy and the two men. "Well, Haveril?" said the Judge again. "What's up? You look like—"

"Oh!" said Barry, and climbed down over the wheel then.

"Anything wrong?" demanded Judge Blue.

"No, sir," said Barry. "I just sort of got to thinking, that's all."

And he still was thinking as he followed the Judge and Lucy into the cool, imposing white palace trimmed in its bright bluebird blue. He knew that queer things did happen now and then, but he had never known a queerer than this: Here in Judge Parker Blue's stable was Tex Humphreys' fancy saddle from which his brother Robert had been shot. The saddle looked at home here, too, with a man shining it up.

V

"You youngsters amuse yourselves for a while without me," said the Judge. "I'll be with you shortly."

"When are we going out to the ranch where my folks are?" asked Barry.

"Right after supper, son. Meantime you can see your sister; I'll send a man with word that you're here."

They passed, the three abreast, through the amply wide door into a cool dim hall. At one side was a staircase, and the Judge ran upstairs like a boy. Barry and Lucy stood a moment really looking straight at each other for the first time. Her brows were puckered into a puzzled frown which might have been only the shadow of her soft brown hair; then a faint lovely smile came into her sweet gray eyes and ever so fleetingly touched her lips. Barry smiled back at her. Instantly they were friends—and friends from the very beginning seem to have the trick of understanding. Each saw that some unsmiling sober thoughtfulness lay behind the other's smile.

"I am afraid!" whispered Lucy, and shivered.

"So'm I!" said Barry and stared at her.

They heard a door slam upstairs; the emphatic sound broke a spell just weaving itself about them.

"Come," cried Lucy swiftly, "and I'll show you your room. Then we can go outside to the summer house; it's nice out there this time of day."

Barry, clutching hat and carbine, stepping with utmost care across carpeted floors, passed through the grandest rooms he had ever seen or even dreamed. The room allotted to him was at the rear looking out on the garden and, beyond, the mountain slope. As she threw the door open and stood aside for him, Barry's heart sank. He knew he'd never dare besmirch a bed like that! Of a sudden he felt horribly ragged and dirty.

"I'll wait for you outside," said Lucy.

He went in and stood looking about him. There was a mirror over the washstand; he seemed inexorably drawn to it. A red flood of shame burned hot in his tanned cheeks as he looked at the wild, Indian-like face that seemed to reproach him with scornful dark eyes, at besmudged cheek and brow and dusty eyelashes, at long black unkempt hair almost down to his shoulders.

He set his rifle aside and washed; he poured out the water and washed again; he cleaned out the basin and dried his hands on the inside of his shirt. He used comb and brush, doing the best he could with that wild Indian hair of his. Then, carrying his battered old hat crumpled in his hands, he went out to join Lucy.

The summer house was a pleasant place under

56

shade trees, and there were benches and in the shrubbery quick darting humming birds no bigger than Barry's thumb gave them something to talk about. They didn't smile again but were as shy as any two wild things. When he looked at her it was when he thought she wouldn't notice; when those expressive big eyes of hers turned toward him it was when he was looking thoughtfully down across the little town in the valley.

Abruptly, out of an uncomfortable silence, she grew gay again and he had the feeling that a lot of Lucy's gaiety was just pretended. Jumping up she exclaimed:

"Do you want me to show you around the place? The flower garden and the vegetable patch and the corrals and barns—"

"Yes," said Barry, and added, "I liked your stable."

So first of all she carried him away to the stable. Barry led the way inside, stalking straight to the harness room where the man who had been doing something with a saddle was back at his work. He was an old stooped gray man; he looked up and nodded and went on with his work.

"That's a pretty fine saddle," said Barry.

Lucy, noting it for the first time, said, "Why, it's the loveliest saddle I ever saw! Whose is it, Andrew?"

"Belongs to a stranger," said Andrew. "The Judge mebbe knows him. He come in late las' night, changed saddles account the cinch o' this one bein' ready to bust; rode on. Said he'd be back tonight."

"A stranger?" repeated the girl, intrigued. "What was he like, Andrew?"

"Jus' a young cowboy, I reckon," replied an unconcerned Andrew. "Lef' his horse here, too. Been ridin' hard, I reckon."

"A man ought to have a pretty fine horse to match up that saddle," suggested Barry.

"Let's go see it," invited Lucy. "Is it in the corral, Andrew?"

He nodded, and as they left was whistling softly, "For I'm a young cowboy, an' I know I done wrong." The two went to the largest of three corrals, climbed together to the top bar and were looking the horses over when the Judge came out to join them.

"It must be that one," said Lucy pointing. "That high-headed black with the white saddle marks. It's not one of ours I'm sure."

Barry didn't say anything. Lucy was right. That was Tex Humphreys' pride among his saddle horses. That was the horse which, only a few days ago, had carried Robert Haveril to his death.

The Judge had a scrap of paper in his hand. He waved it toward Barry, saying as he came on: "I'm sorry you won't be able to see your sister today, young Haveril. There was a note on my study table, sent over by Zachary Blount; he went to Pride's Valley this morning on a bit of business for me, something that looked funny about the deed to a new ranch I just bought. He took his wife along. But they'll be back tomorrow or next day."

Lucy turned so abruptly that she almost lost her balance, and Barry put out his hand to save her from falling. She started to say something but her parted lips closed slowly without speaking.

"What's up, Lucy?" asked the Judge.

"Nothing," laughed Lucy. "You made me jump."

"You're looking at some high-class horse flesh there, Haveril," said the Judge, and stood by Barry, leaning on the corral.

Barry nodded. He wanted to ask about that high-headed black, but hesitated. Blind instinct, subtle intuition—he didn't know what—made him move as cautiously as all his true kindred, forest wild things, moved. They sniffed the air, they listened to silences and were uneasy. Later he might put one and one and one together; now he didn't think about things as much as feel.

But whereas he was content with silence, Lucy was not. She asked of the Judge, pointing again:

"Who's the stranger, Daddy, that owns that one? He's got the most gorgeous saddle I ever saw."

The Judge looked the horses over. "That black?" he said. "Oh, yes. It belongs to a young cowboy who rode in late last night. He had to go on and asked to leave his horse here until he came back. Where'd you see his saddle?" he asked.

"Andrew was fixing the cinch. It's a fancy Mexican saddle, and Andrew gave all the silver work a polish; it hurts your eyes to look at it."

"Let's go to the house," said the Judge. "It's most supper time."

But it was not supper time, and they loafed comfortably on the shady front porch looking down over Tylersville. Sitting up here and looking down that way, Barry noticed, gave one a sense of superiority; it was as though he owned all he saw. The Judge, leaning back in a big armchair, tucked in the corners of his ample, humorous mouth and looked complacent. "It's a great country, huh, young Haveril?" he said.

They were out there when Ed Brawley, the sheriff, came. He did not stay to supper; instead he and the Judge went upstairs to the Judge's study and left the two young people to their own devices, mostly silence and averted faces, for half an hour. When the two men came down, Brawley said bluntly to Barry:

"I come purty close runnin' yuh in today, young feller, account yuh bein' a stranger, carryin' that red gun an', as folks say, bein' heavy with gold. My mistake, I reckon; the Judge tellin' me who yuh are, one of the Sundown Haverils. I guess yuh're on the square; if yuh ain't, well I'll mos'

60

likely be crossin' trails with yuh ag'in. So I'll be steppin'. *Adios*, everybody."

Young as Barry Haveril was, and inexperienced in the ways of men, square as a die himself and straightforward in thought as in act, yet there was in him a native shrewdness comparable to that of his forest friends and enemies. A young bear that had never seen a trap and didn't know what a trap was, yet sniffed at it if not carefully concealed with dead leaves, and gave it a wide berth. And now Barry, looking far beyond the little town and across the hills beginning to withdraw among purple and violet shadows, was mentally sniffing like a suspicious bear.

"How far is it out to the ranch where my folks are?" he asked without withdrawing his expressionless gaze from the melting distances.

"It's inside thirty miles," said the Judge. "That little span of mine will do it in less than three hours. We start right after supper."

But they didn't go right after supper, nor did they go at all. The three were dining at a long table that would have seated a score, being served by the big Negro, when a man rode up from Tylersville for word with Judge Blue. The Judge went out to him, and returned almost immediately. "I've got to see a man in town," he said. "Go ahead with supper; I'll finish when I get back. I ought to be with you in half an hour."

After an hour of waiting Barry was more the

61

sniffing bear than ever. Lucy had conducted him to a pleasant room where there were books and a piano and sofa and easy-chairs, and at first had chattered like a magpie. She had sung for him a little, too, and at first he had listened enrapt and had looked at her admiringly, thinking her the daintiest and sweetest and cleverest little thing in the world; every bit as nice as the other Lucy, he was almost reluctantly admitting. But even her singing or her quick sidelong glances or her shining hair, which he would have loved to touch but would not have dared—none of all these, or the whole slender grace of her, could long hold him. He grew as restless as a man sometimes does when in his bones he feels an imminent break in the weather, a thunderstorm boiling up while the skies are still blue and serene.

Still time passed and Lucy was as restless as Barry, and glanced at him now and then in a queer way, so that he saw the shadowy something again somewhere behind her eyes and remembered how she had whispered, "I'm afraid." When the Judge's voice said, "Sorry I'm so late," both of them jumped, for they had not heard him come in. He tossed his hat to the piano top and looked at his watch. "We'll go first thing in the morning. All right, young Haveril?"

Ten minutes later Barry was alone in his room, confronting a bed with which he meant to have no dealings, not alone because of an earlier dread of disturbing such elegance, but more than that because he was of no mind for any sort of bed now. He extinguished his lamp and went to his window; he stood there a long while looking out at the dim bulk of the mountain under the stars.

Something was wrong and he knew it. It was no longer a mere uneasy suspicion but a positive certainty. Yet he was none the less puzzled; he didn't know what was wrong and he didn't quite dare let his thoughts go the way they wanted to go. Judge Blue seemed to him a fine man; he asked himself what possible unfriendly interest the great Judge Blue could have in Barry Haveril, with nothing that anyone might covet except a red-butted gun and a little heap of gold. It was preposterous to think of the Judge, with his name and fame, with his thousands of wide acres and far-roving herds, giving a second thought to Barry's small possessions.

But little things, each almost negligible in itself, dropped into place like links in a chain, and the chain was not to be ignored. The Judge had befriended him, a perfect stranger, and told him where to take his gold. The Judge had rescued him from arrest. The Judge had invited the Sheriff to supper, had talked aside with him, and the Sheriff had gone, leaving Barry unmolested. The Judge had promised that Barry's sister would come, too; and then had received word she could not. The Judge had promised to take him to the ranch where his folks were, and then had found that impossible.— And Lucy *was* afraid of something.— Then there were Tex Humphreys' saddle and the black horse. The man who had ridden that horse here might or might not be the man who had killed Robert Haveril. Whoever he was, he was a stranger here—to all save the Judge.

"And he never even once mentioned my gold, and he never even once said a thing about my gun," thought Barry.

But as time passed and the house grew utterly still, he swept all these considerations clear of his mind. After all his one concern right now was the saddle out there in the stable and the high-headed black in the corral—and the cowboy who had left them here and was to come back for them.

"I reckon no one will hear me now," decided Barry, and crawled out through the window, dropping noiselessly to the ground.

He stepped softly through the dark, making a guarded circle of the house to assure himself that the rooms were all dark. Then he went to the stable, always moving stealthily and keeping as much as he could under the biggest trees or among shrubbery. His nerves tautened as he fancied that someone was watching him, following from a discreet distance; and he stood stone still for minutes, listening and straining his ears against the silence. He even retraced his steps, seeking the one who for an instant he had "felt" stalking him. Again he circled the house. No one. Well, he hadn't been in the least sure. He returned to the stable. Near the big double doors was a bench under a tree. He sat down and waited. It wouldn't matter if he had to wait all night; he meant to be on hand when the young cowboy who had Tex's horse and saddle came riding back. He slid his hand down to the butt of the new six-gun; he dozed, started wide awake and dozed again a dozen times before the soft beat of shod hoofs stiffened him into alertness.

He saw the dark form of man and horse coming on from beyond the stable, a single silhouette dim against the mountain flank.

The rider came down with a subdued jingle of spurs at the stable door; he was whistling softly and didn't turn Barry's way. When he got the door open and led the horse inside, Barry rose quietly and followed. And this time, were there anyone following him, there was little likelihood of Barry noting him, so intent was he on the man in front.

There was the sound of a stumble, a softly breathed curse, and then the scratch and flare of a match. When the lantern at the harness room door was lighted at first it revealed little but six legs, those of the horse and the two booted ones of its master. Then the lantern was swung up to be hung on a nail, the soft whistling was resumed, and Barry saw that it was Jesse Conroy.

"Hello, Cousin Jesse," he said in a quiet voice, so grave and sober that you'd have thought a man who spoke like that had never known how to smile in his life.

Jesse Conroy whirled, as swift as a cat, and crouched and whipped out the gun riding loosely in its holster. The three motions were like one. Barry saw the gun barrel dully reflect the lamplight.

"Oh, it's you, Sundown!" said Jesse. His hand that had jerked the gun up a little more than waist high was lowered. The gun, however, was not immediately returned to its holster. His next words were spoken with an affectation of levity, but there was an irritable edge to his voice: "Yuh made me jump purty near out'n my boots, Cousin Barry. Y'want to look out, scarin' folks like that, less'n one starts shootin' before he thinks."

"Why should you start shooting, Cousin Jesse?" asked Barry.

Jesse laughed and at last slipped his gun back into its place.

"Yuh shore did make me jump," he said, and sounded entirely good humored now. "I never knowed yuh was friends o' the Judge. I never knowed yuh even ever come to Tyler. What're yuh doin' down here, huh, Cousin Barry?"

"Want to sell that black horse you left here last night, Cousin Jesse?"

"What's come over yuh? I thought yuh didn't go in for hosses yuhse'f, likin' them long laigs better."

"That's a real nice horse," said Barry, and sounded very thoughtful.

"What's on yore mind, Cousin Barry?" said Jesse, and again his voice was edged.

"That saddle, too," said Barry. "I was looking at it this evening. The fancy Mexico one. Where'd you happen to get that saddle, Cousin Jesse?"

Jesse answered in an off-hand way, "That saddle? It's one I picked up down to Laredo one time. Why?"

"When?" asked Barry. "You been down to Laredo since I saw you? It's quite a ways from here."

Jesse's answer hung fire scarcely a noticeable instant. "Hell no," he said. "It's one o' my ol' saddles; I've had it two-three year."

"You lie, Cousin Jesse," said Barry steadily, and pulled his six-gun out of its holster. "That was Tex Humphreys' saddle; so was that black Tex's; and you killed my brother Robert to get them both. Killed him like a dog just for a horse and saddle. Now, if you think you've got any more killing to do—"

He knew while he was talking to Jesse that someone had followed him and was standing right behind him now. But he couldn't turn, nor could he step aside; there wasn't time.

Barry didn't know what happened next. He realized that Jesse Conroy had moved with an almost incredible swiftness, as quick as a mountain cat or a rattlesnake striking out from its deadly coil. But despite that flash of action on Jesse's part, no shot was fired by him. Nor was any fired by Barry.

What happened was this: A man standing close behind Barry already had his weapon in hand| and lifted; it was a Colt revolver, like Barry's, save for the butt. He brought it down brutally on Barry's head, and the boy slumped down where he was and knew nothing at all of who had struck him.

But Jesse knew even before the commanding voice said: "Pocket your gun, Laredo! And put out that damned light. Quick about it!"

"I'm damned!" muttered Jesse Conroy. Slowly he obeyed both orders. Then through the sudden dark his voice came quietly, "What's the game this time, Judge?"

"So you killed young Haveril's brother, did you? Just for a horse and saddle!"

"Yuh're a fine one to talk," sneered Jesse. "Well, I'm not sayin' whether I killed young Haveril's brother or not, but I'd shore shot young Haveril daid if yuh hadn't knocked him out the minute yuh did. It might have been better if yuh'd kep' yore hands in yore pockets, Judge. I know this hombre an' I know what he's like clean through. If yuh ain't killed him already, beatin' his skull in, it's a job for me."

"No," said the Judge, and sounded stern about it. "No. You hear me, Laredo? I've got plans of my own for him."

"Yes?" said Jesse, and sounded frankly mystified. "Want to make me laugh? Judge Blue wastin' time over this kid? What in hell's he got that I overlooked?" He ended jeeringly. "He ain't a prince in disguise or somethin', is he?"

"You might call him that," returned the Judge soberly. "Now look here: you want to get some money out of me, don't you? And you know I've had a tough run of luck and am so damned near broke wide open that your chances of getting it are a lot slimmer than mine of having to fold up and get out on a run. And—"

But Jesse flared up, saying in that deadly cold voice of his: "Yuh don't run out on me an' yuh know it, Judge. Once let me spill my story in the right set of ears an' yore runnin' days is over. If I don't get mad an' burn yuh down first!"

"Some day, Laredo," said the Judge more quietly, yet in just as deadly and cold a voice, "we'll maybe cut loose and kill each other. Now if you'll keep your shirt on I'll tell you about this young Haveril. He blew into town today with a fist full of gold with the dirt still sticking to it. And it's my pressing affair to find out where he got it."

Jesse whistled softly. "An' I might have killed him before yuh found out!" Then, eager and alert, he added, "But Judge, he'll be lookin' up his folks, across to yore new ranch; an' he'll be tellin' the crowd all he knows—"

"He won't be seeing anybody but me for a while," said the Judge. "I'm keeping him shut away. In the morning, if he's feeling like traveling, I'll put him on a horse, tell him we're headed for the ranch, and hand him over to you. And you'll be over at the shack in Encina Cañon. You and I will work this together, Kid. And when we've won it, I'm paying you off, and you're handing back to me what's mine— and after that if we ever meet up again— Well, fill your hand, Kid, that's all."

Jesse laughed tauntingly. "There's one more thing, Judge," he said. "I got a good look at the girl the other day. When I hand yuh back what's yore'n, yuh're goin' to hand me the girl along with the res' o' my pay. I got a hankerin'— Dammit all, Judge, I'd marry her even!"

For a while it was very still there at the stable. After a while the Judge drew a long breath. He said in a voice which was not quite so steady: "You're getting a swell-head, Laredo. It's a disease that's sometimes fatal. Better slow down."

But the Laredo Kid, reckless and arrogant young devil that he was, standing there invisible in the dark, doubtless with his hand tight on the butt of his gun, mocked him drawlingly.

"I fell in love I reckon! If yuh're so damn' smart, Blue, why didn't yuh figger on that happenin'? Soon's I seen this little Lucy o' yore'n, I says as I'll take her in part pay. An' when some day she gets a good look at me— Shucks, Judge, girls go crazy over a feller like me, an'—"

"You fool! She's only a kid anyhow, only sixteen—"

"I'll wait a bit," grinned Laredo. "Until she's, say, eighteen! That's about right, ain't it, Judge?"

"Better be on your way, Laredo. And if you're not just trying to be funny— Marry her? Well, we'll see later. Tomorrow evening early I'll be at Encina Cañon, and young Haveril will be with me. We'll talk. And one thing more: better get rid of that horse and saddle tonight."

"I'm on my way in two shakes," returned the other. "Drag your man off and shut the door so's I can have a light. Mebbe yuh'd better shine a light on him now to make shore whether he ain't playin' possum."

"I've had a hand on him all the time," said the

Judge. "He's out cold. Get going, Kid. *Y adios.*"

"*Adios, amigo,*" laughed the Laredo Kid.

Of all this, Barry Haveril, plunged into the dark depths of utter unconsciousness, heard never a word. Yet much of it he was to know before the already far advanced night was gone.

He regained consciousness lying fully dressed on the bed which earlier he had been adverse to mussing. There was a cold wet towel on his head and the Judge stood over him, waiting for him to open his eyes. The Judge was in slippers and trousers evidently hastily pulled on over the lower part of a nightgown.

"Well, young Haveril," he said. "Alive, are you?"

"What happened?" said Barry, confused.

"I got up for a drink of water," said the Judge, "and thought I saw someone prowling outside under my window. I went out to see about it and was just in time to see you standing in the stable door talking to somebody; and just when it looked like shooting, some other fellow jumped up behind you and knocked you out cold with a club. Then they were off like a shot, the two of them. What was it all about?"

"The man in the barn, with the lantern— Know him, Judge?"

"Can't say that I do," answered the Judge. "He was by here a month or so ago, looking for work. That's all I know about him. Who is he?"

"I don't know much about him myself. I met up with him not long ago; he told me his name was Jesse Conroy and we sort of figured out we were relations."

"What were you two getting ready to fight about?"

Barry shut his eyes and lay still a moment. Without opening them he said, "My head hurts, Judge; it's hard thinking straight."

The Judge nodded understandingly. "Sometimes a man wants to think straight before he does his talking," he agreed. "Well, I guess you're all right for the rest of the night, Haveril. See you in the morning. We'll ride early if you're all right."

"I'll be all right," said Barry, and the Judge withdrew, taking the lighted lamp with him.

It was nearly an hour later when Barry had his second visitor, an hour of a wracking headache and bafflement. He tried to get matters straight and could not. Someone had followed him about the house, and had struck him down when in another second he and Jesse Conroy would have argued matters out in the smoke. He wanted to know who that was. Then he grew aware that he was no longer alone, but that a slim white figure bent over him. It was Lucy in a long nightgown with something thrown over her shoulders. As he reared up on his elbow she said, "Sh!" almost at his ear.

"Lucy?" he whispered.

Lucy, too, whispered. Incoherent at first, her rushing words only perplexed him anew. But he caught, "Go! Oh, go quickly! Get up and go! You must— You can, can't you? You're not hurt too badly, are you?"

He sat on the edge of the bed and Lucy's face was so close to his own that, in what dim light filtered in from the stars, he could see her eyes in a white face, and her eyes were big with fright. Even her voice, whispering as it was, was charged with terror.

He caught her hand and held it tight, himself tense and filled with dread, while he commanded her to tell him what was wrong, what had happened or she was afraid of happening.

It came in a wild jumble of words. There were things which she wanted to hold back, which she had not thought that she could speak of to anyone, and yet in her frantic state before she was through he had nearly the whole story, some of it in such wild and broken fragments that it was only afterward that he could make sense of them. For Lucy was afraid of her father, and did not want to tell that—and yet out it burst, with a sob which shook her from head to foot.

First of all, she had known that the Judge lied this afternoon when he told Barry that Zachary Blount had taken Barry's sister out of town— for Lucy herself had seen Zachary and the Judge

74

together going into a store just before the Judge joined her to drive home. She couldn't sleep; she had heard the Judge when he softly quitted his room, and she had followed. So, while he trailed Barry, she crept after the Judge. And she had seen and overheard what occurred at the stable.

"He—that man—your cousin, he is the Laredo Kid!" she told Barry fearfully. And then she told the rest of it, and ended with her frantic plea: "You'll go! Oh, Barry, I'm afraid— Promise me!"

"Yes," said Barry, and slipped from the bed, groping for his hat and the new carbine. "I'll slip out and go now."

"You can take my horse. No one is apt to notice it's gone. It's the little bay with—"

"No. They could track a horse. They won't be able to track me."

"You'll go to your folks?"

He had thought of that already, but he said: "No. They'd look for me there first of all. I'll go somewhere else." He hastened to the window and put a leg over the sill; then he pulled back to say to her, "But you? Aren't you afraid here?"

She clutched him, and whispered shiveringly. "I'm scared to death. Barry."

"Then come with me—"

She seemed for a moment, while their hands were locked so tightly together, to be of a mind to go with him. But, "No," she said. "I'll be all right. Anyhow, for a while. Until the Laredo Kid comes back and— Oh, Barry! *He wants me!"*

Barry said, "I won't go without you!"

"You must! You must, Barry! And quick!"

"Then I'll come back—"

"Listen! I sometimes ride back on the mountain to look at the sunset. There's a trail up to Lookout; it's a plateau behind the house with the cliffs cutting across it. Meet me there, Barry—at sunset—"

"Tomorrow?"

"N-o. Not so soon. They may be watching for you. In three days, Barry?" He nodded and gripped her hand harder than ever, then slipped out through the window and vanished, a swift silent shadow soon merging among other shadows and then blotted out. The girl shivered and drew her shawl tighter about her, and crept like a little ghost back to her room, no longer the haven it had always been, but a place of dread.

VI

Three years passed before Barry and Lucy saw each other again, a three years which carried both far afield, which left its marks on them, which brought Lucy to the fresh bloom of full blown nineteen and womanhood, and made of Barry Haveril a young man in his early twenties in whose steady eyes was a look far older.

That night Barry fled into the mountains, taking every precaution against leaving a sign of his passing. He traveled more slowly than was his habit because of the throbbing ache in his head, but when day broke he accounted himself safe from pursuit, a good twenty miles away. He did not turn toward his own place, so sure was he that Jesse Conroy would hunt him there; and now that his first meeting with his outlaw cousin had been interrupted, he meant to postpone the second a few days. First, he wanted his head to clear, and that dull ache was still there; also he wanted to see Lucy again; and finally he came to tell himself coolly that right now, if he and Jesse met and drew their guns, there was little hope of Barry even pulling trigger, so incredibly swift was the other. Barry said a hundred times: "I'll make myself just as fast as he is. Then I'll go get him."

The evening appointed for the meeting with Lucy found him at Lookout Point, high on the mountain side above the Judge's fine house, hidden in a brushy thicket from which he could watch the steep zigzag trail. The cool twilight faded just as the little pink and gold clouds on the horizon had done, and dark came and there was no sign of Lucy. He waited an hour, then withdrew higher up into the mountains. He came back each sunset time; on his third coming he saw something which had been here all the time, waiting for him, passing unnoticed. It just happened now that a stiff evening breeze set a corner of the scrap of paper fluttering so that it caught his eye. There was still light for him to read the penciled words:

Dear Barry, If anybody finds this it will be you, because no one ever comes up here. I am writing this the very next day after you left. I am to be taken away this very day—and I don't know why and I don't even know where! Oh, I hope you are all right! And, Barry, I do wish I had gone with you. You will come back when it is safe, won't you? I'll ride up and leave this now—I'm telling him I'm going to say good-bye for a while to Lookout. I'll put it half under a stone and I hope you find it.—Good-bye, Barry.

Lucy

Again he returned to the solitudes, and this time an oppressive sense of apprehension and of an unaccustomed loneliness went with him.

"Tomorrow," meditated Barry, making his swift silent way through a bit of forestland where he crossed a tiny upland valley toward his new hideout, "I'll go see my folks. I've got to tell them about Robert."

But again he reckoned without the changes that these few days had already made. It was to be a long, long while before he was to look into the eyes of any of his own blood. Further, at that instant, he stood in the gravest danger of never having another morrow to reckon with. For as he passed through a small open glade, all without warning a shot rang out and a bullet cleft the air, close to his ear, and with it came an exultant shout:

"Got you, Laredo! Got you, you dog!"

Barry leaped as a deer leaps, clear of the opening among the trees and into a patch of brush, and leaping fell and rolled and brought up crouching, his own gun in hand, in a shadowy gully. He had heard only the voice and the singing bullet, had caught only the red flash of fire, seeing nothing of his assailant. A second shot and a third whizzed over his head. He did not return the fire, though he held himself in readiness; he shouted back:

"Hold it, or I'll burn you down! I'm not Laredo. You've got the wrong man!"

There was a silence out of which finally a puzzled voice, sounding disgruntled, muttered:

"Not Laredo, huh? Who says so? You'd say so if yuh was Laredo."

"Don't be a fool," grunted Barry. "If you know Laredo, you know his voice, don't you? Then you know I'm not Laredo. And if you don't know him—well, what do you want to kill him for?"

Reluctantly the voice admitted:

"Yuh don't sound like him, that's a fac'. But yuh looked sort of like he does— And what the hell yuh prowling around like this for if yuh ain't Laredo?"

"You make me sick," snorted Barry. "You came mighty close knocking me over, you jackass."

"If I was only shore," complained the invisible man. Then he said more brightly: "Step out where I can see yuh good. If yuh ain't Laredo I won't drill yuh."

Barry stirred ever so slightly, still crouching in the hollow, and thus at last was able to make out the form of the other man, standing close to a pine. He lifted his gun and covered that dim form steadily. Then he answered with quiet emphasis:

"I've got you covered! Wiggle your ears and I'll be the one who's drilling you! Up with 'em! High up and quick about it!"

"Damn yore eyes," growled the other, and dropped his weapon. Barry heard it fall.

A moment later the two, standing fronting each

other in the open, amply satisfied themselves that neither was the Laredo Kid. Barry found himself looking down into the upturned face of a dried-up little old man whom, by campfire later and after that by daylight, he discovered to have a wilted and discouraged looking gray mustache, long gray hair in a fringe about a shinily bald dome, and a pair of the most wistful baby-blue eyes he ever saw.

"No, yuh ain't Laredo, dang it," admitted the little gray man, and sounded more disgusted than ever. In the same querulous voice he growled: "Dang it, I dunno how I come to miss yuh like that, nuther. I ought to've got yuh dead center."

"I'd think you'd be glad you didn't," snapped Barry, "seeing that I'm a stranger you've got no grudge against."

"A man likes to hit what he shoots at, don't he?" rasped the other.

"What have you got against Laredo?" Barry asked.

"Aplenty! An' if I never do another deed o' kindness, long's I live, I'm goin' to let the bad blood out'n him, an' that'll be all the blood he's got. That's a vow, stranger; hear me? Mebbe it'll be a long chase, with him on the jump like he is—"

"What do you mean, on the jump?"

"Ain't yuh heerd? Shore, he is. Only I thought yuh was him, an' mebbe he'd snuck back—"

"Where'd he go? When?" demanded Barry. "What's happened?"

"Mebbe yuh're lookin' for him too?" suggested the old man shrewdly.

"Yes," said Barry, making no bones about it. "Now tell me."

"Wait till I go git me my gun." He picked it up, dusted it off against a pair of ragged old overalls and jerked up his head to remark waspishly: "Yuh got your nerve, young feller, to make me throw ol' Maria down like that! Don't yuh know she might of got a sight jammed ag'in a rock?"

"Tell me about Laredo," insisted Barry.

"Come along over to my camp. It's only a short piece back up in the gully. We'll squat an' git acquainted."

"Anybody else at your camp?"

"Jus' Arabella."

Arabella was as small and tough and dried up for a burro as the little gray man for a human being. While Arabella dozed nearby, the two men sat on a log over a tiny fire where coffee and bacon and flapjacks were being brought to a state of delectable readiness. The little old man chewed tobacco vigorously, spat copiously and with amazing inaccuracy for one who must have put in years at the pastime, and talked until his listener finally grew sleepy. But for the first half hour Barry was wide-awake enough.

The old man by his own account was a shiftless

prospector, a nomad, and undoubtedly something of a scamp. What his real name was he never revealed; he conceded that men called him Baldy or Dad or Timberline, and that long ago he had come from Georgia. Why he came in the first place, why he never went back, was left to the imagination.

Yep, he knowed Laredo well, and he'd knowed him a long while. Likewise he knowed Judge Parker Blue, an' knowed him a lot better'n most!

"What do you know about them?" asked Barry, stiff with eagerness.

Old Timberline shook his head and spat sprayingly, so that Barry ducked and sat a bit farther away.

"I keep my mouth shut until I git mad, young feller," he retorted. "Then I'm apt to say things."

He refused to discuss the Judge, save generally, and beyond hinting broadly that he had a fund of secret knowledge about Judge Blue's past which, were it suspected by that worthy, would have him on both knees begging to eat out of old Timberline's hand, he would not go. In the Laredo Kid's case, however, the gates were wide open.

The Kid, said he, had managed to get himself into such a mess that there was nothing left for him but to skedaddle, which he did with bullets pesterin' him like a swarm of hornets. Laredo, it would appear in some unusually reckless, devil-may-care mood, had stirred things up right in Tylersville the other night until before he got through the lid blew clean off hell's bake oven. First time he had ever showed his face in Tyler, too; it had always looked like he was hands-off for this particular town. This time, dangerous and mean-looking, he busted square into the Jamboree Saloon. He held the place up, he cleaned up two poker tables—yes, all alone he was—and before he got clear he killed two men. But he did even more than that. One of the men he killed was Jake Hammond, a man that folks liked real well. And Jake's kid, Jakie, only nine years old, happened in there, sent over by his mama to bring Jake home; and Jakie saw it all and went crazy over it and ran and grabbed Laredo by the legs. And Laredo said, "Yuh want some too, do yuh, yuh little—" and shot him through the head. He went out laughing, the boys said, but he went fast.

Now the whole community was up and after him, and Laredo without a doubt had fled the country.

"You know the little kid he killed?" asked Barry softly. "That why you're after him too, Timberline?"

"Hell, no," said Timberline through an amber spray. "That wasn't done to me personal, an' there's enough fellers that did know Jakie. But Laredo, he crossed my trail close to six months ago; I was out on a desert stretch a consid'able ways from here, southwest. I don't do much talkin' about what happened—but I been after him ever since."

Presently Barry said, thinking about his plan for tomorrow:

"You seem to know a good many folks around here, Timberline. Happen to know anybody out at the Judge's new ranch about thirty miles from Tylersville?"

"Hell, yes," said Timberline. "I was out that way recent, prospectin' them little hills with the red gullies in 'em. There was some new folks out there, a man name of Haveril an' his wife. A real purty little woman she was, too." He pulled at his mustache. "I was goin' back to see her some time, but she's gone now."

"Gone? Why, they were there only three or four days ago."

"Gone now though. Y' see, young feller, whatever happens in this country gets talked about in Tyler, an' whatever gets talked about in Tyler, I find out when I drop in. Three-four days ago the Judge busted out o' here, headed somewheres else. Some folks says he went East an' some says West; it's my bet he's headed Californy-way. Anyhow, he took his gal Lucy with him; an' he took his new hired hand, that Zack Blount, an' his purty young wife along— they say she's a Haveril, too. An' he stopped off at the New Branch, an' told 'em there he'd sold it,

85

an' he chased them Haverils off; an' folks say they for shore headed to Californy." He cocked a blue eye at Barry. "What yuh askin' fur?" he wanted to know.

"They're my folks," said Barry. "Father and mother and brother; and Zack Blount's wife is my sister."

"Hell yuh say," observed Timberline politely. "So you are a Haveril too, huh? Shake, Haveril."

Absently Barry shook as directed, feeling his hand gripped by a small one that seemed old leather on the outside, spring steel within.

"I was going to see them tomorrow—"

"Not tomorrow, Haveril. Yuh'll have a job findin' which way they went. Don't believe myse'f they quite knowed where or what they was headed for."

"Most of all, I want to come up with the Laredo Kid!"

"Yuh'n me, both together!"

"Are you going to tell me what he did to you?"

Timberline squinted at the small fire. "It's somethin' I don't hanker to talk about," he said with his former waspishness. "I ain't ever tol' anybody. But it was like this: I was out in the desert, like I said. He rid in, stranger to me, while I was cookin' supper. I had a fine mess o' beans if I do say it myse'f. I let him eat danged nigh all of 'em, an' I never said nothin' an' he never said nothin' nuther. Not so much as damn-yore-eyes,

86

or a polite thank-yuh-damn-yuh. Nothin'. Then he got up to go. He sees somethin' I got settin' on a rock; he says, 'What's that there?' It was a can o' tomatoes, Haveril; a can o' tomatoes that I'd carried three weeks, an' every day I says, I'll eat 'em tomorrow, an' when tomorrow come, I jus' saved 'em for nex' day. An' I tol' him, an' sort of laughed, I guess. An' he sort of laughed too, an' crawled on his horse an' started off. An' then, quicker'n a damn rattlesnake, he whirled in the saddle, an' started shootin'—an' when I got done rollin' over backwards, thinkin' he was shootin' at me, I seen what the devil done. He'd put six bullets in that can o' mine, jus' shootin' it clean all to hell. An' off he rid, kind o' laughin'."

"And that's why—"

"Can you blame me, Haveril?" asked old Timberline simply, as man to man.

When later Timberline, a man who lived most of his days alone in mountain or desert country with none for companion but one like Arabella, yet who anomalously liked to have a "pardner" with him, again suggested that he and Barry hunt together, Barry shook his head. He liked Timberline well enough; he enjoyed some several hours in his garrulous company, yet he was in no mood to measure his stride to any other. So he went his way and Timberline went his way—and they met up again within ten days. And after that, they met again and again, and after the first few encounters it could hardly have been all chance bringing them together.

First Barry returned to Tylersville. He went openly, in broad daylight, but he was watchful at every step. No one molested him; none seemed to have any memory of him. He saw Brawley, the sheriff, on the street, and thought that Brawley saw him. At the hardware store, then at other likely places, he sought information. He could learn little that his new gossipy friend had not already told him. It was true about Laredo and the furor he had left in his wake as he fled for his life; true, too, that, with no particular explanation, the Judge had "gone on a trip." All were confi-dent it was just some hasty business trip and that he'd come back sooner or later to his great possessions. True, too, that the Haverils had left the New Ranch. None knew exactly why or where they had gone.

Before Barry left Tylersville he drew heavily upon his pocket money and bought the first horse he had ever owned. He purchased the best to be had on short notice, and rode out of town that evening well equipped, his carbine in saddle holster, conveniently at hand. He struck out for his own place, at the head of Sun Creek Valley. It was his thought that Cousin Jesse might have ridden that way, if not looking for Barry, then just because that was the way he had headed the last time a posse was hot on his heels.

"He's likely to have him a hideout up that way somewhere," he thought.

He slept two nights in his own cabin; nowhere could he find any sign that anyone had come this way. The next day, with his small pack behind his saddle, he rode farther up into the mountains. It was like getting home to be in these quiet remembered forests. He rose to many a vantage point, looking for a wisp of smoke above the tree tops, for the trace of a man's boot or a shod hoof. He was hunting as he had hunted since he was big enough to carry a gun.

When he came finally to the ravine where he had watched the two men washing gold, he came too upon old Timberline. Barry had seen his smoke far off; it was twilight and the old man was cooking his supper. Down by the creek, with the din of the water in his ears, he did not hear the horse's hoofs; his back was turned and he was humming contentedly to himself as he stooped over his frying pan. Barry shouted at him:

"I got you, Laredo!" and then sat there laughing as the old man whirled about and glared at him.

"Light down, you ornery cuss," invited Timberline when he saw who it was. "Supper's mos' ready."

"Got any tomatoes?" asked Barry, and swung stiffly out of the saddle.

"Go on," snorted the old man. He forked at some bacon with a green stick, slipped two more slices into the pan, and grabbed at his coffee pot just in time; it was beginning to drool over. "Squat. I got a good suppertime story to tell you while you eat."

"Yes?" said Barry. He unsaddled and was staking his horse out in a little flat not twenty steps from where the fire blazed when he called out, "What's this? What have you been doing here?"

There was a mound, freshly heaped dirt still moist on top of it, the prospector's short-handled shovel sticking in it. Timberline glanced over his shoulder.

"Oh, that. That's what my story was. I jus' finished buryin' a couple hombres."

Barry came to the creek and squatted down to wash his hands.

"Only two?" he grunted. "What did you do the rest of the day?"

"If you don't believe it," Timberline said, and sprayed his usual fragrant amber mist, "jus' scratch off a little dirt an' you'll find 'em. What's left of 'em, that is. The buzzards drawed me this way; them two had been dead more than one or two days. Injuns, I'd guess. Somebody had shot 'em."

"I've seen those two. Right here, Timber. Who killed them, do you suppose?"

"Likely they kilt one another. Anyhow I tucked 'em in. I happened this way 'cause I seen the buzzards. Now, mos' folk don't hanker much after them birdies; me, I sort of like 'em. I been used to 'em out on the desert. Kind of company, times. An' buzzards is always a good luck sign for me. Come ahead, Haveril. Got yore own eatin' tools with you, ain't you?"

Barry dried his hands on a new bandana he had bought in town.

"Laredo, maybe," he suggested. "Looks like Laredo to me. I've hoped to pick up his sign out this way somewhere."

"Nope," said the old man. "He'd not waste time an' ammunition on these greasers. I reckon he does kill just for fun, times he's bored with things goin' slow; but I wouldn't pin this on Laredo."

They ate and sipped strong black coffee. Barry said, setting his cup down and stirring it with Timberline's bacon stick, cooling it:

"You been gold hunting a pretty long time, Timber?"

"Ever since I was old enough to chaw terbaccy," said Timber, "an' I learned that real young."

"Look like a good prospect here?"

The old man snorted disgustedly. "You wouldn't get a show of color if you grubbed around here all your days. It's as unlikely a place as ever I see."

"Going to try it, long as you're here?"

"Nope. Soon's it's light enough to see I'm draggin' Arabella out o' here."

"Where for, Timber?"

He pointed. "Over yander, Haveril; acrost them mountains an' acrost the next ones. It's a hundred mile from here, where I'm headed for, mos'ly west, partly north."

Barry grew interested. "What do you know about mining, anyhow?" he demanded.

Timber stared at him, sniffed contemptuously and—Barry, seeing what was coming, jerked his coffee cup out of the way and dodged back.

"I know all there is to know, young feller. If there's gold around, me, I can smell it."

"Ever find any?"

"Shucks! A hundred times."

"What did you do with it all? Got it with you? Or got it buried?"

"Git funny with me, young feller, and I'll shoot yore eyes out! What did I do with it! What does a man do with gold? Spent it, darn yuh."

"Bought what with it? Arabella?"

Timberline finished his meal in silence—silence so far as speech went, though he made clucking sounds in his throat—got up, scraped out his pan, sloshed cold water in his coffee pot, and rolled into his blanket. Barry sat a while by the creek, looking at the black glow of it with the stars coming out to swim among the pools.

In the morning after breakfast, horse saddled and pack rolled, Barry said: "There's gold here, Timber. That's what those two men were up here for. I reckon Laredo found them with their pockets heavy." He climbed up into the saddle. "With them dead, buried by you, too, I guess it's yours now. So long, Timber."

The old man stared speechlessly after him, then darted down to the creek like a swallow. Barry rode slowly, climbing the mountain. From a point high above, he saw the old man waving his hat; he couldn't hear, but knew that Timberline was whooping to him, calling him back. It was a chill morning, but that warmed him. He waved his own hat and rode on.

He got to thinking of his own gold. Timberline would no doubt grub a while, glean enough of the bright metal to make him think longingly of the delights of town, then go hightailing back to Tyler or some other place, squander his gold dust and end up by getting robbed of his claim. One way or another, there'd soon be other men flashing their shovels and picks and pans throughout this wilderness.

So Barry stopped at his own creek and went soberly to work. Day after day he labored all day long with sand and gravel, washing his gold in a deep frying pan. Encountering one pocket after another during three consecutive days, each as rich as the one he had come upon the first day, he accepted his good fortune quite as a matter of course; he experienced the same satisfaction he would have felt on a hunting trip on coming into a good game country.

All this was merely by way of preparing for a long pursuit. If he was right that the Laredo Kid had come this way, well then doubtless the Kid had gone on ahead in the same general direction. Only you couldn't tell how far he might go, whether he'd turn back or press on into Arizona, California, Nevada. What Barry did know was that money, a thing to which he had given so little thought all his life, was needful to get a man over the ground swiftly.

He couldn't estimate how much gold he had, save by comparing the final heap of it roughly with that which he had taken with him to Tylersville. He said to himself, feeling a first touch of wonder, "Say! this is a lot of money!" He broke it down into half a dozen piles, each representing approximately the amount carried to the scales at the store. "Must be more than two thousand dollars already! That's more than I'm going to need. I'll get started tomorrow morning."

When he departed at daylight, still heading north and west, but beginning to swing a bit more westwardly, he carried his gold inside his bed roll.

Down in a long valley at the head of a vast, rippling, grassy plain—cow country, this was—he tarried at the boisterous little town of Five Springs. Here he got word of Laredo; at least he assumed it was Laredo. Some days before, a young man answering his description, three others of his stamp with him, had stormed into town from no one knew where, had paid his wild way in gold dust, had gotten into a brawl and had stormed out of Five Springs again, headed west. Barry followed on.

Whenever he heard of depredations, of lawlessness and cruelty and wanton killing—and these were not uncommon—he sought his Cousin Jesse in the neighborhood. But Cousin Jesse, as though he knew that unrelenting retribution rode tirelessly after him, still rode on, ever westward. So the weeks passed. And so came a third meeting with old Timberline. Barry, riding into the dusk of a lonely region of sandy hills and sage and gray green cactus, saw the bright light of a campfire and turned down into the hollow thinking there would be water there. Old Timberline, squatting on his heels over his frying pan, looked up.

"Supper's mos' ready," he said as he saw who it was. "Light down an' j'ine in."

"You're the easiest man to find I ever heard of, Timber," laughed Barry, and was surprised to discover how glad he was to see the old fellow.

"It's always easy findin' what yuh ain't lookin' for," said Timberline. He put in more bacon. "Reckon yuh'n me's sort of pardners ever since we met up."

"What about the mine back there in the mountains?" asked Barry as they ate and drank the strong black coffee.

"Shucks, that wasn't no mine; jus' gold sprinkled from hell to breakfas' in the sand an' gravel, an' too darn much work to git. I stuck a few days, washed out enough gold to buy me a new outfit an' come along."

Then Barry noted that Arabella was replaced by a stout, bandy-legged black horse. He asked what had happened to Arabella.

"Died on me," said Timber. "Leg all swole up. A feller comes by an' says a rattlesnake done it. Shucks. Mosquitos was bad that night; that was how it started."

"Go on with you, Timber! No mosquito—"

"In the night Arabella lost her temper an' was snappin' at 'em. I could hear the click o' her front teeth. Must of bit herself."

The two appointed no rendezvous, but as months went on Barry began to think that it was in the cards, as the old fellow insisted, that they were cut out to be partners. They met near the California-Arizona border line; they met up near Stanislaus; they met months later, when both had turned back to New Mexico. That was something more than three years after the beginning of this long pilgrimage in which Barry Haveril always sought his cousin, and Timberline sometimes sought gold.

Also this meeting came after Barry at last came up, all unexpectedly, with Lucy Blue, and at the same time with—was it the Laredo Kid?

VII

Both Barry Haveril and the home country back into which he rode had changed during three years. Barry was a good two inches taller; his was a sinewy slim figure, swaying gracefully in an accustomed saddle; he jingled spurs with the best; he used a revolver as though it were a part of his own body, as much so as his hand; and his steady keen dark eyes were the eyes of a man who had gone his solitary way even when he moved among other men, and who knew at first hand what privation and hardship and danger were. He had known that thirst that torments just before it kills; he had smelled burning powder; there was a tiny white scar, like a little new moon, on his jaw from a Mexican's knife cut. There were humor and kindness in those dark eyes of his, but there was also that sternness bred of the life he had led and of a stern purpose. His home country, his old mountains and high valleys and cascading waterfalls—had they been conscious entities as a man is—would have been hard beset to know him again.

Just so it was hard for Barry Haveril to recognize the once familiar high country through which he rode now. He came to a town of a thousand rip-roaring inhabitants in a valley he remembered as a haven for deer and small game. He passed on, and found that this was rapidly becoming cattle country; looking down into the lower lands he was always seeing herds, and occasional cowboys. His eyes clouded. He didn't like it. He felt that he could smell cows in the air, that the air grew tainted. He spurred on.

Within half a day's ride from the wild creek where he had found gold, he came upon the phenomenon of the mountains in labor, giving birth to a brawling, squalling, lusty raw brat of a town.

This was Red Rock when first Barry saw it one late summer noonday.

There was a road of sorts down in the valley, a single track with turn-out places to pass when teams met, and he saw wagons of all sorts— old Democrats, spring wagons, Studebakers, buckboards—crawling along it, the farthest looking no bigger nor livelier than squash bugs. The town was a clutter of shacks of raw green boards, of log cabins and lean-tos and some queer tent affairs like Indian wigwams translated into canvas. Everything was commotion and dust and excitement, with the hum of cross-cut saws, the thud of hammers and the raucous voices of impatient, sweating men.

Barry had headed back this way because, two months before, out in Nevada, he had heard a rumor of Jesse Conroy that made him believe that

Cousin Jesse had turned toward New Mexico before him. Here was a likely place to tarry and seek. So he rode down into Red Rock.

The first house built here was the place of Tinker Joe, and it was only a dugout; Tinker Joe had staked the first claim. The second building was naturally a saloon, a sort of crooked barn with dirt floor, crazy walls, planks for a bar, and unlimited, always augmented, bad whisky. Here men gathered and here first of all Barry Haveril quested.

Barry tarried twenty-four hours in this bedlam and was glad to get the noise of hammering and sawing and cursing out of his ears, the smell of the place out of his nostrils. The town nursed itself to sleep on its whisky bottle; Barry rode out of it while it still sprawled sleeping in the clean dawn. Tonight, he thought, he'd sleep in his old cabin, alone with the mountains he loved— unless it, too, had gone the headlong way of such places as Red Rock.

He began to see landmarks on every hand that he knew as well as he knew his own boots. But over the first ridge, looking down into Pleasant Valley, he encountered the unfamiliar again. What had been a bit of wild Eden remained Eden, but tamed. The waterfalls down the steeps, flaunting their spray like wind-blown manes of runaway white horses, were the same, and so were the noble old pines and the wide sweeps of grassy meadow; but with them the accustomed ceased. There were glimpses of a road down in the bottom lands; at a distance, mere specks, were grazing cows and horses; more guessed than seen through the dark green of a grove were the white walls of a building of some pretence. And down a winding trail, riding like a man in some sort of new-fangled riding habit, a girl with hair flying like the waving water-manes was the final note. Think of a girl up here! The vast domain that had belonged to deer and bear and mountain cat, to grouse and wild turkey—and to young Haveril—had been taken over by mankind with a vengeance.

The trail was steep and crooked, he high above, she far below. Almost as soon as he saw her he lost sight of her around a bend. His horse minced downward, sure-footed, with Barry leaning back in the saddle. He thought, "I'll pull out pretty soon and let her go by." Once he heard her horse's hoofs clanging against the rocks, though he could not see her. Then he did glimpse her at the exact instant when she pulled her horse in so sharply that it slid on four bunched feet. That was because three men had suddenly appeared before her in a little open place, the three abreast, blocking the way.

He saw her whirl and start back toward the valley. He heard a man's voice shouting; he saw one of the three forcing his horse after her; he saw the widening noose of the man's rope circling above his head—and heard the girl's scream. The noose flew through the air, sped unerringly. It settled about her upper body, drawing her arms down close to her sides. Had she not sharply reined her horse in she must have been dragged from her saddle.

Barry Haveril shot down that steep trail with all the speed of the merry mill-tails of hell. When he came up with the quartette, two men were down on foot, dragging the girl down with them. Barry, sliding his horse to a standstill close behind them, had his gun out while the dust puffs were rising from under his horse's hoofs and began shouting things really not meant for a girl's ears at all. The two men holding her were so utterly taken by surprise that they stood stupidly and gawked; the third, slightly behind them and thus nearest Barry, young and bleak-eyed, whipped out his gun and fired, and his first bullet struck Barry's saddle horn and whined off into the forest like an angry bee. His second bullet went almost straight down into the ground as he was toppling from the saddle, for Barry had fired as he saw the other's gun flash out, and found its target unerringly. The man dropped his weapon and pitched from his saddle into the trail whence he rolled down the sharp slope and lodged against a tree trunk.

The fallen man's horse, crazed with fear, bolted

down trail, stirrups flapping wildly, and crashed into the little knot, human and equine, blocking the way. In a moment of utmost confusion, with the girl almost breaking free, Barry saw the two men reaching for their guns. One of the two jammed the muzzle of his gun between her shoulders.

"You shoot, damn you, an' I shoot!" he called out.

"Call it a draw then, so you clear out," Barry retorted. "I can drop either one of you gents at the push-up of an eyebrow. If you want to fork saddle leather and get to hell out of here, get going fast."

"Give us a show to pick up Sarboe," said the man. The girl looked at Barry appealingly. She said, frightened, "Do what he asks."

"What's left of Sarboe may be of more use to you than it is to me," said Barry, and kept one eye shrewdly on the third man who he knew was itching for a chance to drop him. "Suppose you get going?"

Sarboe, looking white and sick and sullen, was helped by his companions into the saddle, and the three, with Sarboe swaying, rode down trail and at the first cluster of young pines were out of sight.

Barry really looked at the girl for the first time. Now, he had gone for something more than three years thinking that little Lucy Blue was the prettiest thing, the sheerly loveliest thing, that ever lived. Her one brief letter found at Lookout Point was in his pocket now, in a leather wallet he had long ago bought just to carry it. Lucy Blue had been divinity to him. And here was this girl—

His eyes were a mountaineer's eyes; they pierced great distances, they fed upon the glories of sunrise and sundown, upon ineffable blueness of mountain skies, upon the play of shade and sun among yellow aspen leaves, the black and green and silver of running waters, the vast sweep of plains, an enamel with the rich colors, blues and reds and yellows, of wild flowers. His eyes, since he was a mountain man, were truly windows of the soul—windows letting the beauty of light come in.

This girl with the wind-blown hair and violet-gray eyes and the lines of her that fitted into his ideals like a beloved one in a lover's arms, was the loveliest thing he had ever seen. At that instant Lucy Blue, like a little wistful, vanishing ghost, began fading out of his life.

She lifted her head. She looked at him, her eyes and his eyes talking together, and then she said:

"How can I ever—"

"You're beautiful!" said Barry.

Her face from white flamed red. So recently in danger from strangers handling her brutally, she quite naturally misunderstood his tribute which, be it conceded, was a bit over bold.

"Oh!" she said.

Her horse had started to run; its dragging reins had got underfoot and it had stopped, restive and uncertain yet waiting.

He watched her gather up the reins, making the horse step over, and swing lithely into the saddle. She started to ride away, then turned to him and found him sitting there motionless waiting for her to speak or to ride on, just as suited her.

"I do thank you!" she cried out then, unnerved. "You, one man against those three devils! And— and—"

"I'm going to see you again, you know," said Barry.

She pointed.

"I live down there. You can't see the house; it's hidden by the pines. Yes. You will come to see me."

She spurred off down the trail. He went on his way, headed for his lonely cabin and thinking of her.

Then at last he came into a country where nothing had changed. The still forests were as he had left them with now and then a glimpse of a deer or the russet brown of a lusty young gobbler. When down a long shadowy aisle among the pines he sighted his own place, something leaped up within him and took him by the throat. It was good to get back, to find things as they had always been and to be alone—

And then he saw a little trickle of bluish-gray

smoke making its thin wisp upward from his chimney! He rode up to the cabin and dismounted, throwing open the door violently, of a mood to give some interloping stranger a piece of his mind.

Squatting before his fireplace, busied with frying pan and coffee pot, was old Timberline.

"Howdy," said Timber, as though they'd parted yesterday. "Jus' in time for supper."

When Barry went straight to his bunk and threw himself down and laughed, and kept on laughing, Timberline could only suppose that he was drunk.

"Yuh're always trackin' me down, ain't you?" said Timberline.

"Whose cabin is this, anyhow?" demanded Barry.

"Mine. I found it. The man that made it must have left the country. There ain't been nobody livin' in it for more'n a year; yuh c'n tell by the way the brush has growed up. What yuh laughin' at, Hyena?"

Barry sat up and felt glad that he hadn't come back to a deserted cabin. It was good to see old Timber again. He said:

"I reckon we've got to be pardners whether we like it or not."

"We always was," said Timberline.

"Haven't found your gold mine yet?"

"Nope. Not yet, Kid. But I'm headed right this time." He waved a new long-handled fork Barry had never seen. "Over yander. About two hundred mile from here."

"They've found gold near Red Rock."

Timberline cackled derisively. "Them tinhorns would call Boot Hill a gold mine, gettin' gold out'n dead men's teeth. Me, Sundown, I want me my bonanza or nothin'."

"Pardners, huh, Timber?"

"Shore. Always was."

"Tomorrow morning I'll show you where the gold is."

Timberline looked unimpressed. "Scratch like a wild squirrel inside a boy's shirt, an' mebbe git a dollar a day?" he scoffed.

"About five hundred a day for me," said Barry. "You ought to do twice that."

Timber began lifting slices of brown crisp bacon from his pan.

"It don't happen to be back towards Red Rock, do it?"

"Yes. Why?"

"That's lucky," said Timber. "Yuh got to go to Red Rock anyhow tomorrow. That is, onless— Yuh didn't happen to see her today, did you?"

"Who?" said Barry.

"A real purty girl. Name of Lucy," said Timberline. "Got to know her purty good when I come through. She's had a sort of come-down in life since yuh seen her last. Look in at the Gold Nugget lunch counter. Yuh'll find her there. Ain't run up against Laredo yet in your travels, have yuh?"

They turned in early that night, turned out early in the morning. Barry thought, "Strange how things work out." Today he would see Lucy—but yesterday he had seen that other girl. It was he who made the fire for breakfast. He used a piece of paper to start the blaze, a piece of paper splitting along its creases from two years folded in his wallet. The wallet itself, a splendid affair in red leather which had cost him ten dollars, he threw into the fireplace. He no longer needed it.

Timberline now had a pack mule he called Alfred, and a spotted, blue-eyed vicious looking brute of a mustang named Heliotrope that he rode. After breakfast he and Barry rode off to Barry's creek.

"It's got to be good," said Timberline, when he crawled down out of the saddle. "Else I'll jus' skin off a few dollars an' mosey on. If I ain't here when yuh git back from Red Rock, yuh c'n figger I'm somewheres else. *Adios, compadre.*"

Barry, feeling queer about it all, rode on into Red Rock, looking for the Gold Nugget lunch counter. To see Lucy again after all this time— He thought, "We were just kids, both of us." And he thought further: "We didn't know each other; saw each other just one day. I'll bet she has forgotten all about me." That thought wouldn't have occurred to him twenty-four hours earlier; now he welcomed it.

Then he thought, "The Judge must have cracked up— Or did she run away and leave him?" It was hard to think of her brought down to this, running a lunch counter in a tough mining town. "Poor little devil," he thought compassionately.

Lucy, behind the counter, was cutting an apple pie when he came in. He stood there and stared. Lucy! Not Lucy Blue at all, his little sister Lucy!

"Barry!" she cried, and dropped pie and knife, and came running into his arms.

Her eyes were as he remembered, blue as forget-me-nots, and as sweet. She and Barry clung to each other. Then they sat down at a corner table, with their elbows on the oilcloth, and truly looked at each other.

"Tell me, Barry—"

"Tell me, Lucy—"

"Mama and papa—"

"Where are they?"

"And you!"

"And you!"

They fell to laughing, and tears gathered and spilled over in little Lucy's forget-me-not eyes, and Barry's eyes too were wetly bright.

Her husband, Zachary Blount, was dead; a horse had trampled him and pneumonia had carried him off. She had tried so hard not to be glad! For he had been a brute to little Lucy, and she had found him to be as crooked as a stake-and-rider fence. Zack Blount had it in him, perhaps, to be ruggedly honest; certainly he grew to be the opposite. That was due to the influence which came to dominate him, Judge Parker Blue.

"I found out so many things," said Lucy in a hushed voice, both her little hands hugging one of Barry's big brown ones. "Judge Blue—he is a terrible man, Barry. Nobody knows it; everyone thinks he's grand. But he is the worst man in the world."

They chattered for half an hour and didn't get said half the things they wanted to say, asking questions which went unanswered because other questions cut across. Barry rode back to see Timberline at the creek, promising to return the next day.

There were so many things to think about: Their father, mother and brother had moved on "west." Just where, Lucy did not know. She hadn't told him where the other Lucy was, Lucy Blue, because he hadn't even thought to ask. He had told her that their brother Robert was dead; he did not tell her that he had been murdered. It seemed to him that already Lucy had suffered enough; intuition told him of that hell that had been her life with a brute named Zachary Blount. Still he felt that all Lucy's hell was behind her;

there had been something shining in her eyes.

"Another man?" thought Barry. He was almost jealous about it. He thought grimly, "If there is, and if he isn't good to her, I'll kill him."

Arrived at the creek he found Timberline's two companions, Alfred and Heliotrope, browsing contentedly, but no Timberline. Barry lay on his back under a pine, looking up at the blue through the dark shellacked green, thinking about things, and most of all he thought of the girl who had caused him to burn Lucy Blue's letter.

Then Timberline came down through the brush.

"It's a bonanza, young feller!" shouted the old miner. "We're goin' to call her Sundown Mine, an' she's goin' to make us a coupla kings." He executed a sort of tap dance; he sailed his battered old hat skyward and shot at it with his old belt gun, missing it a mile. "Let's go get drunk," said Timberline.

Barry remained thoughtful. There was little Lucy in Red Rock running a lunch counter. Somewhere, "Out West" were his mother and father, their hands calloused, perhaps their hearts weary. There, too, was the girl of the trail; she looked like a million dollars, and Barry wanted gold nuggets for buttons on his shirt when he went to see her.

"Look here, Timber," he said soberly. "We're pardners. But I don't know as much about gold mining as a pig knows about a fiddle, and while you're a man who ought to know it all, all you do is jump around like a grasshopper in a hot skillet. Let's go get us a third pardner, some man that knows about making a mine pay, and that we can depend on, protecting you against my ignorance, protecting me against your damfoolishness."

Timberline promptly caught fire and exploded. He even clapped on his battered disreputable hat and started saddling. "Pardners, hell, you an' me!" he snorted indignantly. "I'd ruther had ol' Arabella for a sidekick." Barry sat under a pine and watched him and waited. Presently Timberline threw his rope, came over and sat down too, wolfed at his plug and began spraying misted amber.

"Shore," he said, mollified with never another word from Barry. "Shore, Sundown. Don't I know it? They's a young squirt name of March, Ken March, son of ol' Big Moments March, an' he knows sassafras from gumbo anyhow. He's a minin' engineer, born o' minin' daddy an' granddad, an' he's in town. I'll go git him."

"Grease the trail and slide," said Barry.

Timberline slid. Barry eased back under his pine and stretched out and looked at the sky. It was blue with a few fleecy clouds in it. He saw neither the sky nor the clouds, but through some necromancy of the moment, a pair of eyes. "If I storm in on her so soon," thought Barry, "she'll be sure to think I came to get thanked some more." And then he thought also: "If I don't show up, she'll think it's because I don't want to. And I'm not going to have her thinking that!"

He opened his roll, got out his razor and went briskly to work on the stubble on his face. He washed at the creek; he had an extra shirt and put it on. His hair was rather long, but men in these mountains didn't bother much with barbers, and he didn't want to waste time going all the way into Red Rock. He pulled on his hat, studied his reflection a moment in a still pool, shrugged and went for his horse.

When again through the pines he glimpsed the rather imposing house he turned straight down the slope toward it, approaching it by way of the barn and corrals. For the first time he saw the building clearly and fell to staring at it as he might have done if he had never seen anything like it. Yet it happened that he stared that way because he had seen a house very much like it! It was big and square, with walls gleaming white, with portico and columns—and with a bright bluebird blue trim to doors and windows.

He stopped his horse near the barn. A voice said, "Lookin' for somebody, stranger?"

Barry didn't turn. He just said crisply, "Whose place is this?"

"Judge Blue's, o' course," said the stable hand.

Of course! Then—

"There's a girl lives here," said Barry. "Who is she?"

"Why, Miss Lucy, o' course!"

"Judge at home?" asked Barry, and was glad to receive a prompt "No," in answer. So he asked next: "Miss Lucy? She's here, though?"

Yes, Miss Lucy was there. Barry left his horse at the stable and walked on to the house. As he mounted the steps to the front door he heard voices, first the voice of the girl of the trail, the sweetest of rippling music, and he called himself a fool for not remembering better; of course that was little Lucy Blue's voice. It, too, had changed a bit, but not as much as she herself had. If he had just heard that voice, now, this afternoon, and hadn't seen her at all—

Then he heard a man speaking, and Barry stiffened to a dead stop. This, he thought was a voice he would never forget, one that had something of arrogance in it even now at what he was swift to realize was a tender moment. For the man in there was making love to a pretty girl, and sounded in dead earnest—and there was not a doubt in Barry Haveril's mind that at last he had come up with Cousin Jesse, the long sought Laredo Kid.

Barry didn't even think of stopping to knock at a closed door. He simply threw it open and burst in upon the two people in the big living room.

VIII

The two sprang apart. Barry, his eyes blazing, cried hotly:

"Got you, Laredo! You—"

He broke short off, and the hand that had slid down to his gun rested there, fingers gripping but making no move to draw the weapon. He stared at the man facing him and fell into utter confusion.

He had been so sure of Jesse Conroy's voice— *but was this Cousin Jesse?* He could not for the life of him be sure. Had it not been for the voice he would have never looked twice at this man when seeking the Laredo Kid.

Almost as tall as Barry, and of Barry's supple slenderness, he was dark and wore a small black mustache that curled upward at the ends, and a tiny imperial, as black as ink. Handsome and devilish, he had a pair of fearless steady black eyes which stared insolently into Barry's. Dressed rather extravagantly for this part of the world, he was obviously one of fastidious tastes. He wore the finest and tallest of shiny black boots; he wore a clean white silk shirt and scarlet neckerchief; his dark trousers were ornately belted; a pair of showy gauntlets were in his left hand. He wore, as so many did, crossed belts;

the gun butts were ivory and silver-mounted.

The girl, flushed and indignant, broke the brief electrical silence.

"What do you mean by this sort of thing?" she demanded hotly. "What right have you to break into our house like this?"

Barry said, looking not at her at all, but steadily at her companion:

"You arc Jesse Conroy."

The other, whether Jesse Conroy or a stranger, laughed in his face, yet his eyes remained as watchful as a hawk's. Also his ungauntleted right hand, like Barry's, was on his gun. He said drawlingly:

"Just now you called me another name. Laredo Kid, wasn't it? Suppose you make up your mind."

"You are Jesse Conroy," said Barry. "You're the Laredo Kid."

The girl looked from one to another, to her companion only fleetingly to take swift stock of the faint smile upon his lips, to Barry searchingly, not knowing what to think.

"You are the man—" she began.

Barry nodded. "On the trail, yes. And you're Lucy?"

Up shot her brows at that.

"I am Lucy Blue, yes," she said quite coolly.

"Then we used to be friends," said Barry. "Friends for one short day anyhow. I am Barry

Haveril. It was three years ago, at Tylersville."

She gasped and her eyes opened wide. Then she studied him harder than ever.

"I—I wouldn't know you," she said slowly. "You have changed a great deal."

"Sometimes a few years make differences. I didn't know you either. And my cousin here, Jesse Conroy, has changed more than we have, I think. But I knew his voice—"

"Is that why you thought him your cousin?" At last she laughed a little, but even so there remained a tenseness in the room. "Well, I can tell you that you've made a mistake. This is Tom Haveril— Oh!" she exclaimed as she seemed to see light dawning. "That explains it! You are both Haverils, and if that Jesse Conroy was a cousin, all three of you must be related!"

"Tom Haveril?" said Barry frowning. "I never heard of any Tom Haveril."

"One of the Texas Haverils," came the answer, more drawling than ever. "I reckon you're one of the Panhandle branch?" A faint sneer made his lips contemptuous. Then he added, still further insulting, "If you're any Haveril at all!"

"Why, damn you!" cried Barry.

The other shrugged. His eyes dropped fleetingly to Barry's side.

"That gun you've got your grip on now," he said coolly. "I've heard of one like it; most everyone has. It's like the one they say the Laredo

Kid used to tote. For all I know, you might be Laredo yourself!"

Lucy drew farther away from Barry and, as though for protection, closer to the other man. Then, before Barry could answer, the man who now retaliated by naming him Laredo, added swiftly:

"Miss Blue was telling me how some men attacked her today; how a stranger, who seems to be you, appeared at the dramatic moment! Did you really shoot the chap who tumbled out of his saddle? Or was it just arranged to impress Miss Blue?"

Barry was saying to himself: "I'm right; it *is* Cousin Jesse!" But before the contemptuously drawling voice died away he grew uncertain again, admitting that Cousin Jesse didn't use to speak like this; Cousin Jesse would say laigs for legs, daid for dead, shore for sure, and all that sort of thing. Yet three years—

Barry said to the girl, "Anyhow you know I'm Barry Haveril, don't you, Miss Lucy?"

Lucy looked distressed; further, she looked alarmed and suspicious. She said: "I—I don't know! You don't look like Barry Haveril. It's not only that you're so much taller, older looking; your eyes don't look the way his did, you don't carry yourself the same."

"Haven't I told you that you've changed too?" he countered.

"If you should happen to be a Haveril," said the other man smilingly, "I suppose you know someone hereabouts who can vouch for you?"

"Why, of course!" exclaimed Barry. "My sister! You know her, too, Miss Lucy! You knew her in Tylersville; she has the same name as you. Lucy Haveril she was, then Lucy Blount."

"Oh!" exclaimed Lucy. "Of course I know her. She's my dearest friend. If—if you should really prove to be her brother, I'd be so happy!"

She used the word "prove" without thinking. But Barry caught the implication. Due to the shrewdness of this man, whether Laredo or Tom Haveril, he'd be damned if he knew, he was shoved into the position of proving who he was. Well, that shouldn't matter (though somehow it did). The vital question was: Who was this fellow anyhow—Laredo, whom he should shoot dead in his tracks, no difference in whose house and in whose presence found, or Tom Haveril?

A dull, baffled rage seethed within him: He *knew* this was Jesse, the Laredo Kid—only the sheer hell of it was that he *didn't* know!

"I'll be going now," he said slowly, and felt defeated. To the man he said, "If you're Cousin Jesse, and I think you are, then you're Laredo too, and I'm going to kill you." To Lucy he said queerly: "Remember the letter you left for me at Lookout Point three years ago? I kept it—"

"Oh!" said Lucy the second time, and now

eagerly extended her hand. "If you really did keep it—and I don't know why!—" but the color came flushing up in her cheeks again—"then—"

She was asking him to give it to her, and he could only mutter, cursing himself for having mentioned it: "I burned it—just after seeing you on the trail. You see—"

She stiffened and stepped back. As Barry turned and went out he heard her companion's quiet laughter.

He headed straight to Red Rock to see his sister and have her go out to Judge Blue's to talk to Lucy. Also he meant to learn what he could of "Tom Haveril." The first man he encountered was old Timberline, just starting back to camp.

Timber greeted him with enthusiasm, inspired, Barry suspected, by a drink or two. The old man said:

"I seen young Ken March, Sundown, an' it's all fixed. He was jus' lookin' aroun' for a chance like this. You see, he's a minin' man an' always was, but not like me. Minin' engin-eer, is what he says he is."

Barry said "Fine," rather absently, and started to ask his partner if he knew anything about Tom Haveril. But Timberline was full of his subject, if of nothing liquid and more potent, and hadn't finished. He had a lot to say about young Ken March. He was "loaded for bear" and was in the midst of his garrulity when Tom Haveril—or

Laredo?—rode up, headed into Red Rock. Barry reined his horse about sharply to block the road. Tom Haveril—or Laredo?—eyed him coolly, sat loosely in his saddle and said crisply:

"Well, stranger? What's on your mind this time? If you want trouble, just fill your hand."

Barry said quietly, "I want my friend Timberline to meet up with you. Know this gent, Timber?"

Old Timberline squinted narrowly at the darkly handsome face regarding him arrogantly.

"It's Tom Haveril, ain't it?" he said. "Seems I've seen him a time or two."

"You've seen the Laredo Kid, too, Timber. This fellow look anything like him?"

Old Timber scratched his head and sprayed. "Danged if I know!" he said in a troubled voice. "I never thought about it before. I'd say off-hand that he does, an' he don't!"

"Take a good look at him," Barry insisted. "Allowing for that new mustache and chin-whisker—"

"Well," said a thoughtful Timberline, "he does kind of look like Laredo. Not much more'n you do, though, Sundown."

Tom Haveril laughed and said, "I reckon that'll hold you, stranger," and rode on, Barry reluctantly letting him pass.

The old man's face puckered as though he were going to cry. "I wisht I knowed, Sundown!

I wisht I knowed. Look at him, the way he rides! That's jus' the way Laredo rode off from me that time, laughin' like that, too!"

"I think he is Laredo," returned Barry. "I've got to find out for sure."

He rode on. A few minutes later he saw the many yellow lights of Red Rock down below him, and heard Red Rock roistering. He thought: "I'm going to get Sister Lucy out of that place. She can keep house for Timber and me—when we get a house."

As he rode into town it was to the accompaniment of both music of a sort and of voices; an orchestra of violin, banjo and guitar made for added hilarity in the barn of a saloon, and men going up and down, most of them headed toward the music and the bar, had to call out greetings to friends as far as they could make them out. Barry passed through this to Lucy's lunch counter.

Lucy wasn't there, and her assistant didn't know where she was or when she was coming back. Yes, he had seen her go about an hour ago, but it was when he was at the back end of the place, near the stove, and she was standing near the door looking out. He thought someone had called her outside, that she'd just stepped out on the sidewalk for a minute. But she hadn't come back. N-o; he hadn't rightly seen anyone call her out; it was just that she sort of went like that. Where did she live? Back yonder a piece, with the Prices. Price was an old teamster, and Miss Lucy roomed at his place, being a friend of Mrs. Price's.

But Mrs. Price, sitting on her porch when Barry rode up, hadn't seen Lucy and wasn't expecting her; it wasn't time for her to be coming home. Mrs. Price couldn't understand her being away from the lunch counter; and there wasn't any place to go, that she could think of—not for a girl like Lucy Blount in a town like Red Rock.

Barry left word that he'd be back, and returned to the main street, making sure as he rode by the lunch counter that Lucy wasn't there. There was a long pole hitching rail in front of the saloon; he left his horse to companion the many other horses stamping or dozing, and went in. Before he left town he meant to learn something about the man who called himself Tom Haveril.

There were perhaps forty men in the place, yet almost instantly Barry's roving eye found Tom Haveril, and marked who it was with him. It was Judge Blue. The two at the far end of the long bar were slightly withdrawn from the rest of the crowd, full glasses set before them, while they spoke together. It was long since Barry had seen the Judge, yet those three years which had so altered others appeared to have missed him altogether. He was the same imposing figure Barry had first seen in Tylersville; there was not an added line about those bold leaf-brown eyes, and the old dominant carriage was the same—as were the broad dove-gray hat and glistening high boots and blue frock coat and striped trousers. Most of all a quality of sheer force which was about the man like an aura was unchanged.

Barry strode through the long room making a bee line to the two at the far end of the bar.

"Hello, Judge," he said quietly.

The Judge regarded him a moment without speaking, taking him in from head to foot. Then, "Do I know you?" he said. "Don't seem to place you."

"I hoped you'd remember me. I'm Barry Haveril. Three years ago, over at Tyler—"

"I remember that day. I remember Barry Haveril. Changed a lot, haven't you?"

"Not more than most folks around my age do in three years. I was just a kid then, I guess. I came into town with some gold dust. You sent me to the hardware store to get it weighed; then you had me up to your house on the hill."

The Judge's eyes bored into him. "And you— if it was you—walked out on me that night without a word!"

"There were reasons," said Barry.

The Judge nodded slowly, as though not to deny that any man might act with reason without necessarily stopping to explain. He gave the impression which he customarily gave, of being a fair-minded man.

"My daughter Lucy," he said presently, "was beset by some ruffians on the trail. If it was you who gave her a hand, I have you to thank. And if you can ever lead me to the ruffians—"

"One was called Sarboe," said Barry. "But I didn't come here to talk of this, and I don't want any thanks. But maybe you can tell me who this man is that you're drinking with?"

"Why," cried the Judge, and sounded heartier, "it's my friend Tom Haveril! By thunder! If you are Barry Haveril, you two might be related!"

"I'm not hunting any kinship," said Tom Haveril—or Laredo? And Barry said shortly:

"I think we are cousins, and that this is Jesse Conroy. They used to call him the Laredo Kid. *You'd know, Judge!*"

"I'd know Laredo?" said Judge Blue mildly.

"You saw him that night, didn't you? In the barn, when I went out to see who it was that owned a certain saddle and horse. I figured the man that outfit belonged to was the man who murdered my brother Robert. And it turned out to be Laredo. You saw him, didn't you?"

The man at the Judge's side said, never more drawlingly: "Look at his gun, Judge. Like one the Kid used to tote, isn't it? It's in my head that he arranged that attack on Lucy yesterday. It's in my head he's Laredo himself."

The Judge fell to frowning and plucking thoughtfully at his lower lip.

124

"You're a stranger here," he said to Barry. "Tom Haveril isn't. Many know him for one of our up-and-up young ranchers; many will step up and vouch for him even though he hasn't been here all his life. How about you? Who in hell can step up and tell us who you are?"

The up-and-up young rancher spoke swiftly:

"He says Lucy Blount is his sister. He says she can tell us."

"Well then," exclaimed the Judge, and sounded hearty once more. "Let's step over and see Lucy Blount! Anything she says goes with me. Come ahead, boys—"

"She isn't at the lunch counter right now," said Barry.

The Judge looked astonished. "No? That's funny; she's always there this time of night; I usually run in, pretending it's coffee I want when I'm in town. Where is she?"

"I don't know," said Barry. Then he let his hand down to his side, close to his gun. For it flashed on him that he was in some sort of trap. He just said, "And she's not over at Mrs. Price's. They don't know where she is."

The Judge looked at him a moment, then downed his drink without a word. He moved as though to leave the room, turning his back on Barry. Barry, grown watchful, noted that every man in the room was looking his way. He saw, too, a sudden tightening of muscles about their

125

eyes and knew, just when it seemed too late to do anything about it, that the Judge had flashed them some sort of signal, and that they had understood. Evidently they had been half way expecting some-thing of the sort.

The Judge's voice boomed out sonorously:

"Watch him, boys! It's my bet and it's Tom Haveril's that he's the Laredo Kid! Don't kill him unless you have to—but don't let him get away!"

Barry sprang back, to get the wall behind him, and snapped his gun out of its holster. But as he did so he saw the lamplight glisten on some two score other guns, and every unwavering barrel was turned upon him.

IX

"Go slow, Laredo, if that's who you are!" called the Judge, resonant and commanding. "Make a wrong move and you're dead forty times! Steady does it, and you've got a chance."

Barry did not stir hand or foot, or any muscle. From where he stood he could see every man in the room.

"You boys can get me if you want to," he said steadily, "but I'm betting drinks for the crowd that I'll get two of you, and that's twice as many as you'll get of me—and those two will be the Judge and the man who says he's Tom Haveril."

"If you're the Laredo Kid," said the Judge sternly, "you won't last until morning. If you're Barry Haveril, no one's going to lift a hand against you."

"I'm Barry Haveril and not Laredo," said Barry.

"These are fair men," said the Judge. "Strangers to you? Well then, they've got nothing against you. They'll give you a fair trial; I'll see that they do."

Barry thought, "All I want is a fair trial. Will I get it?" He saw that the many men watching him were the type to be expected here; they were all hard or they wouldn't have lasted to get to Red Rock, and some of them were harder than hard. Among them there would be friends of Judge Blue, friends of the cool, contemptuous Tom Haveril leaning against the bar.

He said drily: "I don't hanker to peg out tonight. You see, boys, I've got a couple of jobs I'd like first to finish. One is to nail a certain hombre's hide to my barn door—and I haven't got any barn yet!—Now keep inside your shirts! I'll have the barn and a few other things when I get through with my second job: that's to develop a gold mine that's been waiting for me more than two years."

"You're doing a lot of talking," said the Judge.

Barry thought: "He's already got this meeting by the throat! That's what he's good at. That's how he got him his title, making himself judge over a lynching."

He said, and not even the elegant Tom Haveril was ever more drawling: "Give me a fair trial, with every one of these men in on it, and I'm with you."

A headlong fellow standing close to the Judge shouted: "Listen to him! He'll tell the whole room full of us what he'll do or won't do!"

"You're damn right, stranger," Barry shot back at him swiftly. "If you don't like it, why just fill your hand and start things!"

"Go slow, you hot-heads!" roared the Judge. "This is going to be orderly or I walk out on you, and there'll be more than one man killed, and you'll never know the right of it." He nodded approvingly at Barry. "I like your talk, young man, and I'm here to see you get a square deal. Shed your gun, and we'll handle things according to Hoyle."

"Like hell, I will," said Barry mildly.

Some laughed and some growled and some simply stared; feet shuffled and even the Judge didn't know what to say.

"I'll take mine standing up," said Barry. "Right where I am, and with my hand filled. Take it or leave it."

A young fellow, big and blond, came shouldering forward.

"He's right and he's playing his hand straight out," he announced in a profoundly deep bass voice. "Until we find out the rights of it, I'm chipping in on his side."

"Better go slow, Ken," said Tom Haveril, speaking up for the first time. Barry didn't miss the thinly veiled threat nor did he fail to catch the name, "Ken." This blond young giant then might be Ken March, the new partner whom old Timber was taking on.

"Why should I go slow, Tom?" demanded Ken March. "I've already said I like the way this lone wolf plays his hand. Then," and a slow, good-humored grin played across his heavy features, "there's something else. You heard him say he's got his pick into a mine? Well, I believe it, and what's more, maybe he and I are pardners!" He turned to Barry. "You're the fellow Timberline told me about?"

"That's so," nodded Barry, regarding Ken March narrowly and feeling inclined to approve of him.

"You haven't asked me to chip in," said March, "and from the look of you, you're not given to yelling for help. Just the same it seems you're a stranger here—and I'd be glad to line up along-side the Judge in seeing you get a square deal."

Instantly Barry made up his mind. He grinned back at March.

"Thanks—pardner," was all that he said.

Then, having at the top of his mind the thought that the Judge was overweeningly the great influence here and that the Judge could be bought for gold, he recklessly played a high card, win or lose. He suddenly shoved his gun back into its holsters, ignored the many guns trained on him and stepped to the bar. From his pocket he jerked the small buckskin bag containing the major part of his golden gleanings of two years ago; he poured the little dully gleaming heap out on the bar.

"There's more where that came from, boys," he called out cheerily. "No reason we should all go dry; step up; it's on me."

"If he's Laredo—why, damn him!" someone shouted.

"It's a funny thing," drawled Barry, "but no gent has actually stepped up and said I'm Laredo. You haven't, have you, friend?" The man muttered and subsided. Barry called to the Judge, "You haven't said I'm Laredo, have you, Judge?"

The Judge answered slowly: "No. I said I had a notion you might be."

Barry swung toward Tom Haveril. "How about you?" he demanded. "Naming me Laredo?"

The answer came deliberately. "You accused me of being that yellow-bellied rattlesnake, and all these men know I'm not. Then I took a good look at you. You're toting Laredo's gun. You look like Laredo to me. That's all I know."

Barry laughed and called again: "Step up, gents. Name your poison. Does it look like I had enough here to pay for a round or two?"

Thus he strove to center their interest on his gold, knowing well enough that in any case a few hours would spread talk of it. But Tom Haveril, still leaning lazily against the bar, was single-purposed. He said:

"A while ago you said you had a sister here, Lucy Blount, and that she could settle this."

"Why, so she can!" cried Barry.

"*Bueno*," nodded Tom Haveril. He glanced about the room. "Suppose a committee of you boys goes and puts it up to her? I reckon we'll all take her word."

131

Ken March looked at Barry, and Barry nodded. But he had to add: "The only trouble is that I don't know where she is. She doesn't seem to be anywhere in town."

March's brows came down in a frown; plainly his thought was the same as voiced by some man saying with a laugh, "Not in town, huh? Where'n hell would she be this time o' day then? Out in the hills visitin' with the timber wolves?"

Another man spoke up sharply. "I seen her just a little while ago, when it was hardly more'n dark. She *was* ridin' out o' town. A couple o' boys was with her. One of 'em was Dick Longo, that Johnny-come-lately that's been ridin' with Sarboe."

Sarboe! The name rang bells in Barry's brain, and thoughts clicked away like mad. Sarboe, one of the gang that had attacked Lucy Blue! Tom Haveril had tacitly accused Barry of setting those wolves on her; if Tom Haveril *were* Laredo, what more likely than that he himself had been at the bottom of the thing? What next? Tom Haveril—*Laredo, damn him!*—had heard Barry say that Lucy Blount was the one person here who could identify him!

"This damnfool trial is postponed," Barry shouted aloud. "If you want me I won't be hard to find. If you think you can stop me now, try it! I'm on my way to find Lucy Blount."

For once in his life Judge Blue was uncertain. He started to speak, then held his peace. A swift glance passed between him and Tom Haveril; the younger man permitted a shadowy smile to touch his lips, then shrugged.

"Here, you're forgetting your gold!" called Ken March.

"Scoop it up for me—pardner," Barry called back. "Or let it lie. There's plenty more."

"I'm coming with you if you want me," said March almost hesitantly.

"Why, that's fine!" cried Barry heartily.

The two, shoulders all but brushing, stalked through the crowd that fell aside to right and left for them. Ken March called back to them: "I left enough of Sundown Haveril's dust on the bar for your drinks." Then, as he and Barry came out to the horses, he said curiously: "I've got into the way of thinking Tom Haveril a friend of mine. I caught a look on his face just now— Friends with Tom Haveril? I'm not so sure!"

Barry stopped and looked at him thoughtfully.

"Hard to be sure of a man, isn't it?" he said.

"A man's never sure—"

"Just what I was thinking! Now, if I could only make out whether you are a man to tie to, or—"

"Why, damn you!" roared out Ken March and

glared at him and swung on his heel, going straight back into the saloon.

Barry went straight to his horse. "A man gets where he's going all the faster when he rides alone," he grunted to himself, but was nonetheless piqued at March's loss; he had thought he was going to like that fellow. It was only after he had swung up into the saddle that he thought, "Huh, he forgot to fork over my gold." Well, that was nothing.

He rode up and down the street, asking every man he met if he had seen Lucy Blount that night. He found three who said that they had, and each bore out the tale told by the man in the saloon; each of them said that they had seen her riding out of town with two men. One of his informers didn't know who either of the men was. One said, "She was with Ike Pennel and another hombre." One said, "Sure I saw her; she was with Longo and Pennel." All agreed that the trio had ridden hard, as though in a hurry to get somewhere, and that they had taken the North Road. And all that anyone could say of the North Road was that it was the continuation of Red Rock's one street, leading up into the mountains to the new mines—and forking off into a hundred trails on both sides.

Barry looked ahead gloomily into the heart of the mountain district, thinking of the countless small valleys and cañons and dense copses wherein a cabin might lie hidden while a man sought it within a few yards. As he pondered he rode slowly, striking into the North Road.

He came to the first clearly defined off-shooting trail, all but passing it in the dark. He stopped a moment, shook his head and rode slowly on. He came to the next, stopped again. He knew then that he had entered on a hopeless task; worse than that, it was a fool's errand. He was simply rushing hotheadedly into the impossible. A star slid down the sky. His eyes followed it absently until it was gone.

He had scarcely sat there pondering five minutes when he heard a furious pounding of hoofs, and a rider came racing out of Red Rock. Whoever it was, this man rode in the wildest haste. As he came close and then shot by, Barry saw what was more like a black shadow blurred than a horse and rider.

"Now, who the devil's that?" he wondered. Someone headed on an errand similar to Barry's, someone looking for Lucy—or going to Lucy, knowing where she was? Tom Haveril, perhaps?

The one way to find out was to follow, if follow he could without losing the other in the dark or being discovered by him. He glanced back toward the little town; no one else rode this way. He looked again after the speeding horseman just in time to catch a glimpse of him swerving around a bend in the road. Barry dipped his spurs and sped after him.

For perhaps three or four miles Barry had no trouble in following his quarry, but he kept telling himself, "Sooner or later he's bound to turn out of the road, and then if I don't look sharp I'm going to lose him." But as it chanced, even when the man ahead did forsake the road for a side trail, Barry was not for an instant thrown off the track, for this occurred almost at the top of a long steep pull, and Barry from a hollow below saw the dark form when it swerved off to the left. Coming himself to that place he saw a well-defined track leading windingly among the pines; pausing a moment to listen he heard the hammering of hoofs, fainter now on dead pine needles, a muffled thudding swiftly growing dim. He swung into the narrow way and spurred on.

He forced his horse at a run up a steep hill, came for a moment into a clear space among the pines and of a sudden saw a light ahead.

It was but a dim yellowish glow, and he lost it almost as soon as he saw it, but he knew it for the window of a cabin lighted by a lamp or candle. There was no longer any danger of losing the man he had followed. He saw him scurry across a little clearing, riding up to a cabin squatting on the mountain side under a cliff. He heard startled voices, a rapping at the door and voices again, sharper now.

"What the hell?" somebody shouted from within.

The answering voice gave Barry Haveril a distinct start. Why, this was not Tom Haveril at all! It was the booming voice of Ken March saying commandingly:

"Open up, Longo! Hell's to pay in town. Open up, damn you!"

There was a brief silence. Barry rode on, slowly now, out into the clearing. If the man at the door, Ken March, turned his head, he would be sure to see. But he did not turn. Again someone spoke, Longo no doubt, and March answered and the door swung open. For a second Barry saw the wanly lit room, then the door slammed shut—

And then, when he was almost at the door himself, he heard a roar of rage—that was Ken March's thunderous voice for none to mistake!—and after that inarticulate roar there came the crash of pistol shots. It sounded to Barry like the gunfire of a dozen men.

He hit the ground running, threw the door open and burst into the room, gun in hand. He saw in that one photographic instant a place of feeble light festooned in powder smoke, with Ken March against one wall, firing as fast as he could pull trigger, with two men he recognized from yesterday on the trail, Longo and Pennel no doubt, against another wall, pumping hot lead at March—with Sarboe on a bunk, propped up, blazing away at March—with Lucy crouching in a corner.

"I'm with you, Ken!" roared Barry, and cut down on both Pennel and Longo.

With five men fighting in a room not above fifteen feet square, the thing was of necessity over almost as soon as it started. Of them all Barry, the latest comer, was the slightest wounded, taking a bullet grazingly along his outer thigh while a second carried his hat off his head. Longo, a look of consternation in his bleak eyes, let his arms fall to his sides, let his guns slip from his lax fingers, half-pivoted slowly and melted down to lie prone. Sarboe lay writhing on the bunk. Pennel started to run to the window, turned to fire again, dropped his gun and screamed and tried again to get through the window, in the end hanging there grotesquely like a limp bundle of rags. And Ken March, standing a moment against the wall, with both arms out as though crucified, finally simply sat down and rolled over and lay still.

Lucy, shaking pitifully and as white as death, her eyes enormous with horror, stood straight up and swayed a little and at first could not speak. Then she cried chokingly, *"Barry!"* And then she ran and went down on her knees over Ken March, and put her arms about him, calling desperately, "Oh, Ken! Dear, dear Ken! Look at me, Ken!" And Barry understood that it had been a man who had put that shining look in her eyes when he had first found her again, and that that man was Ken March.

"Ken's going to be all right, Lucy," he said as one who knew that also. "He's too good a man for these polecats to kill."

They were still trying to find all Ken March's wounds, to see which were the worst, when again a rattle of hoof beats rang out. Barry, swiftly reloading his gun, stepped outside; at what he saw he muttered under his breath, "If they're friends, fine; if not, we're done for." For here came at least a score of riders.

They were Red Rock men who had followed Ken March when with sudden inspiration he had stormed out of the saloon, calling back to them where he was going. At their fore rode Judge
Blue and Tom Haveril.

"What's going on here?" demanded the Judge, peering at Barry through the dark. "What's happened?"

"A good deal has happened. We've got Lucy back, but I'm afraid Ken is pretty bad hurt."

There was a hasty dismounting as men pressed forward to the door. First of all out of the saddle, first by a long leap into the cabin, was Tom Haveril. Barry, watching him at every step, saw that Tom Haveril's bold black eyes darted to Sarboe, Pennel and Longo before they took fleeting stock of either Ken March or Lucy.

By this time Ken March, in great pain yet fully conscious, was propped up against the wall, and Lucy's strong young arms were supporting him. As some of the men looked down at him he tried to tell what had happened; Lucy finished the tale for him. She told how two of the men, Pennel and Longo, had tricked her out of town, using an ancient and infallible ruse, making her think that Ken March had been shot.

Men looked at one another, then at the three who had fought it out with Barry and Ken March.

"We got plenty rope with us," said one drily. Another, a young fellow looking white about the mouth, burst out: "My God, Bill! They're near dead now; Longo hangin' there in the winder is dead, looks like! You couldn't—"

"We must somehow get Ken to the doctor right away!" cried Lucy. "He is terribly hurt."

Ken March said that if they'd bandage him up a bit to stop the blood, and would hoist him into his saddle, he could ride all right. They carried him outside; Lucy ran and gave Barry a frantic little hug, then hurried along after Ken.

Someone called from just outside, near a corner of the cabin: "Here's a good tree. We want another rope."

Longo "hangin' there in the winder" was dead,

yet they hanged him up by the neck just the same. Pennel was dying, dying fast, too, yet he kicked his life out alongside Dick Longo's limp, gently swaying body. As for Sarboe, as they dragged him out of the bunk and toward the door, he fell to screaming with terror, begging for his life.

Barry Haveril did not enjoy looking at all this; still he did look. He watched Sarboe's face, hung on his words as men dragged him out to the tree already bearing its dead fruits, a noble old pine that towered serenely over all these men, dead or alive.

Sarboe screamed: "Save me! You save me, Tom!"

Tom Haveril struck him in the face. But Sarboe screamed the louder and a new note got into his voice, like the snarl of a coyote, and Barry heard his words bubbling out:

"I'll talk! I'll tell—"

Barry leaped forward, shouting: "Let Sarboe talk! Give him a show to tell what he knows. There's somebody else in this—"

A man dropped a noose over Sarboe's head; it was Tom Haveril's hand that jerked it tight, stopping short Sarboe's words and his breath along with them, making of a sudden his face a purplish congested horror.

"Damn you, Tom Haveril!" shouted Barry, and tried to break through the men surrounding

Sarboe. But he could never make it in time. A dozen hands were on the rope and Sarboe swung, kicked and clawed along with Dick Longo.

Tom Haveril shouldered his way to where Barry stood.

"Sounded like you said something to me," he said.

"Looks to me like you were in an almighty hurry to shut Sarboe's mouth," said Barry hotly.

Tom Haveril thrust his face so close that Barry could see the expression of his eyes. They were bright with triumph and hard with some determination. And in their hard brightness was something of sheer devilish mockery.

"Wonder what Sarboe might have had to say?" he drawled. "Anyhow he won't do any talking now; none of this bunch of scorpions will. Too bad, huh, Sundown?"

He turned away, laughing. Barry caught him savagely by the arm.

"Sundown, am I? Who taught you to call me that—Cousin Jesse?"

"Didn't you tell us back there in town that you were a Sundown Haveril?" Tom Haveril shook his arm free and went on his way to his horse. He was still laughing as he swung up into the saddle. And beside stiffening Longo, Sarboe and Pennel were still twitching.

Men took their departures. Some of them, the younger men, were in an almost scrambling haste to get away from this place, to rush back to a warm room and lights and companionship and heady liquor. Last of all to go was Barry Haveril. A man called to him asking if he was hurt much; did he need any help. "I'm all right," said Barry.

He was so deliberate that by the time he had toed into the stirrup he was the only man left here. He stood a moment with one foot up, one on the ground. Then he pulled his boot back out of the stirrup.

The cabin was dark; someone had taken the trouble to blow out the light. The door was still open; Barry looked at it curiously It seemed to invite.

"Now, I wonder—" he mused.

He tied his horse again, made sure that none of the departing riders was hanging back, then went into the cabin.

X

There was but the one window; he hung a blanket over it before he struck a match. The lamp stood on a shelf; as he lighted it and looked about him his shoulders twitched involuntarily: the place reeked like a slaughter pen and there was a feeling of unquiet ghosts in the air.

"Best get it over with in a hurry," he thought distastefully. "And I reckon I'm a fool for hoping to find anything."

To look here for something, he knew not exactly what, was one of those darting inspirations which come to men, the sort of things we call hunches. Some day maybe we'll know what a "hunch" is.

He had long known that the Judge feared Laredo, that Laredo "had something" on the Judge. He suspected that Tom Haveril and Laredo were one; that there was something between Tom Haveril and the three men now dangling from the big tree; that this hideout was therefore a place that might have been used by Tom Haveril him-self. Surely Tom Haveril had shut Sarboe's mouth! Surely Sarboe had wanted to talk. Well then? It was just possible that there might be something left here that would aid Barry Haveril in seeing through a smoke screen.

There was a faint breeze stirring; he had closed the door but the blanket puffed in and out over the window. In so still a house it caught his attention. He thought how the night wind was just rising now, how later it would set the three bodies swaying rhythmically out under the pine.

With scant hope of finding anything, still he began ransacking the place. He pulled the blankets off the bunks and shook them out, then tossed them into a heap on the floor. He peered under the bunks; they were low, close to the floor, so he tried to drag them from their places. One came freely; nothing under it but foul scraps. The other was nailed to the wall. He gave it a powerful wrench and succeeded with it. Nothing there, of course.

He went to the shelves, scattered the articles, looked among them; he looked up at the rafters. He turned to the door. With his hand on the latch he stopped. The blanket over the window, seeming to move stealthily now, was not what held him. He was of no mood to let graveyard fancies haunt him; he was asking himself of a sudden: "Why was that bunk nailed down? Didn't need to be." He stared at the two benches. As far as he could see they were just alike, rough-and-ready affairs slung together the easiest way, planks nailed together and mattressed with tips of pine boughs. Each stood on four sturdy legs, sawed-off sections of young tree trunks. "Just alike. One's nailed to the wall, the other free. Why?"

So it was to the bunk that had been nailed in place that he returned. He tried to pull up the floor boards in the space it had covered; they were down solid and it would require some tool to remove them. He regarded the portion of wall that had been behind the bunk; he noted how a short section of log had been slipped in. He began working at that short section. When it came free in his hands he found a hollowed space in the wall; his groping fingers came in contact with a small box of some sort; it was of iron or steel, a slight flat thing a man could have shoved into his pocket.

Once there had been a lock on it, but the lock had long ago been broken or shot off. Barry opened it; it looked to contain papers. He stepped closer to the lamp. There were papers or some-thing of the sort, wrapped in a newspaper. The newspaper looked old; he noted that it was the Laredo *Blade*, dated twelve years ago.

What it contained turned out to be an amazing number of photographs; he thought there must be hundreds of them. The first picture he looked at was of a little girl, perhaps six or eight years old. The next was the same girl; the picture might have been taken the same day. Another of the same little girl—another and another. He flipped over to the last of all. It was Lucy Blue.

The one next to it was Lucy Blue. So was the next. And the next—

Lucy smiled at him, Lucy looked at him thoughtfully, Lucy coquetted with him in a hundred garbs and poses. Lucy in riding habit, Lucy mounted, Lucy riding full tilt, Lucy about to toe into stirrup, Lucy in swimming suit, Lucy in dress for fancy ball, Lucy in high boots and big sombrero. Lucy when she was younger than when he had first seen her, Lucy as he saw her yesterday.

Barry Haveril pulled off his hat. Perhaps because he was so overwhelmingly in the presence of Lucy Blue, perhaps to scratch his head—

That damned blanket-curtain over the window kept stirring, breathing like a live thing—a screen to shut ghosts out—or to keep them in here along with him? He jerked his head up to stare toward the window. The blanket at a lower corner had been shoved aside. Barry saw a face wanly lit up by the pale lamplight. It was the dead face of dead Sarboe.

For a second he felt ice in his blood. Sarboe's eyes protruded, his tongue came out horribly and ran along his white lips, his mouth writhed as though a dead man would talk—but there came not so much as a dry whisper of sound.

Barry was standing with his hat clutched in one hand, the thin flat steel box in the other, when

147

he heard the door open. That everyday sound brought him back in a flash to an everyday world. As he dropped hat and box together, as he jerked his gun from its holster, the door was flung open. He saw Tom Haveril confronting him, a gun in his hand.

They shouted at each other at the same split second, and as they spoke, they fired. There was no missing at a distance like that. Still standing, both beginning to sway, smoke filling the small room and flashes of flame stabbing through the smoke, each man of them emptied a six-gun.

As Tom Haveril slumped down and then fell forward across the doorsill Barry sagged against the wall and crashed to the floor. The spinning world went black and empty for both men.

XI

Tom Haveril, never before so flashily dressed, with tiny black mustache and imperial trimmed to a hair, rode jauntily up to Judge Blue's mountain home. Lucy Blue heard his horse's hoof beats and was on the porch to meet him. He ran up the steps to her, catching her two hands in his gauntleted ones. Lucy laughed and after a tussle broke free.

"But Tom! Remember you're scarcely out of the hospital!"

"Call that place a hospital?" laughed Tom Haveril, and tried to recapture her. His face was still white from some seven weeks of being shut up in a room, the first few weeks of which the doctor said he had one chance in a hundred.

Lucy must have been expecting him. She wore a pretty new dress which left her lovely arms bare, and there was a little cluster of blue field flowers at her breast, one solitary flower like a blue star in her high-piled hair.

"Lucy!" he said. "You—you drive a man crazy!"

"Do I?" laughed Lucy.

"If you don't marry me now," he said, all eagerness, "right away—"

"Then what?" teased Lucy.

"I'll steal you! I'll grab you off your feet, throw

you across my saddle, and gallop off with you."

"Won't you come in, Mr. Haveril?" invited Lucy demurely.

They went together into the big living room, and Lucy tamed him in a time-honored fashion, eluding him when he grew reckless, singing to him over her guitar, provocative and—uncertain. She didn't quite know.

"I wish I knew!" she cried suddenly, breaking off with a sweep of fingers across the strings. "What did happen to him?"

"Who?" demanded Tom Haveril.

"The man who shot you. And what about that other man?" She shuddered. "The one that was hanged—Sarboe. Why did someone carry him off, a dead man?"

A frown caught his brows up in a dark cloud. He, too, wished that he could come at the answer to that last question of hers! Then he smiled.

"If some crazy fool wanted to go out there and snatch the bodies of a couple of dead men, what of it?" he demanded. Then he added briskly: "I didn't come out here to talk about that, Lucy. I'm well, now. I'm going back up to my place. How about coming along?"

Lucy wanted him to ask her—but she wished that she didn't have to answer. Not now. She was always postponing it, always about to slip into his arms and whisper, "Yes, Tom!" yet eternally withholding that yes, always praying for something to happen to postpone the moment.

And always it seemed that prayer of hers was answered. Certainly it was now. Tom Haveril had been with her but a few minutes, and the trail had seemed clear when he rode through the pines to the white, blue-trimmed house, but before Lucy had to answer with more than a flush and a dimple or two, here into the yard came someone riding hot-haste. It was a man she didn't know, a young fellow who looked and rode like one of the Judge's many cowboys. He came running up the steps, clanking his big-roweled spurs. When she hurried to the door Tom Haveril was just behind her, looking over her shoulder.

"Hello, Bendy," he called sharply. "What's up?"

"I want to talk to you," said Bendy excitedly.

"Well then, talk! I said, what's up?"

"It's about Sarboe!"

"Sarboe! He's been dead nearly two months!"

"Jake sent me. He seen two men back up in the hills, beyond Cool Crick. He says one was Sarboe. The other was the feller that shot you— that you said you shot down. Jake says—"

"Never mind!" said Tom Haveril shortly. "I'll come out and talk with you. Back off and wait." To Lucy he said, looking puzzled: "I'd better find out what this is all about. Those two, if they're alive and are ganging up—"

"Yes!" cried Lucy. "Go and find out. See Jake. And let me know—"

He hurried off; she saw him talk earnestly with the messenger, then go to his horse. The two rode away. She turned back into the house.

She felt strangely excited. Sarboe alive! And that other man—Barry Haveril! She knew that he was really Barry Haveril, because the other Lucy, Lucy Blount, had told her, "It's Barry, my brother." She remembered him so vividly well, how when just a boy he had stopped at her father's house, how she had seen the Judge strike him down, how she had gone to his room to warn him, to urge him to flee. For a full year, for nearly two, she had even fancied herself in love with him! She, sixteen, falling in love! Then handsome Tom Haveril had come—

And after all she knew nothing about Barry Haveril. He well might be the desperado that both the Judge and Tom Haveril proclaimed him, he with that darkly saturnine face of his, those black piercing eyes, that freebooter's carriage of his whole body.

And yet—she thrilled strangely at the thought: "He's alive!"

The late afternoon merged gracefully into dusk. She strummed her guitar absently, she hummed a few of the haunting old airs; abruptly she put both instrument and music aside and went impatiently out to the porch, down the steps, out among the brooding pines. She saw the Judge come home, riding hard; she caught a glimpse of his face and so did not call out to him, he looked so worried, so ready to fly into anger. He swore at the stable hand who took his horse; he went striding in a sort of savage way to the house. Lucy sighed and curled up in the hammock in the grove of young pines.

She saw Andrew close the stable doors, and presently a light, like a little earthbound star, winked out from the loft where he had his room. The black boy who presided over the kitchen came out on the stoop, rattled a pan and went in, slamming the door.

A rider came up through the pines, and Lucy sat erect, thinking it was Tom Haveril returned already. When she made out that it was a stranger on a white horse, she lay back in her hammock. The man went to the house, knocked, was invited in by the Judge, speaking brusquely. The two were in the Judge's study for ten or fifteen minutes. Lucy drifted far from them, wondering about so many things.

The door opened, a bright rectangle in the night that had fully come, and she saw the stranger and the Judge together. The Judge clapped the other man on the shoulder. He said jovially, "Fine, Joe, I knew I could count on you. So long, and ride happy."

Joe went down the steps and along the path toward his white horse down by the barn. The door closed. Lucy thought that her father had gone inside until suddenly his bulky figure loomed up blackly on the path. He was stealthily following Joe.

There was a light in the kitchen window; a stray beam struck in such fashion on something in the Judge's hand as to make it gleam. Again she sat up, fascinated though she did not altogether know why. Then she heard the shot. And she saw the ugly spit of fire from the Judge's hand. The stranger, Joe, did a half spin and crumpled in the path. He had turned as he heard steps behind him; he had fallen shot just beneath the heart.

If ever there was cold blooded murder, she knew that this was. "Fine, Joe. I knew I could count on you. So long, and ride happy." And then a shot to the heart.

She all but fainted, cowering in her hammock. She heard two more shots fired; they didn't sound like the first, were from another gun. Still she lay powerless to stir.

But when Samson came running out from the kitchen, and Andrew came clattering down from his loft, and other ranch hands gathered—they came ominously, strangely, she thought, like wide black wings out of a clear and empty sky when death occurs—she forced herself to slip out of her hidden place and to stand up and even to hurry around the house, out of sight and to her room.

She threw herself face down on her bed; she wished that she were dead. Would she ever understand ever so little this man, Judge Parker Blue? A shudder shook her from curly head to slippered feet. Had she been articulate then she would have cried out in her desperation: "He is my father and I love him—and I fear and hate him! He is my father, and so I am a part of him, like him, the same somehow as he is! And he is a murderer! I saw him creep up behind Barry Haveril long ago and hit him over the head; I heard him talking with the Laredo Kid, the robber and thief and killer—and Laredo said some day he would come back and marry me—when I was eighteen! And I'm over eighteen now— And he—my father—is a murderer, and the friend of a bandit, and is afraid of Laredo because Laredo knows of other crimes he has committed. My own father!"

When after a while Tom Haveril came riding back she heard him, but she did not get up from her bed. She heard the Judge, as hearty as ever, greet him at the door.

"Come in, Tom; come ahead in. We're a bit upset here. A drunk fool, Joe Hosmer it was, came out making trouble. Shot at me twice; nearly got me. I had to blaze back at him. Wanted to wing him; damn it, killed him."

Tom Haveril's answer escaped her. She wasn't sure that he laughed. Later she assured herself she had imagined that, she with her jangled nerves; a man *couldn't* laugh at such a thing, couldn't make a mockery of it as Tom Haveril had seemed to do. The two men were walking toward the Judge's study; she heard the door slam.

But she could not overhear what was said behind that heavy closed door. Tom Haveril sat on the corner of the Judge's table, his leg swinging so that at first he looked casual and careless. But the expression of his narrowed eyes, as hard now as black agate, was anything but inconsequential. The Judge, once their eyes met, stiffened in his chair.

"So you thought you better kill him, huh, Judge?" said Tom Haveril.

"Self-defence," said the Judge, and reached for tobacco.

"Sure," said Tom Haveril, and shrugged. He caught his knee up between his clasped hands and put his head back and looked at the Judge through almost closed eyelids; his rather long black lashes made inky shadows on his pale face. "I'm telling you something, Judge," he said drawlingly. "All hell's loose on the range."

Blue's bushy brows jerked upward. "What hell on whose range?" he demanded.

"Sarboe's alive. We saw him shot to death and then strung up. He's alive."

"That means nothing to me," said the Judge, and rested easier in his chair, preparing to smoke.

"It means a hell of a lot more than you know! You want to know on whose range hell has busted

156

loose and I'm telling you—on mine! Something else has happened that is none of your damn business! Now, get this: I am going to marry Lucy —*and I am going to marry her tonight!*"

"Like merry hell you are!" snorted Judge Blue.

"I've fooled with you long enough, Judge," said Tom Haveril, as cold as ice. "More'n four years now, I reckon. Well, I'm at the end of the tie-rope right now. I marry Lucy tonight—or you're just a hunk of barbecue meat."

He came down from the table like a mountain cat, landing neatly on his nicely booted toes. The Judge surged up from his chair, his face purplish red—

When Lucy heard Tom Haveril calling to her softly from the living room she went to him. First she called, "I'm coming, Tom; just a minute." Then she bathed her face and brushed her hair and looked for a little while at her eyes in the mirror; she hoped he wouldn't see the look in them.

When she came slowly into the room lighted by two coal oil lamps, so that there were shadows everywhere and less of true light than a mere thinning of the dark, he chanced first of all upon the few simple words which at the time could most of all avail him. He said quite simply:

"Lucy, I love you so!"

"Do you, Tom?" she returned softly, wonderingly. For his words as he spoke them were almost like mothering arms about her, gathering her comfortingly close.

"You know I do, Lucy. And I want you to marry me now, right now. I want you to come away with me, to my place. Will you, Lucy?"

The Judge came in and said, "Ha! What's going on here?" And then he laughed genially—quite as though he had never killed a man in his life.

"He—he wants me to marry him—right away!" gasped Lucy.

"I thought I saw it coming," said the Judge. He came to her to put his fatherly arms about her; she shrank back and ran headlong to her room. But she laughed back at them when they knocked at her door—hysterically, and they thought that they understood a girl's laughing like that, and after a while she said, without opening the door: "Yes, Tom. I'll marry you tonight—if you will take me right straight to your place."

"I'm off for the preacher!" shouted Tom Haveril joyously. Then she heard him and the Judge walk away together.

She looked again at herself in her mirror. Her face was as white as death, yet seemed to grow whiter. Then all of a sudden it flamed red. Her eyes were like the eyes of a sleepwalker.

And Barry Haveril, miles away in a secret and hidden glen in the mountains, was thinking of Lucy and of the Judge and of Tom Haveril as he saddled and made ready to return and take up his active part in the world of the living, returning like a man from the greatest beyond. He had been very near death, he had lain like Tom Haveril near death for weeks. But they were hard killing, men like the Haverils.

He called and Sarboe came shuffling from the place they had used a shelter, a rock-bound hollow under beetling cliffs, with a brushy growth in front like a wall.

"I can't wait any longer, Sarboe," said Barry. "I've got to see my sister and Timberline and Ken March, and let them know I'm alive. And there's someone else—"

He was thinking of Lucy Blue. Sarboe naturally supposed he spoke of Tom Haveril.

"Come with me, Sarboe? Or waiting here?"

Sarboe answered with a grimace and a shake of the head. Barry had got into the way of reading the meaning of Sarboe's slightest gesture. That was because Sarboe had not spoken a single word during the weeks they had spent together up here in the solitudes. He wanted to speak, he was anxious to speak—his anxiety was such that at times the swollen veins in his forehead stood out like purple cords under the skin; but from the time he had been dragged out under the pine where Pennel and Longo swung, he had not spoken a single word. That was because he could not.

What had caused this loss of voice, Barry did not know. Perhaps the grip of the rope about his throat when he had been left there hanging, with the fear of death, death's certainty rather, worse than a tight rope about his heart? From the way Sarboe mouthed, twisting his lips fearfully and sputtering and catching his breath, and from the wild look in his eyes, Barry judged that the explanation might lie elsewhere. Sarboe was like a man who stuttered not through any physical impediment but because of something in his brain. He had been dragged away to be hanged when he was pleading so hard to speak! He had wanted to say something, hoping to save his life by saying it. His last thought as they swung him clear of the ground was, "I've got to talk!" And as he swung, perhaps his thought was, "I'll never say another word." Certainly he had not said a word since then.

That he had lived through the experience was understandable enough; his gestures showed Barry how it was. They had thought that he was mortally wounded when in fact he was but little hurt. He had managed to smear blood all over his face from a mere scratch of a wound on his jaw; he had been doubled up on his bunk with both hands at his middle making others think as he thought himself, that a bullet had gone through his abdomen. A bullet had struck there, but had been deflected by the big silver Mexican buckle

at his belt; besides gouging him superficially, it had done no damage. As things turned out, it had saved his life. For men trussing him up to swing had thought him already as good as dead, had taken no care to bind his hands; and as he began choking, he also began clawing his way to liberty.

Barry rode alone, but he called back, "I'll come back, Sarboe, or I'll send for you." For had it not been for Sarboe, Barry must have bled to death that night nearly two months ago on the floor of the lonely cabin. Sarboe, seeing both Barry and Tom Haveril drop under a rain of bullets, at first thought them both dead. He found a flicker of life in Barry; hating Tom Haveril with a young, green and terrible hate, he had elected to do what he could for Barry through an impulsive gratitude. He had managed to heave the unconscious man up across a saddle and, afraid of death himself were he discovered, had borne him away to this place which only Sarboe knew. He had labored hard over a man who surely must have died otherwise; he had saved a life for once instead of spilling it out, and as Barry grew stronger, Sarboe became almost his dog.

Of all this Barry was thinking as he rode down a winding deer trail. But soon his thoughts shot on ahead. He wondered if anyone had ever gone back to the cabin? Surely someone had, some of the younger men the very next dawn no doubt, to look awesomely upon the gruesome work of

their hands. They would have found Pennel and Longo, swinging dead; they would have found dead Tom Haveril. And they must have wondered not to have found Sarboe, and must have asked since, "And what became of Barry Haveril?" Timberline and Lucy Blount and Ken March would have wondered too.

So first of all he rode straight to the spot where he hoped to come on old Timberline, from whom he might get news before showing himself in Red Rock. He made this first excursion of his in the late afternoon, starting a little before sunset, wishing to come to Timberline in the early dark and not to be chance-seen by others until he had the lay of the land.

So it was long after dark when he came upon, not Timberline alone, but with him both Barry's sister Lucy and Ken March. It was not much of a coincidence that they were talking about him when he appeared so suddenly before them. For all these weeks they had talked of little else, save of the new log house building here and of developing Barry's mine. They had learned, as had all this mountain country, that dead Sarboe had mysteriously vanished; that Barry Haveril had vanished, too, after coming close to killing Tom Haveril—after having been shot to death, as Tom Haveril swore. Tonight they spoke of Barry, and Lucy, her pretty blue eyes wet, spoke too, both in sorrow and in anger, of the other Lucy.

"I think that poor Barry loved her," said Lucy. "And for a while I thought that Lucy Blue loved him."

"Hell's bells an' turpentine," muttered Timberline, and glared angrily. "You folks make me sick. You're always talkin' about my pardner like he was dead. He ain't."

"But Timber, dear—"

"Don't call me 'dear,' Miss Lucy," snapped old Timber, "an' then go on in the nex' breath sayin' what Barry *was* an' *used ter be*. Dead men don't git up an' walk, do they?"

The place in which they found themselves was the largest log cabin in the mountains. It remained unfinished within and without, a rambling skeleton of logs, roofed over here and there, still open to sun and stars in most places. It was to be the headquarters of the Baron Haveril Mines, with living quarters, rooms for Timberline, second owner, for Ken March, third owner and general manager, for Lucy Blount, housekeeper and general ornament—and for Barry "when he comes home." Already Ken March had a score of men at work, housed down in Red Rock.

There was in this big room a fireplace; Timberline sprayed tobacco juice in its general direction, pulled on his ragged old hat at an insolent angle and stalked out; the two left alone looked at each other and smiled understandingly. Then Lucy sighed again and said unhappily:

163

"And so she is marrying Tom Haveril tonight! After he k—after he tried to kill Barry!" Her eyes suddenly hardened. "I hope she'll suffer for it as long as she lives!" she broke out passionately.

They heard the shuffling of Timber's departing boots, his tuneless old voice raised in a song all his own, consisting mostly of, "Ti de di, te-di, te-daddle." They smiled at each other again.

"He *is* an old dear," said Lucy, "and if Lucy Blue had only loved Barry half as much as he does— Listen to him, Ken, singing to keep his blessed old heart up—or just to make us think he isn't worried!"

The next they heard of old Timberline was some ten minutes later. They heard his voice sounding casual and unconcerned, talking with someone in an off-hand chatty sort of way. Footsteps came on to the house and up the puncheon steps, Timberline's voice running smoothly on; they thought he might be talking with Juan, the Mexican cook. As he pulled the door open he was saying,

"—an' the beans, I keep tellin' 'em, is full o' weazels, an' if you could of saw the sow-belly we got las' time. You know, pardner, I been thinkin' of puttin' up a store m'self, right out here, an' startin' in teamin' an' afore I got through I'd have a town, an'—"

The door open, Timberline still talking, Lucy and Ken March saw who it was with him, and for a moment neither could stir or speak. Then Lucy fairly screamed, "Barry!" and bore down upon him like an altogether lovely young avalanche.

"Shucks, I tol' you Barry wasn't dead," said a scornful Timberline, rather brightly and suspiciously unmoved.

They talked for half an hour, at times all four of them at once, there was so much to be said all round. Lucy wanted to tell Barry about Lucy Blue; there is an explosive quality about news good or bad that makes it so hard for its human container to hold it in; but she thought that she knew how it was with Barry and didn't want to hurt him. It was Ken March who chanced to open the subject. He brought it up by saying,

"Tom Haveril didn't die, either, you know, Barry, he—"

"He's not Tom Haveril," said Barry. "He is Jesse Conroy. He is the Laredo Kid. I know now."

Ken March scowled. "It's going to be merry hell for Lucy Blue then," he said. Barry's brows shot up. What about Lucy Blue?

So his sister Lucy, with her arms around his neck, told him after all.

"They're getting married tonight, Barry. Tom Haveril and Lucy. I—Lucy sent a man over late, after dark, asking us over. I—I guess they're married by now."

Barry sat staring at her like a man carved out of stone and decorated with black jewels for eyes.

"Tonight? Now? Lucy marrying Laredo? Good God!"

"But, Barry—"

He flung her arms away and jumped up. "When? Where? Tell me all about it!" he shouted, his voice rough with anger.

Lucy started telling, but he did not wait for it all. He learned that the ceremony was set for tonight, as soon as the preacher could be brought to Judge Blue's house. As he ran down the steps to his horse, old Timberline went out on the porch, looking after him. He returned thoughtfully worrying a plug of tobacco. Pocketing that fragment which he had failed to pouch, one cheek bulging until it glistened, he spoke his mind.

"I'll go git me my hat," said Timber. "Likewise a horse an' Juan's new-fangled shotgun. If Barry says Tom Haveril's Laredo, why Laredo he is. An' I'm not goin' to stan' for Barry, pardner as he is, nor for no other man to take Laredo apart. Not after what Laredo done to me!"

He snatched up his hat and departed. Lucy burst out hysterically:

"Tomatoes! Oh, Ken; do you hear him? Laredo spilled Timber's tomatoes!"

From the outer dark came a sort of coyoteish yip from Timber. His words were:

"He'll wish he hadn't ever saw a tomato!"

XII

Barry never rode harder than now, rushing along dim trails to come to the Judge's house before it was too late. He was going to put a stop to that marriage though he had to shoot Lucy Blue's scoundrel of a lover dead before her eyes. To think of Lucy Blue about to give herself to Tom Haveril—Jesse Conroy—Laredo!—was like seeing her standing on the edge of a crumbling precipice. Lucy, so purely sweet, so brightly lovely, like a flower whose satiny petals had never been smirched—to come into the arms of a man like Laredo!

"Laredo—and Judge Parker Blue! The two damnedest cutthroats in the world—and little Lucy Blue at their mercy! Oh, no, you don't, you two! Your hides are just as good as stretching in the sun—and Lucy belongs to me. She always did!"

When from the ridge back of the Judge's place he caught glimpses of many lights winking through the pines, his heart leaped up. He thought, "I am in plenty of time." Still he sped on, demanding of his horse all the speed in it, and presently he thought apprehensively: "Maybe I'm too late! Maybe they're just merrymaking— after the wedding. Well, I'm going to kill him.

She'll be widowed before she knows rightly that she's been married. And, Judge Blue, damn you—you, too—"

He dashed through the pines behind the barn, swept headlong around the corral, plucked his horse to a slide and stop at the steps of the house, flinging himself to the porch before his horse stopped sliding. And now his apprehension was greater than ever; he had seen no tethered horses outside, and the barn was dark, and he heard no sounds of music and light laughter and dancing feet. The house, though lamps seemed lighted in all the rooms, was strangely still.

He hammered impatiently at the door, found it unlocked and flung it open without waiting. As he stepped in he saw Judge Blue coming from another room, looking startled.

"Barry Haveril!" exclaimed the Judge. "So you're alive after all!"

"What's all this I hear about Lucy getting married tonight?" demanded Barry.

"What about it?" retorted the Judge.

"She's not to marry that devil, do you hear me?"

Those clear leaf-brown eyes of the Judge, so clear and bright and steady and piercing, regarded him with no hint of emotion in them.

"Have it your way," said the Judge. "She's not to marry him."

That puzzled Barry. He said, "What the devil do you mean? Why do you talk like that?"

"She's married him already. A good hour ago."

"You're lying to me!"

"Take it kind of hard, don't you, Kid?"

"Married already?" Barry stared at him incredulously. The Judge merely nodded and looked back at him in frank curious interest. "An hour ago?" The Judge nodded. "Where is she now?"

"Gone." He added, with a flick of malice, "On their honeymoon."

"Damn you!" cried Barry.

"Certainly," smiled the Judge. Then his voice hardened and at last his eyes grew expressive of a purely murderous anger. "And now you can get the hell out of here!"

Barry shook his head. "No, not yet. Pretty soon, Judge. First I am going to tell you something. After that you are going to tell me where they have gone."

"You are going to tell me something?"

"I know that you came to Tylersville about twelve years ago," said Barry, "and that you were a rich man when you got there."

"Yes?"

"I know that you came from Laredo, and that you came on the jump!"

The Judge's eyes were no longer leaf-brown clear pools; they became mere shadowed slits between narrowed lids. He didn't make any retort this time; he simply waited.

"The Laredo Kid too came from Laredo,"

said Barry coolly. "When he found you again at Tylers, he found a gold mine! You have been afraid of him ever since. And I happen to know why, Judge Blue!"

"You're a damn liar," said the Judge.

Barry laughed at him, but his was not pleasant laughter.

"The Kid has made a ring-tailed baboon out of you, old fox that you think you are!" he jeered. "You lost something, didn't you? A flat steel box with about five hundred pictures in it! And the pictures nicely wrapped up in an old newspaper, more than a dozen years old now! *And you thought, damned old jackass that you are, that Laredo still had all that!* Well, he hasn't got it, and he doesn't know where it is—and you've let him browbeat you into stealing Lucy!"

Slowly as the Judge's jaws bulged, his face whitened.

"You'd better spill all you know, Kid," he said harshly.

"I've got that box and everything in it," snapped Barry. "I got it the night your damned Tom Haveril and I shot it out and both went down. So he has made you let him marry Lucy in a hurry, before you could find out—"

"If you've got that, Barry," said the Judge, eying him, "I'll give you fifty thousand dollars—"

"You'd give the shirt off your back, damn you!

170

Now, where's Lucy? Where's the man you let her marry?"

"I'm going out and kill him," said Judge Blue. "And I'm going right now."

"You'll kill nobody tonight—"

The Judge's eyes were just then the cruelest, wickedest eyes Barry Haveril had ever stared into. The Judge said quietly:

"I've already killed one man tonight, Haveril. Just a little runt who didn't know everything, but did smell out an inkling of the truth, who came skunking to my door tonight. They carted his body off to town shortly before the wedding. I killed him in self-defence, you know! Having dropped him, do you think I am going to stop at him?"

"Where did they go, Judge?"

"I'm riding alone tonight, Kid," said the Judge. "I'm going to knock at the door; he will open up, his hand on his gun as he says, 'Who's there?' He'll see me and he'll say, 'Come in.' That will be my chance. I'll stick a gun into him, right under his heart—I'll give him a minute to know what it's all about—"

Barry caught him by the shoulder. "I'm in a hurry, man! Do you think I want to wait? Look here, Parker Blue; I've got that box and all that's in it; I've got you over a rain barrel, like Laredo used to have you! And I say: *Where are they now?*"

The Judge glared at him, then shrugged. "After all, why not?" he said as though communing with himself. "But I want to be in on this! Suppose he had the luck and killed you? It's an even break. Then he'd have Lucy—"

"Damn you!" roared Barry. "Where did they go?"

"I'll go with you," said the Judge. "Wait for me out at the barn. If we take the short cut we can come up with them before they've much more than got there."

He jerked free and ran back into his study. Barry frowned after him, then turned and went thoughtfully to his horse. He had never thought to ride with Judge Blue, hunting down Tom Haveril. But, as the Judge had said, why not? It was necessary tonight to make sure.

Barry heard him hurrying through the house, calling out some sharp command as he went. A voice answered, "Yas suh, ya-as suh!" and then the kitchen door slammed and Samson went running to the barn, calling out to Andrew from the first jump. When the Judge rejoined Barry his horse was saddled and ready for him.

"He's taken her to his ranch," said the Judge as their two horses jumped under them.

"I don't even know where it is."

"They drove in my buckboard; I let him have my span of sorrels. They'll make lively time, but we'll cut across the ridges; we'll make it in

172

two hours, two and a half anyhow. Hello, who's there?"

Another rider, seeming in haste like themselves, was bearing down on them. Old Timberline's voice piped up: "Hi, you fellers! One of you Barry Haveril?"

"I'm in a hurry, Timber," said Barry, pulling down reluctantly. "What's wanted?"

"Where you goin', Barry? Who's that with you?"

"It's Judge Blue. We're riding over to Tom Haveril's ranch. He— Damn him, he has taken Lucy over there."

"An' you two was goin' without me," muttered Timber reproachfully. He waved the shotgun he was carrying across the saddle in front of him. "Ain't forgot, have you, Barry, how it was my feud an' Laredo's long afore your time?"

"Come ahead then," said Barry, and again he and the Judge shook out their reins. Timberline drove his heels into his own mount's ribs and fell in behind; above the thudding of the hoofs Barry heard him mutter contentedly, "You're danged right I'm comin'."

Their way led them through the notch just above Red Rock, along the high ridge and down into the first of several parallel valleys. The Judge led the way and, though Barry was forced to follow, he could find little fault with the pace that was set. Timberline, doing his best to keep up, began to lag, then to yell at them to wait. They paid him not the slightest heed, and presently failed either to see or hear anything of him.

A sort of madness seethed in Barry Haveril's blood. It seemed to him that they would never come to the end of that ride. Tom Haveril's ranch—how far was it anyhow?

At long last he saw a dim light, far away, looking far below them.

"That's the place," said the Judge over his shoulder. "It's the ranch house. We'll be down there in no time now."

"You think they've got there ahead of us?"

"Sure they have, or there wouldn't be a light. But it won't be long until we run in on them."

All this while Barry had followed because he did not know the way. Now he spurred by the Judge, done with following any man on an errand like this! All this time he had been obsessed by visions which tortured him, Tom Haveril taking Lucy "home"; Tom Haveril's arm about her as they went up the ranch house steps; Tom Haveril —Laredo, damn him! carrying her in his arms across the threshold—

But when they got down into the valley the Judge easily rode abreast of him because his horse was fresh and Barry's was not; and when they came under the cottonwoods in the shade of which the ranch house had been built, the Judge was ahead again. He had dismounted when Barry came up with him.

"You're a hot-head, damn you," said the Judge sternly. "You're over young, so you're a damned fool. Leave this to me!"

"I'll leave it to no man!"

"How'll you get in? The door will be locked. Yell at him that you're Barry Haveril come to burn him down, and what'll happen? He'll keep the door locked, won't he? And he'll pour lead out at you through a window. Keep inside your shirt. This is my play."

He went straightforwardly up the steps, his spurs jingling, his high boots thumping. He knocked at the door and called jovially:

"Hey, you young folks! It's the Judge, bringing you a wedding present he ought to have thought of sooner. Open up, Tom. Open, Lucy."

If Tom Haveril had ever heard the expression, "I fear the Greeks bearing gifts!" he would have quoted it then. As it was his voice rang out sharply, demanding, "Who's with you?"

"One of the boys. He's helping me tote your surprise, Tom."

The door opened only a little; the Judge's bulk thrust it farther back as he shoved on in. And close behind him came Barry.

In the bare ranch house room were only Tom Haveril and his new bride. Incredibly quick, Tom Haveril placed himself behind Lucy. His hat was off, he was coatless, his right hand sped the familiar way to his gun while his left arm about the girl held her tight in a snug embrace.

"I thought so!" he said in cold anger. "You and Barry Haveril, huh?"

When the Judge laughed, "It's nothing, Tom; just a friendly visit," Lucy came near fainting with cold horror. So short a time before, in the same jovial tone, he had remarked: "Fine, Joe. I knew I could count on you. So long, and ride happy!" and then had killed him.

"Tom!" screamed Lucy. "They've come to kill you! They're killers, both of them! Cowardly killers!"

"Why, Lucy!" exclaimed the Judge.

"I saw you!" she cried back at him. "I heard you tell Joe Hosmer good-night—and slap him on the back! I saw you follow him. I saw you kill him!"

"Sure," said Tom Haveril. "Sure." His gun was in his hand now, nosing past Lucy's waist; his eyes, burning with rage and hate, gleamed over Lucy's curly head. "Think you can fool me, Judge? Well, I guess you don't want Lucy killed, do you? Not yet! And you, Cousin Barry? Kind of sweet on her yourself, ain't you? Want to start shooting now—or postpone it again?"

"You cowardly rat!" Barry roared out at him. "Step out like a man. You must have *some* Haveril blood in you. Let's see the color of it!"

"No!" screamed Lucy, and threw an arm backward, trying to get it around Tom Haveril. "No,

176

Tom! They'll kill you. They are the cowards—"

He just laughed, but he remained as watchful as a tiger about to pounce.

"Looks like a draw, don't it, Judge," he said coolly. And then he added, drawling out the words as though he had all night for a casual remark: "Ever notice, Judge, how I always have an ace in the hole? Well, I got a couple of 'em this time. Think about that and go slow."

"Put a name to it," snapped the Judge, his eyes as watchful as Tom Haveril's, watchful for trickery as well as the chance for a snap shot if his enemy showed a vulnerable inch from behind the girl.

Tom Haveril's glance, flamelike, licked back and forth between the two men threatening him.

"You two come at me in double harness," he said. "That means you've got together about things, don't it?" He laughed again. "I can see through a hole if it's big enough," he jeered. "When Cousin Barry and I last met up, he had a flat iron box in his hands, Judge. Next day when they found me out there, he was gone and so was Sarboe—and so was the box. So Cousin Barry got away with it, did he? And he runs yipping to you about it!"

The Judge nodded grimly. "Fire ahead," he said.

"What he got," said Tom Haveril, "was a lot of pictures and an old Laredo newspaper! I guess he told you that? Well, that's a loss that might lose you a nice pot of money, but it wouldn't stretch your neck, would it? *Might* lose you the money, I said—but wouldn't if you played along with me! String your chips with Barry Haveril, and where are you?"

Barry saw the old familiar mockery once more brightening the handsome devil's eyes; he saw too Lucy's lovely eyes distended with alarm. The Judge, whatever he saw or thought, said merely:

"You started out like you were going to speak quite a piece, Tom. Bogged down, though, didn't you? I don't hear anything that makes much sense."

"You're listening for it though!" jeered Tom Haveril, and sounded triumphant. "Your ears are wide open, and you're beginning to think already that you came pretty close making a bad mistake! Well, you did. Barry got those things— but he didn't get the ace I have in the hole. You bet I've still got it. And if you had the bad luck to burn me down tonight—well, it would be just too bad for Judge Parker Blue, formerly of Laredo! You'd hang, just as sure as crab apples grow on a crab apple tree."

"You talk big, Tom Haveril, and ever did," scoffed the Judge, but sounded uneasy.

"You've got nothing to gain here tonight, Judge," said Tom Haveril swiftly, "and everything to lose. I might get killed—Lucy might get killed—*and where would you be?*"

Right there Barry knew that Tom Haveril had as good as won the trick.

The Judge cleared his throat. He said gravely, "Here, let's talk this thing over." He shoved his gun back into its holster; he said in that tone of his which implied that he counted confidently on being agreed with: "Suppose you two mountain cats stick your guns away for this time? As Tom just said, we don't want Lucy hurt. Also, if the three of us get down to cases we might fix things up."

"Sure," said Tom Haveril. "How about it, Cousin Barry? Want to call the party off for this time?"

"I've been looking for you more than two years, Laredo," said Barry angrily. "I've followed you all the way out to California and back. Come into the open and fight it out."

"On my wedding night?" grinned Tom Haveril, and exulted as the fiery flood of rage rose in Barry's tanned face.

"Lucy!" pleaded Barry. "Don't let these two men trick you. As much as anything else I was coming to you tonight to tell you—"

"Let me have a half dozen words alone with Tom Haveril," put in the Judge swiftly. "We'll step into the next room. You can tell Lucy whatever you want to. All right, Tom?"

Without the least hesitation Tom Haveril answered: "Anything you say, Judge. Sure it's all right with me. Suit you, Sundown?"

Lucy cried out, frightened, terribly mystified: "No! No, Tom, they are tricking you! And there is something here I don't understand—it's all so— Oh, I don't know! Like walking on quicksand."

A look flashed from Tom Haveril to Judge Blue. Barry, keyed up to such a notch that he would have heard a pin drop or have seen the quiver of a shadow, could not fail to see it. And he read it aright. Tom Haveril, ensconced behind Lucy, was simply making sure that the Judge would keep out of it; if the Judge nodded ever so slightly, if his guarded eyes said, "Yes," Tom Haveril was hair-trigger set to start shooting. He could not have failed to kill Barry, nor could Barry possibly have fired back.

It was just then, not a second too soon, that they were given brief warning of interruption. A board creaked—not in this room, but in the room beyond it, which happened to be the kitchen—as a door opened from behind Tom Haveril's back.

Barry, fascinated, watched the door open; he saw the barrel of a shotgun thrust into the lamplight; he saw old Timberline's shrewd eyes squinting along the barrel.

"I been listenin' a coupla minutes," said Timber acidly. "Seems like it was about time a man with a shotgun showed up. Am I right, pardner?"

"If you're wrong no man was ever right!"

cried Barry. "Now, you listen to me, Tom Haveril!"

Tom Haveril's lean jaws bulged from the strain he set on them, and his eyes glittered feverishly out of a slowly whitening face.

"Any man who shoots is sure to kill Lucy," he said quickly.

"Hell, no," said Timberline, and the boards creaked again as he came a step nearer. "I c'n shove the muzzle close up to the back o' your head, snugglin' it up, say, under your left ear—"

"Call him off, Sundown!" yelled Tom Haveril. "Quick, or I start shooting— And I'll get you if I die the next minute!"

Barry was tempted then to shout to his old friend, "Blow his damn' head off, Timber!" But Lucy had spun about and her arms were around Tom Haveril, and her two hands were lifted to protect the back of his head. So what Barry said was,

"Hold it, Timber! These two want a word or two together. Let them have it, out in the kitchen! Kill the first one that bats an eye. And I'll have two words here with Lucy!"

The Judge then spoke up. "Call it a draw for tonight, then, Barry?"

"Yes—damn you!" snapped Barry.

"Don't listen to them, Tom!" expostulated Lucy. "They're trying to trick you. They are murderers, both of them."

"Keep steady, Lucy," commanded Tom Haveril, and jammed his gun back into its holster. "You're giving me your word on this, Sundown?" Barry nodded somberly. Tom Haveril turned then, looking along Timberline's shotgun barrel and into Timberline's unblinking eyes. "You, too, Timberline? There's to be no more trouble tonight if we do what Sundown says?"

"It goes ag'in the grain," sighed old Timber. "But, things being as they is, what with Miss Lucy here an' all—yep; it goes like Barry says, only you two got to shed your guns right here."

Tom Haveril freed himself from Lucy's arms, called, "Come ahead, Judge," dropped his guns to the floor and moved into the kitchen. Timberline backed off slowly, always keeping him covered. The Judge stepped briskly after him, likewise leaving his weapon behind. Lucy would have followed but, at the same moment Barry said, "You're to stay here," Tom Haveril said: "Give the fool a chance to talk, Lucy. I'd like to know what he's got to say to you."

So a moment later she and Barry were alone, and Timberline was guarding his two prisoners in the kitchen. She stood with her hands down at her sides, her face lifted defiantly, her eyes blazing into Barry's.

"If you've got anything to say to me," she said hotly, "please say it—and go!"

"Lucy," he pleaded earnestly, "I've come here just to save you, can't you see?"

She scarcely flicked her eyes scornfully at him; there was nothing but contempt in her bitter smile.

"You've got to believe what I'm going to tell you!" he blurted out, his own temper uncertain.

"I'll never believe a single word you ever say! If you're waiting for that time to come— Oh, why don't you go!"

In the next room he could hear the Judge and Tom Haveril speaking hurriedly; he could not see them but saw Timberline, his shotgun gripped with hard, competent hands. He thought: "If I could just make her listen to me! If I could tell her the whole thing—"

He gathered up the weapons which the Judge and Tom Haveril had "shed" at Timberline's staccato command, and threw them as far as he could out through the door into the dark.

"Timber!" he called sharply.

"Here I be, Barry. Want me to kill the two buzzards after all?"

"Herd them out on the back porch! Then get on your horse; I guess it's there handy, isn't it?"

"Never handier," said Timberline.

"I'm not going to talk all night to this girl. And when you and I go—well, we'll go fast."

"Suits me," said Timberline, and then barked out to the Judge and Tom Haveril: "Yuh heard it? March, yuh two. I reckon what Barry's got to say to the lady can best be said tater-tate."

His orders were obeyed; Barry heard Tom Haveril laugh and the Judge curse, and then there was the sound of boots thumping out through the back door. Lucy was about to run after them when Barry caught her by the wrist. As he did so he holstered his gun.

"Lucy," said Barry, "first you've got to believe this: Tom Haveril *is* the Laredo Kid."

She scoffed at him. Then she said, brightly beautiful, as she, so much smaller than he, gave the impression of looking down on him from some lofty height, "Tom told me all that he knows about you as we drove here tonight."

"He's tried to make you think that I'm Laredo?"

He heard the three men out on the back porch; he heard a door close. A moment later Timberline called out, "Ready to ride when you are, Sundown."

At that Barry suddenly caught Lucy up in his arms and ran with her. She tried to scream; he clamped his big hand tight over her mouth. She bit him but he kept her still. He threw her up into the Judge's saddle, held her with one hand while he managed his own horse and mounted, then roared out to Timberline:

"Ride, pardner! Sock your spurs in and *ride!*"

He started his own horse and the Judge's off at a run, heading back toward the mountains. He rode so close to Lucy that his knee crushed into hers and he knew that he hurt her, also that he hurt her with his clutch on her arm, holding her in her saddle. That just couldn't be helped; it was hard work managing her, as fierce under restraint as a wildcat, and the two running horses.

It was a mad thing to do, but mad ventures have a way of being won. After them, not knowing what it was all about, yelling like a Comanche, came old Timberline.

. . . It was at a much later time that Barry said to Timberline, "I was afraid, you bloodthirsty old pirate, even after we'd promised Laredo not to burn him down that you'd weaken and kill him anyhow."

Never before or after did he hear old Timberline laugh as he did then.

"Hell, pardner," he gasped. "I didn't find out till I come sneakin' up the back steps that that damn gun o' Juan's wasn't loaded!"

XIII

"I love you, and you'd better know it," said Barry.

"Oh, do you!" laughed Lucy, but hers was laughter of a sort made for the occasion, made to sting him with her contemptuous mockery.

"Yes, I do. I always have. I'm always going to."

"I am Tom Haveril's wife," she reminded him, no longer laughing, as cold as ice.

That was a good half hour after they had raced away from Tom Haveril's ranch house. There'd been no chance for talking; it had been just about all Barry could do to keep the two horses running, to keep her from throwing herself recklessly out of the saddle. He had promptly abandoned the road and all trails, heading into the thick of the wilderness, welcoming rugged slopes and brush patches and the darkest bits of forest.

Timberline, riding as hard as he could, had never caught up with them. Once, some fifteen minutes ago, Barry had heard him down in the bed of a cañon from which he and Lucy had but just climbed, and had shouted down to him.

"Hi, Timber!" he yelled. "Shove along back to camp. Tell Ken March to have anyhow a dozen men on our payroll to take care of the Judge and

Laredo if they come out that way looking for us."

"What about you?" yipped Timberline.

"Don't know. Don't much give a damn. Oh, I'm all right, and I'm taking good care of Lucy here. See you sometime later, Timber."

Whatever else Timberline had had to remark had been lost in the rattle of their horses' hoofs upon the rocks of the ridge as they rode on and over it. Now that Barry said to the girl, "I love you, and you'd better know it," the two were several miles on their way.

Barry stopped to blow the hard-ridden horses; he had also a thought to Lucy whom he had put through a difficult thirty minutes. They were in an upland meadow, ringed about by the black wall of the forest, with the glittering brilliance of stars above them and a cool night wind whispering and lightly fingering the strands of the girl's loose hair.

"I'm not afraid of you!" said Lucy, defying him.

"I'm glad of that, Lucy," said Barry gently. "Of course there's no reason why you should be afraid of me, but I thought you might be anyhow. I'm glad."

That made her defiance seem a small, unnecessary thing, and so it angered her.

"Let me go!" she cried furiously. "I say, let me go; do you hear me? I am going back to Tom— to my husband."

"He's not your husband, Lucy. You know that.

A preacher just came and said a mouthful of words. Nothing could make you and him man and wife. And if he was your husband, you wouldn't have him long. I'm going to kill him."

"Murderer! Coward and murderer!"

"No, it wouldn't be murder," said Barry calmly. "Not even if I came up on him from behind and killed him before he knew it. It would be what they call execution, Lucy girl."

He could hear her breathing; even in that dim light, so sharp were his eyes when there was Lucy to look at, he could see the tumultuous rise and fall of her breast.

"You—you say that you love me! Then let me go, Barry."

He shook his head. "No. I can't let you go. Not as long as he is alive."

"What are you going to do with me? Where are you taking me?"

"I don't know," he said, very thoughtful. "I want a good long talk with you—"

"Talk to me now. Then let me go."

"We'll ride along," said Barry. "First we'll go to a place I know back a piece farther in the woods. Not only am I going to tell you something; there's something I've got to show you, so you'll know I'm telling you the truth."

She rode along with him again, making no attempt to escape. In the first place she knew that he was at every instant too watchful to permit of her eluding him. Then, too, it was true, what she had said. She wasn't in the least afraid of him!

Now, that struck her as strange: Why shouldn't she be terrified? Tom Haveril had assured her that this man was a murderous scoundrel; in fact that he was none other than the Laredo Kid. And certainly he had been ruthless tonight, a high-handed devil who ravished a young bride out of the arms of her groom of a few hours. Here, too, was he leading her at every step deeper and deeper into the black maw of the wilderness. She could summon up a shudder as she massed these facts—and yet it remained that she was not in the least in fear of him.

"I thought that you were going to talk, to tell me things, as we rode along," said Lucy.

"Remember that night more than three years ago, down in Tylersville?" said Barry. She nodded; they were mounting High Boy Ridge, and he could see her head with its aureole of tumbled hair against the sky. "I went out to the stable, waiting for the man that owned that fancy saddle," he went on. "The Judge sneaked on out behind me. You followed us both."

"Well?" said Lucy, distant, reserved—but alive with piqued interest.

"You saw a good deal of what happened, but you didn't hear all that was said, did you?"

She had heard nothing at all that had passed

between Barry and Cousin Jesse; for, though Barry for one spoke clearly enough, she was too far away, at a safe distance behind Judge Blue, to catch what was said. Then, after she saw the Judge strike Barry down, such was her wild flurry of terrified astonishment, she had heard words almost as a sleeping person might hear sounds, disturbed by them but attaching little logical sense to them. It was all a blur after these years, and had been little better than a blur that first night.

"You saw what happened," continued Barry. "You saw the Judge hammer me over the head. You heard some words, because you told me that night. You didn't see the man in the barn, but you heard the Judge call him Laredo, and you knew he wasn't talking to me! It was the other man that he called Laredo. That man was Jesse Conroy, my Cousin Jesse; and he is Laredo and he is Tom Haveril."

"I don't believe it!"

"You understood that the Judge took a hand when he did, putting me out, to keep me from the chance of being killed if Laredo and I fought it out as we were bound to. And you knew why he cut in, to save my life long enough to find out where I'd got a fistful of gold."

He gave her her chance to speak but she had nothing to say.

"You knew him that day for a liar, for a robber,

for a man to run in double harness with the killer, Laredo. You came pretty close that night to running away with me, Lucy; with me, a stranger. You were scared and you were sick with the whole business. But things ran along—the Judge was always good to you—you covered things up, didn't you? Then tonight."

She spoke up then, and sharply enough. "What about tonight?"

"You saw him kill a man. And you knew it was murder. That got under your skin, Lucy. That gouged deep, all the way into your heart. And Tom Haveril came along, the good-looking, murdering hound-dog, and you married him! And I tell you," and his voice rang out fierce and strong, "it wasn't because you were in love with Tom Haveril; it was because you just had to run away from that damned big white house with its Judge Blue trimmings."

"No!" said Lucy. "It wasn't that—"

"Don't you lie to me, girl! And don't you lie to yourself! *I know!* You, Lucy Blue, daughter of a crook, a liar and murderer! That was just simple hell for you, wasn't it? More than you could stand? And so you ran out on it, and didn't give much of a damn even if you did have to run into the arms of another killer."

"He's not!" She almost screamed it at him, and jerked her horse to a standstill. "You've got to let me go, Barry Haveril."

"I'm going to let you go—set you free—turn you loose," said Barry, and she detected the deep tenderness in his voice. "Not from me, Lucy girl. Not free from me ever. You're mine. But free from something else. Free from the horror of the whole damned thing. I'm going to make you happy with just three or four little words. Ready, Lucy? Hang on to the horn of your saddle. Get ready to be happy."

"Have you gone crazy?" demanded Lucy, wondering at him.

Barry said simply: "Judge Blue isn't your father. That's true, dear. You're not Lucy Blue at all."

"Barry!"

"That's a part of what I've got to tell you," he went on. "I didn't know until that night Tom Haveril and I shot each other. He knew. He had proof of all this hid out at that cabin where we were, where they hung up Pennel and Longo and Sarboe. He came back there to make sure no one got what he had hid. He saw me with it in my hands. We tried to kill each other. I got away with what he'd hid. As soon as he could, he tried to make sure of you, marrying you—"

"He loves me!" said Lucy, trying to sound defensive, but her voice faint.

"That's natural," conceded Barry. "Any man would."

"But tell me—"

"You're going to ride with me. I'm going to show you."

They rode on, Lucy for a while in the most profound meditation of her life. Not Lucy Blue at all—not the Judge's daughter—not the flesh and blood of one who, she knew, loved her, and yet who, she knew too, was a sort of ravening beast of a man. Why, if this were true, she was free, as Barry had said! Free from a dread and a horror which, fastening on her more than three years ago, had at times been a crushing incubus which nearly maddened her, which had made her moan a thousand times, "Oh, dear God, why can't I be dead and have it all over with?"

"Barry! Tell me everything!"

"I'll not tell you everything because I can't; because I don't know it all. But I'm going to show you what Tom Haveril had hid at the cabin in the mountains; and you'll know as much as I do."

"But we're not going to that cabin!"

"Of course not. I've another place, where I've been hid out, getting over the attack of hot lead I caught from Tom Haveril. I left the things there that I want to show you. Sarboe's there, too."

"Sarboe! But Sarboe—"

When she stopped so suddenly he supposed she was just going to say: "But Sarboe is dead! They hanged him!" and so he answered: "Yes, Sarboe is still alive. He saved me from dying.

193

I've been with him all this time. He wasn't even badly hurt; just scared to death, I reckon, and fainting from fear when they swung him up."

But Lucy had been on the verge of saying something altogether different about Sarboe! She came close to blurting out that already she knew about Sarboe; that Tom Haveril knew too; that as she and Tom Haveril drove tonight from the Judge's place to his ranch house he had told her that he had sent out all his boys, a half score wild young devils of his own kind, with Jake Goodby, his foreman, to round Sarboe up. They knew where Sarboe was; they thought that they knew where Barry Haveril was; they were to get the two of them. And this was what Lucy came very close to disclosing the instant Barry told her where they were going—to join Sarboe.

They rode for a time in silence. Even the tremendous news Barry had imparted to her, a thing to sing and thrill through every fiber of her emotional being, must for the moment stand aside for this fresher consideration. It was terribly hard to think clearly! If she only knew where the truth was, if she could but isolate and be sure of all the lies! The things that Barry Haveril said about Tom Haveril and the Judge—the things they said about him—the things which she had found out for herself, not in any clear-cut fashion at all but glimpsing them like a lot of writing forms through smoke—all she knew so dimly, all she hoped so frantically, made together an inferno of doubt. If she was not Lucy Blue, then who and what was she? She wanted to ask that; she wanted to ask other questions and to probe among Barry's answers for his honesty or villainy; and now the question of Sarboe came up!

Something urged her almost beyond her resistance to cry out: "But, Barry, by now they have captured Sarboe! There are eight or ten or a dozen of Tom's men. They've caught him; they're waiting for you!" And while the words seemed actually forming on her lips there was another something which stopped them.

After a long while, "Barry," she said in a small voice. In fact she spoke so faintly that he did not even hear her. So again they rode on in silence. She kept watching him all that she could; whenever they were in some sort of clearing where there was enough light to make out anything at all, she kept looking at him, noting how he carried himself, erect in the saddle, how his head was so fearlessly up; at times she even made out vaguely the firm, masterful profile. She liked the way he wore his hat—

"Barry!"

He heard her this time and said, "What is it, Lucy?"

"You say that you love me, Barry."

"You know I do, Lucy."

She sighed. "Love must be a funny thing. I always thought it would make one good and kind to the other one—"

"I am being good to you tonight, Lucy."

"Barry, let me go back. Don't take me where Sarboe is."

"I can't let you go back, not as long as Tom Haveril is alive. I am taking you where Sarboe is to show you a bit of proof that I've told you the truth."

"I'll wait for that proof. You can bring it to me some other time. Tomorrow, Barry. And tonight— Well, if you won't let me go free, take me somewhere else." Sudden inspiration came to her. "Take me to your sister Lucy!"

He shook his head. "No. They'd look for us there first of all. And it would make trouble for her and for Ken March, and wouldn't help you and me."

"Then—" She didn't know what to say next. They were climbing a steep slope again, and she leaned back in the saddle, one hand wreathed in her horse's mane. She ended uncertainly: "Just don't take me where Sarboe is. Not tonight, Barry."

He thought that he understood, and tried to laugh her fears away. He remembered now how Sarboe had been one of the three men who had closed in about her on the trail that day when he had seen her first after so long a time. He said: "Shucks, Lucy, Sarboe would eat out of your hand now. He's not half the bad man he used to think he was. And—funny, isn't it?—during these last few weeks since he saved my life, he's got to be a real friend of mine. You'll be safe enough with Sarboe and me."

She had a queer sense of having done some vague sort of duty. She had tried to warn him, tried to keep him from running headlong into a snare. She strove to be content with that. She kept telling herself: "I *didn't* marry Tom just to run away from home! I really do love him." She had been fascinated; many girls felt the rollicking fellow's charm. She said: "It isn't just fascination with me. I do love him!" Perhaps she protested too much. She felt a flick of angry resentment, and it was all against Barry Haveril.

After a long, long while of threading devious ways through wilderness intricacies, Barry lifted his arm to point; she saw a flicker of light across an inky hollow, on the far side under cliffs.

"There's Sarboe," he called cheerily.

He was riding so close at her side that she could have put out her hand to rest on his arm. She did lift her hand—

She let it fall again to her side and they rode on down into the dark hollow.

Before Barry had the vaguest inkling that anything was wrong, men sprang up all about him;

rocks and bushes of a moment ago seemed to turn into men. He saw here and there the faint glint of starlight upon their weapons.

"Both hands up, high, Barry Haveril!" shouted an exultant voice. That was Jake Goodby, Tom Haveril's foreman, a man after Tom Haveril's own heart, a slack-jawed, slope-browed killer who ruffled it in these later days as perhaps his forebears had done since the dawn of their being. "High up, an' quick, or you're dead mutton."

Barry obeyed, saying nothing, his eyes darting everywhere at once, seeking to make out how many there were, looking for some avenue of escape.

Lucy felt a gun barrel driven into her side. A man called sharply to her, "Get your paws up too! Who the hell are you, anyhow? Want a bellyful of lead? Get 'em up!"

"Jake!" cried Lucy. "Oh, Jake Goodby!"

"My God," said Jake. "It's a female woman!"

"I'm Lucy Blue. I am Mrs. Tom Haveril. Tom Haveril's wife. We were married just tonight."

Jake muttered, "I'm damned." Lucy ran on excitedly: "You've got Sarboe? You're not to hurt him, you know."

"Sure I know! Tom wants him to talk first. I'm wonderin' if Sarboe'll ever talk again! He's so damn scared he can't say a word. This here is Barry Haveril, ain't it?"

"Yes," answered Lucy hurriedly. "And you're

198

not to hurt him either, Jake. Tom wants him to talk, too."

Jake Goodby began to laugh.

"You helped fetch him along into our trap, did you?"

"Yes! *Yes!*" she exclaimed. "I'll tell you about it later. But you are to hold him and Sarboe until Tom comes."

"Say! You're all right!" laughed Jake Goodby. "Mrs. Tom now, huh? Say, that's fine."

Then, mindful of duty, he laid a hand on Barry's bridle.

"Keep 'em up, feller, if you want to go on breathin'," he said, no longer jocular. "Hey, Slim; you an' Red close in on him an' make sure you get all his hardware. He fancies himself, this hombre; thinks he's a lead-slinger. Better draw his claws afore he hurts himself."

Disarmed, Barry came down out of the saddle and stood still as a rope was double-hitched about his wrists and his hands were tied at his back. He didn't even look at the two or three men busied at making sure he was snugly bound; his smoldering eyes all the while were on Lucy, as slim and sweet against the skyline as a graceful young moon. She was laughing and saying some-thing lightly to Jake Goodby when six or eight of Tom Haveril's young hellions, making gay over the whole thing, dragged him off to join Sarboe where the latter, bound like himself, half lay and half sat propped up against a big rock at the foot of the cliff.

He jammed his shoulder against Sarboe's by way of companionable greeting, since he hadn't a hand free to clap on the other's shoulder, and spoke for the first time.

"They got us all right, Sarboe," he said disgustedly. "Like a fool, I rode with my eyes shut."

Sarboe, writhing in his bonds, could only grunt. The several men who had deposited Barry here laughed and made their joyous and profane comments, then went over to the fire where Lucy had just dismounted, aided from her saddle by Jake Goodby, surrounded by the other men who wanted to know about everything. So she was now Mrs. Tom, was she? But Barry noted that always they were looking toward him and Sarboe, keeping an eye on them.

He could hear Lucy's voice, and it seemed to him that she had never been so gay. He couldn't catch all the words, but few of them in fact, but after a while he heard her say: "Jake, I want to talk with you. And while we're talking have two of your men watch over Tom's prisoners for him; we mustn't take any chances on their getting loose."

So a couple of Jake's commands came lounging over to stand guard, and Barry saw Lucy and Jake Goodby move somewhat apart, toward the farther rim of the uncertain circle of flickering firelight, to sit on a log and talk together.

XIV

Jake Goodby had blue eyes set too close together, and long lashes like a girl's. His yellow-gold hair curled about his ears and lay low on his forehead in little tight ringlets. Not over twenty-two, already he was known to have killed three men. The killings were all "in fair fight," it was generally conceded; it happened that he was one of those men, talented in one thing only, and that was destruction, who could have the fight look fair enough and yet remain cold murder. There have been musicians like Blind Tom; there have been all too many "killers" like Jake Goodby. With a gun in his hand he was lightning, swift and deadly. Else he had never been fore-man for Tom Haveril.

But Jake Goodby, like many of his sort, though preening himself with enough vanity to outfit ten men, did not have it in him ever to be anything more than he was now, some other man's hired hand or paid killer. Just about all the brains he had must have been in his two agile hands. He could take plain orders and carry them out; he could put a bullet through a man's heart or between his eyes; with that said, there's not much more to be set down to the man's ability. He had had a father who had made him go to school; three years the shifty-eyed boy went, and at the end of the third year the first reader was an utterly blind mystery to him.

Tonight he sat on a log in the firelight and talked with the boss' wife—talked, incidentally, with the prettiest girl Jake Goodby had ever seen. He looked at her as he looked at all women, his eyes crawling over her.

Lucy smiled at him. Jake shoved his hat back and swelled visibly and touched up the pale gold ringlets on his forehead, making sure that she noticed them.

At that moment Lucy was in a panic. She had ridden knowingly into this trap with Barry because it was the only way, because Barry had dared carry her off by force, because she meant to go free. Even so she had been tempted to warn him—and that though he was so avowedly her husband's enemy, so high-handed with her, so hateful! Had there been more time to think things out, perhaps she could have managed so that she could have escaped without seeing him in his present predicament.

Now she had to ask herself just how serious that predicament might prove to be, and that was what started up sudden panic in her breast. He would go back, fast bound, to Tom Haveril and Judge Blue. If these men strung him up as men like them had done with Sarboe and the others, it would be at least in part her doing.

Barry had said, "You are not Judge Blue's daughter." He said that he had proof; that he was bringing her here to show it to her. And he had sounded as though he meant what he said; it rang so true, not like a lie at all! And he had said that Tom Haveril knew—and always he was saying, "Tom Haveril is Laredo."

She said to herself, "If he could be free, to go his own way; and I could be free from him—"

So she sat on a log with Jake Goodby and even smiled at him, and strove to give Barry back his freedom, keeping her own meantime.

Jake had Barry's gun, dangling it by its heavy belt.

"Let me see it," said Lucy. "How would I look, wearing a gun like that?"

Jake admiring, let her buckle the weapon about her slim waist so that it banged low down on her thigh. "Say, why didn't you'n me ever gang up afore now?" he said playfully. What if she was the boss' wife? She was a girl, wasn't she? And didn't girls always shine up to Jake Goodby? "We'd of made a great team," he assured her.

"You musn't forget that I'm married now," laughed Lucy.

And there, she thought, both frightened and exhilarated, she had set her hand to the plow. She even said to herself, "I am making myself as cheap as a dirty rag doll." Well, what of it, so she might save a life tonight—perhaps more lives than just Barry's?

"Aw," said Jake, "yuh ain't scercely married yet. Jus' married tonight, an' already Tom lets you fly loose? Me, if I was Tom, I wouldn't of."

Lucy looked at the knot of men loafing beyond the fire. Already it was growing late and these men, like all other ranch hands, were up at daylight and asleep shortly after dark, except on their more or less periodical wild nights. They weren't prepared for bivouacking; with their "chore" done they grew at once restless and sleepy.

"There's no need for them to stay any longer," said Lucy. "With those two men tied up, there's no danger from them."

"Might as well all of us be ridin'," said Jake, and added comfortably, "but there ain't any hurry. They'll be a moon later."

"No; we're to keep the two men here until Tom comes. They have something hidden here that he wants. Better tell the boys, Jake, to scatter as they head back, so they'll be sure not to miss Tom. He'll be riding this way, and he doesn't know the exact spot, does he?" For Tom Haveril had told her that all he knew was that Sarboe and Barry had been reported to him as being some-where hereabouts.

"How about you?" asked Jake. "You'll stay here, waitin' for Tom."

There were many ways in which she might have said yes. Still thinking of the rag doll, she answered, "If you want me to, Jake."

His hand crawled along the log like a crab and fastened on hers. For just a single loathsome second she let it rest there; then she slipped hers out from under it. At that moment fortune favored her, as fortune does seem to have the way of favoring those who run at least half way to meet it. One of the men beyond the fire called through a yawn: "Hey, Jake! Come alive, will yuh? What're we doin', squattin' here all night?"

Jake got up and went over to them, pulling his hat low over his eyes again, slouching up to them like a tiger cat, a bold figure in his own eye and sure of being no less in the gray eyes which must be following him.

He spoke in a low tone to the others. What he said Lucy could not catch though she listened intently. They laughed and one of them slapped Jake on the back, and off they went, dragging their spurs clankingly. Lucy thought: "He's such a big fool! I'll have no trouble at all." Then she noticed that as Jake came slouching back and the others went to their horses and rode off with a whoop and a rush, one man had remained behind; and this man went straight to where the two prisoners leaned in such helplessness against their rock. She saw him squat on his heels so close to them that he could watch their slightest movements.

Lucy thought: "I must be careful. Jake isn't as big a fool as I thought he was." She thought too that she'd best keep a firm hand upon the tiller of conversation; if she didn't steer strongly she knew which way he would drift. She said quickly,

"What do you suppose it is that they have hidden out here, Sarboe and Barry Haveril, that Tom is so anxious to get?"

"I didn't know that part of it," said Jake. "Well, shucks, it don't make no difference to us, does it, Lucy?"

"I'd like to know what it is," said Lucy thoughtfully enough. "What do you think?"

"What would it be?" he mumbled, not particularly interested as yet. "What would a bum like Sarboe have? Or Barry Haveril?"

"They say that Barry Haveril has found a rich mine. Do you suppose—"

Then Jake did take an interest. Gold and liquor and women, outside of his pastime of murder, constituted his trinity. And with gold you bought the rest!

"Say! That's right. His old pardner, Timberline, an' young Ken March, his other pardner, look like gittin' ready to open the earth up over to that crick o' their'n. But shucks, what would he have any gold hid way off here for?"

"I'd like to know. Wouldn't you like to know, Jake? Before Tom gets here?"

Jake laughed. "You little devil you, Lucy!"

"I think I can find out something, Jake! I already have an inkling. But we'll have to hurry.

Let's see. You call your cowboy back over here where he can't hear." She said "your" cowboy to stuff still further that swollen vanity of his. "Let me have five minutes— I'll bet you, Jake Goodby, that I can find out!"

"But you look a-here," he began.

"Oh, they can't hurt me!" cried Lucy, jumping up. She laughed and clapped her hands down on the butt of Barry's gun. "They're tied up, and look at me wearing this!"

She called the weapon to his attention in haste, rather than have him begin to think about it later. She knew that he had not the least reason to suspect her, since it was she who had led Barry into all this. And she knew he wasn't thinking about any harm coming to her at his prisoners' hands.

"How'd you make him talk?" wondered Jake.

"What if I let him think maybe we might let him and Sarboe go—that is if they told us where they had it hid—and if there was enough to make it worth our while? Don't you think they'd talk— rather than have to talk to Tom when he comes?"

"Say! an' you an' Tom jus' married tonight!"

"Is that any reason why I can't do some things for myself?" scoffed Lucy.

"I don't think you better—"

"I'm going to anyway! You can't stop me, Jake Goodby. If you won't help me, if you won't just call that man of yours away from them for five

207

minutes— Oh, all right for you, Jake Goodby."

"Well," said Jake slowly, "it won't do any harm for you to find out what you can. I'll bet they don't open their traps. But go 'head."

"Call him over," commanded Lucy, and her heart, already racing, began thumping wildly. She thought all of a sudden, ready to break down; "Oh, I am the fool! This is crazy. It won't work. It can't—"

"Hey there, Bunce!" called Jake. "Come here."

Bunce grunted and got up and stretched his legs. "What yuh want, Jake?" he asked as in high heels he clumped and stumbled over the uneven ground, coming through the firelight to the log.

"Squat, Bunce. We'll chin. Miss Lucy's steppin' over to ride herd on them two hombres a minute or two."

"It ain't no job for a girl," said Bunce. Then he saw the gun dangling from its belt about her waist and grinned.

"Gun woman, huh?"

Lucy made some light rejoinder, she didn't know quite what, and started walking slowly through the firelit circle to the two men leaning back against the big rock in the shadows at the foot of the cliff. She was praying mutely at every step, praying to a compassionate God to help her; somehow to aid her in coming between Barry Haveril and Tom Haveril.

Barry watched her wonderingly as she came

toward him. When the fireglow shone reflected from his six-gun swinging at her side, he stiffened from head to foot; could she have seen his eyes then, she would have been startled by the look that leaped up in them.

She came on until she stood over him, looking down into his upturned face. At first, she realized, she must say something for Jake Goodby to hear. His suspicions might wake at any moment.

She found it easiest of all to laugh. Her nerves were so on the stretch that she wanted to scream anyhow, and so she stood and laughed, and none of the men who heard knew that she was on the edge of hysteria.

"So it's funny, is it?" said Barry savagely.

"You were so stupid," cried out the girl, still laughing. Then she grew suddenly still, then said in a queer stiff sort of voice, "Tom Haveril will be here soon, Mr. Barry Haveril—or is Laredo the name? And when he comes—"

"When he comes?" said Barry, and pulled his legs up under him, as though to ease cramped muscles.

Lucy stepped a little closer. She was just shaping her lips to whisper hurriedly: *"Barry, I'm trying to help you!"* But she didn't whisper a syllable. There was no time. She was never so surprised in her life; she had never dreamed that anything human could be as incredibly swift as Barry Haveril was then. He came up standing like a snake coming out of a coil. The two strong hands she thought so securely tied behind him flashed out and caught her up, swinging her clear from the ground. At a single bound he was around behind the big rock, and she was huddled at his feet, and his gun was again in his hand. At the same instant out of the corners of her eyes she saw Sarboe surge sideways and launch himself along the ground on hands and knees, so that now he and Barry Haveril and herself were all behind the boulder. And Barry, armed again, was roaring like an angry bull.

"Jake Goodby! You, Bunce! Up with 'em or I'll kill the two of you!"

They were no less astounded than Lucy, the thing had happened so all without warning. Further, they were in the light, uncertain though it was, and Barry was scarcely more than a voice and an invisible menace behind his bulwark. Add to that that Goodby and Bunce, did they take to flight, had a log in the way to be scrambled over, and that Killer Jake Goodby was horribly afraid of death. The two men got slowly to their feet and put their arms straight up.

"Here, Sarboe," said Barry. "Hold this girl down where she is. Don't let her wiggle out of your hands; she's as tricky as a cat."

"Barry!" cried Lucy, desperate.

"Shut up!" he snapped back at her. "I'm busy now."

Then he gave his undivided attention to Goodby and Bunce.

Barry Haveril's hands felt numb and awkward, like somebody else's hands; the rope about his wrist, so recently removed, had been blood-chokingly tight. He meant to take no unnecessary chances, and so stood where he was behind the rock. If it came to a gun fight with Goodby and Bunce he would need all the odds he could get until his blood ran normally in his fingers again and that feeling of thickness went out of them.

"Step this way, you two," he commanded sharply. "And better not try any funny business."

Bunce started forward, then stopped to glance sideways at Goodby. Jake had not moved. He answered Barry's command stammeringly:

"Yuh want to k-k-kill us! Yuh—"

"Well, there's no law against it, is there?" retorted Barry. "It's always open season on varmints like you two. Now step lively. Come ahead, Bunce; come ahead, Goodby."

Bunce started again; this time Goodby came fumblingly along. Barry, watching him narrowly, saw him stumble slightly; well, that was natural enough for a man walking with both hands high above his head, with his eyes fixed straight ahead. But almost too swiftly for the eye to follow his movement the next minute he accomplished the unexpected. Thoroughly convinced that Barry Haveril was going to kill him, just as he would have killed in Barry's place, he sprang nimbly to one side, snapped out his gun, and started shooting over Bunce's shoulder. His first bullet came so close to Barry's head that its angry hiss was loud in his ear.

Bunce yelled out in rage and terror, then jerked out his gun and started blazing away at all that he could see of the man behind the boulder. But poor Bunce never had a chance; Barry's first answering shot broke a leg for him and he fell lurchingly. Jake fired again, but his aim was disturbed and his shot went wild. He was letting the third shot off when he like Bunce went down, shot through the body.

Sarboe and Lucy were standing up now, Sarboe with both arms about the girl holding her tight, she with no thought of escape as she stared horrified at the two figures lying huddled together there in the firelight. She thought that both men must be dead already, so starkly still were they.

Then she saw one of them move. Bunce threw his gun from him, out into the brightest lighted of the firelit space, and called out pleadingly: "I'm done, Haveril. There's my gun. An' I wouldn't of started this anyhow. It was that damn' yellow dog Goodby."

Goodby stirred slightly, as though in an effort to rise, then lay still again. Barry came forward, gathered up both men's weapons, then asked curtly of Bunce, "Where are you hurt?"

"I got it in the leg," groaned the cowboy. "The bullet smashed my leg bone; I could feel it smashed all to hell."

Barry called to Sarboe: "Come along here, Sarboe. And bring Mrs. Tom Haveril with you."

So Sarboe came and Lucy with him, one of her wrists clenched tight in his hand, her face white, her eyes looking enormous and brilliant in the firelight.

"Is he dead?" she whispered, looking down on Jake Goodby.

"If he is, he asked for it," snapped Barry. He gave into Sarboe's keeping the weapons taken from the two wounded men. "I'm going for the horses," he said and hurried off, merely adding over his shoulder, "Watch both of 'em Sarboe; and don't turn that girl loose."

Sarboe grimaced rather horribly, strove to speak and made only a queer groaning sort of sound; muscles stood out rigidly in his neck and the veins on his forehead looked to be about to burst.

Barry returned hurriedly with the horses, his and Sarboe's and the one that Lucy had ridden here, the Judge's. Also he brought something else, but they did not see it, the flat steel box which he had unearthed from its hiding place and tied to his saddle strings.

"You are not going to take me with you!" cried Lucy as soon as she saw her horse, and began struggling with Sarboe. "Barry Haveril, you have no right!" Then, seeing how stern and expressionless his face was, grown afraid of him all of a sudden and for the first time, she began begging him to let her go. "You will let me go now, won't you, Barry?"

"I don't know what to do with you," he said heavily, staring at her.

"Then let me go! Oh, please, Barry!"

"That's what I ought to do; send you back to Tom Haveril. It would serve you right. And I've got a notion— No! You're coming with Sarboe and me. Now get on your horse. We're in a hurry."

She strove to temporize.

"What about these two men, so terribly hurt? You can't go off and leave them like this!"

"Get up on your horse!" he commanded her, and when she saw the look on his face and saw that in another moment he was going to make her do what he wished, she scrambled into her saddle. Barry and Sarboe, one on each side of her, were mounted almost as soon as she. Barry sat a moment frowning down at the two men on the ground. Then he shrugged.

"There's nothing I can do for Goodby; he'll want a doctor if he can live long enough to get one. Bunce is all right. And it won't be long until Laredo and his pack get here. Come ahead, Sarboe; we're riding."

"And you're taking me with you!" exclaimed the girl.

"Yes. God knows why; I ought to be through with you for good and all after what you've done for me tonight. Come on; let's get going."

"Bunce!" Lucy cried back as the three horses started. "Tom Haveril will be here soon. Tell him; tell him which way—"

Sarboe leaned toward her as though he was going to take her throat in his hands. Barry said: "Leave her alone, Sarboe. Let her yell. We're riding."

They rode for hours, so long and up and down such trailless slopes that Lucy was drooping wearily in the saddle long before Barry called a halt. She lost all sense of direction. They turned down into deep dark ravines; they threaded endless forest solitudes; they zigzagged along mountain flanks so that after a while she gave up trying to guess which way they were riding. And when at last they stopped and she slid down stiffly, she had not the vaguest idea of her whereabouts. Sarboe, too, was a bit mystified, this being new country to him. Barry had brought them to his old, first cabin, or rather into the grove just behind it. Here he was first to dismount.

"Barry," said Lucy faintly. She was ready to burst into tears from sheer weariness and strain of all that she had endured tonight; horror and hasty marriage and stress and horror again. During the long ride Barry had not once spoken to her, and somehow his bleak reserve chilled her unaccount-ably. She began telling herself, "He was trying to help me. He did think he was saving me from something. And now he— Oh, I want him to know that I'm not the little cat that he thinks me."

"Well?" he demanded coldly, staring up at her.

She tried to tell him. "Tonight when we rode into that trap—"

"Yes? What about it? You knew, didn't you?"

"Yes. But you had no right to force me to go with you—"

"Let's not talk about it. Sarboe, hold the horses here a few minutes; I'm going forward on foot to make sure everything is clear. And keep your eye on Mrs. Tom Haveril." Then he laughed shortly and said: "Mrs. Laredo. Let's give her her true name and title, Sarboe: Lady Laredo!"

"Listen to me!" said Lucy. "When I came out to the rock where you were, wearing your gun—"

"It was you who did the laughing then!"

"I had planned— You see, I couldn't guess you had gotten the ropes off—"

"Sarboe's work. They'd had him tied an hour; he worked free, got me free." He looked up at Sarboe, looming dark and silent in the saddle. "Guess you saved my life tonight, old-timer. Maybe it's twice you've done that for me. And all I ever did for you was to shoot you!"

"Would you believe me," asked Lucy, and

braced herself and unconsciously hardened her voice, "if I told you that I was coming to try to get you free?"

"No," he said promptly. "Maybe I've just got to knowing you tonight Lady Laredo! I saw you on that damned log with Jake Goodby—"

Suddenly, without finishing what he was going to say, he moved off through the grove, lost to them before he had taken a dozen of his long strides. He saw the cabin looking dark among the trees, its rear wall almost indistinguishable in the shadows. The moon of which Jake Goodby had spoken was not yet up, though the first softly glowing promise of it brightened the mountain tops in the east. He turned a corner, going softly, to come to the door on the other side.

Under the closed door he saw a thin thread of wan light, a light that ebbed and throbbed and waned and was never strong. A blanket was hung over the one window; there was but the vaguest hint of light along the top. He judged that someone must have had a fire going in his fireplace; that it had all but died down now.

He stood, listening. Not a sound came to him from within. Still he stood, listening and pondering.

"Asleep, probably, this time of night. Unless—"

Unless it was Tom Haveril or men he had sent here on the off chance that Barry Haveril would come this way. That could easily be. Tom

Haveril—Laredo, damn him! Jesse Conroy— would remember this place.

"Just the same I'm going in. I can't make that girl ride all night. She's at the end of her rope now."

He stepped softly to the door and lifted the latch slowly, guardedly, making not so much as a whisper of sound. Then he began shoving the door open. Slowly, stealthily he forced it back. It hung on its ancient rawhide hinges, and these could give out no sound. It would have scraped the floor and given out some whisper of sound, but he lifted it clear. Opened an inch it gave him a glimpse of the cabin's interior; there were dying coals on the rock hearth, the red lump of a chunk of wood farther back turning into vivid coals, melting down into a bed of ashes. The light was wanner than weak moonlight, yet he looked in from the dark and could see some of the things inside.

He could see the foot of the bunk against the wall; he opened the door another inch and saw a man's booted feet. Some fellow asleep, just as he had thought likely—

He threw the door wide open. The man on the bunk did not stir. Barry stepped into the room, making sure with a quick glance about him that there were no other men concealed in the shadows. Then he called out:

"You, there! Who are you?"

Still the man did not move. Barry came closer; the fellow lay on his back; he had drawn a scrap of blanket up about him. His face looked white in the dim light. His eyes were closed.

Barry saw a small ragged pile of wood by the fireplace and threw some scraps of pitchy pine on the coals. They sputtered and sizzled and burst into flame. Then at last the man on the bunk did stir. So he wasn't dead after all, as Barry has begun to suspect. He muttered something; he twisted about and suddenly was sitting up, his feet on the floor, his two hands braced on the edge of the bunk, his eyes wide open and staring.

The pine flared up into higher brighter flame; the cadaverous face of the man on the bunk seemed to start forward out of the dark into the light. Barry Haveril, spellbound, slack-jawed in amazement, stood staring back into those staring eyes.

The man, looking ready to drop dead, laughed instead. Then he said thickly, speaking with difficulty: "So it's Cousin Barry, huh? Make yuhse'f tuh home, Sundown!" and flopped over on his back again, one lax hand hanging to the floor.

Yes, it was Cousin Jesse.

It was Jesse Conroy.

It was the Laredo Kid.

And it was not Tom Haveril.

XV

To Lucy, beginning to shiver with cold as the night wind stiffened and as an utter weariness bore her down, it seemed that Barry Haveril was never coming back. She crawled out of the saddle; Sarboe struck the ground the moment that she did, vigilant as Barry had commanded. She said faintly: "I'm tired to death—I feel like dying. Let me lie here." She lay flat, her arms loose at her sides, and Sarboe stood over her. She saw the pines looking as black as funeral cypresses against the sky, she heard the wind rustling through them, she saw a handful of stars swimming dizzily, and shut her eyes. She didn't know whether she was fainting or going to sleep or really dying, and it didn't seem to matter.

And still time crawled by, and even Sarboe, grown restive, began to wonder, and Barry did not come back to them. Sarboe couldn't see the cabin; he didn't know where it was or even that there was a cabin; all he could do was wait and make sure that the girl was here when Barry came back for her.

Then at long last Barry stepped out of the shadows.

"There's water right over there, Sarboe," he said. "Give the horses a drink, then unsaddle and put them on their tie ropes the other side the water hole. Then come along to the cabin."

Already he had seen Lucy where she lay, his eye caught by something white at her throat. He stooped over her. When he spoke his voice was gentler than when he had stalked away from her.

"Tired out, Lucy? Well, it's been hell for you, hasn't it? Want to walk a hundred yards to shelter and sleep?"

"I want to lie here and die," said Lucy miserably. "I hate everything; I hate living. Leave me alone."

So he gathered her up into his arms. She struck at him but he did not seem to notice, and certainly did not mind.

"You're such a beast," she panted.

"Yes," said Barry Haveril heavily. "And a damned fool. But I won't hurt you."

Again she was not in the slightest afraid of him, he carried her so tenderly, as a man might carry his first born, his truly own, to its sleepy-time place. She could have dozed with her head against his shoulder; how strong his arms were and how comfortable it was to rest within them. It was like a blessed floating through space.

He set her down on a bench against a log wall, and she pressed her palms against her heavy eyelids, and shook her head and then looked about her. She had never been in so primitive a human habitation. Yet it was not without its homey charm. But when she saw the bunk and the man on it, a white-faced, dead looking man, all the peacefulness of Barry's cradling arms and of this quiet, simple place were wiped out by fresh stark reality.

"That's why I had to keep you waiting," said Barry. "I thought for a while he was dying. I had to find where he was hurt and bandage him up. I'm not going to let him die."

"Who is he?" she asked.

"Look at me, Lucy!"

She looked at him, no longer heavy-eyed but with excited interest. He said, talking distinctly and slowly and somehow altogether like a man at the end of his tether:

"He is Jesse Conroy. The Laredo Kid. And he isn't Tom Haveril—and I've been a damned fool."

"You shot him?"

"I wish I had," he muttered somberly. "No. I found him like that."

"Then—"

"Haven't I told you already that I've been a damned fool? He and Tom Haveril were as alike as two shells out of the same gun, except for Tom's little devil-beard. And except that Tom talks different— Not his voice, just his way of saying things. I thought he'd changed with three years, that was all. Well, I was wrong."

"Didn't I tell you all along that you were wrong?" she exulted over him. He had nothing to say, not even a shake of the head for an answer.

She stood up and took a deep breath. If ever in her life she had, not only the opportunity, but the excuse as well, to give Barry Haveril a thorough tongue-lashing, it was now. But, about to speak, she fell silent.

"If it wasn't so late, and you so tired," he said, "I'd take you right back where I got you, back to Tom Haveril. We'll have to do the best we can for tonight. I'll cut you some fresh pine tips and make some sort of bed for you, and you'll slip right straight off to sleep. You needn't be afraid of anything. And it'll be day before you know it."

She looked fearfully at the man on the bunk. "He is dying now. He looks like—"

"No, I tell you! I won't let him die! Not now. I've been looking for that man for three years. I've sworn I'd kill him if I never did another thing."

She drooped down on her bench again and a shudder of nausea shook her.

"Why don't you kill him now?" she said bitterly. "It would be so easy! He's half dead anyhow. If you're so fond of killing, what are you waiting for? You'll never have a better chance—"

He glared at her, then muttered something under his breath and went out.

Among the young trees, he started hacking ends off their boughs to make her a bed, and cursed himself for a fool at every hack.

When he came back Sarboe came with him, and

both men were carrying armfuls of pine tips for her comfort. She had her first good look at Sarboe's face, and her thought was how worn and ill he looked. Then she remembered. How little one thought of other people! Sarboe had been shot; she had seen Barry Haveril shoot him out of his saddle. Then he had known all the unthinkable horror and torment of being hanged! He had swung by the neck, under a dark tree, thinking that it was the end, such a horrible end; alive he had lived through death. He still lived, but that horror had caught him by the throat so that he could not even talk now, could not voice any of those chaotic mutterings welling up within a darkened soul.

From him she looked at Barry Haveril. He, too, had been near death those few weeks ago; his face was white and drawn; there were ghosts haunting his dark eyes.

As the two men came in, Sarboe's eyes, grown eloquent of late, having photographed the room, flashed from the gaunt, pallid form on the bunk to Barry, demanding explanations.

Barry's answer was a mere: "I don't know. I found him like that. He's had a bullet through him."

They built up the fire; they did what they could to make Lucy comfortable for the night. She snuggled down in her nest of a bed—and instantly was as wide awake, of as little mind for sleep, as any child on Christmas morning. There were those words of Barry Haveril's, "You are not Judge Blue's daughter." She couldn't think of a madder thing than to tell any girl that her father was not her father—yet Barry's voice had somehow carried conviction, if only short lived. And he had said that there was proof of this—and that Tom Haveril knew of that "proof," some tangible thing which he had kept hid out by the lone cabin where they hanged Longo and Pennel and Sarboe.

Sarboe had brought in a small pack of food. Lucy wouldn't eat; Barry merely shook his head at it. So Sarboe ate a few bites alone and lay down in a corner beyond the fireplace and went to sleep. Lucy, on her elbows, looked at Barry brooding by the chimney.

"There was something you were going to tell me," she reminded him.

He looked at her blankly. Then: "It's late and you're done in. Better go to sleep, hadn't you?"

"Sleep! Without knowing what it was that you said you could explain! You said I wasn't Lucy Blue at all—"

"I know how you feel." His own mind had been groping; there were questions he wanted answered before he could think of sleep. One was already answered for him: Tom Haveril wasn't the Laredo Kid. But shutting one door to speculation seemed to open a dozen others. Tom

Haveril did know a good deal about Laredo; he had for a time at least been custodian of the flat steel box which Barry was sure Laredo had originally stolen from the Judge. Yes, he and Laredo were linked together somehow. But how?

And how much of it did the Judge know? Why had he allowed Tom Haveril to marry Lucy, unless there was a pretty clear understanding between the two? Did Laredo have anything to do with their arrangement? Had he handed the flat steel box over to Tom Haveril voluntarily, or had it been stolen or wrested forcibly from him? Here was Laredo now, badly hurt, perhaps dying; who had done that for him?

His somber eyes trailed back to the man on the bunk; for a time he forgot Lucy and his promise to tell her what he could of the amazing news concerning herself. Now he could think only of Laredo, a man whom he had hunted for years, lying now only a few feet away—and instead of killing the dog, he had already, forced by ironical fate and his own humanity, started trying to nurse him back to life!

"If there was a single word of truth in what you told me—" said Lucy.

He looked at her absently, then nodded and went out. Returning he brought the flat steel box with him. There was a sort of table he had made long ago, shoved into a corner. He placed it nearer the fireplace, so that the dancing light of blazing pine would illuminate it; then dragged the bench up for Lucy to sit on. She was all eagerness at his elbow as he opened the box.

"Why!" she gasped, seeing the hundreds of pictures. "They are all of me! I know them; papa —the Judge—used to take one of me every Sunday almost!"

"Ever strike you as a funny thing to do?" he asked.

"No. Well, it does seem sort of queer, but you see I've always been used to it. He started it before I can even remember, when I was five or six years old. I've looked over them a hundred times; I used to laugh at what a funny little tyke—"

"They're all dated on the backs," said Barry. "They're arranged in order. If you hold them in a pack, like a pack of cards—"

"I know," said Lucy. "Like this!" She held them with thumb and finger of her left hand; with her right she bent the pack backward, then released the pressure slowly so that the various pictures flipped into view one after the other and swiftly. Packs of pictures of dancing girls in various sequential postures used to be made like that, so that when riffled smartly the girls appeared to be alive, dancing.

"Yes," he nodded. "Like that you seem to see a little girl of six grow right up to your age. The last picture doesn't look much like the first, does it? But when you take them straight through, you can see it's the same you, can't you?"

"Of course," said Lucy, and looked at him with a puzzled frown. "But I don't understand—"

"Here's something else. It was in the box when I got it; I guess it's been there always, for a dozen years. It's an old newspaper. The Laredo *Blade.*"

He opened it for her carefully; from years of being folded it split along the creases. It was a small, two sheet affair; banner headlines across the first page had to do with a crime the enormity of which had horrified the community not unused to violence, had turned Laredo into a sort of hornets' nest with all its citizens for once stirred by a common irate impulse—to make the murderer sorry that he had ever been born, before they gave him the death he would be begging for.

Briefly, this is the gist of the newspaper article:

Colonel Dave Hamilton, his wife and three other members of his household had been shot to death. The Colonel, a newcomer to Laredo, but already immensely popular, had arrived with his family from Virginia, intending to buy a vast holding hereabouts and make this his home. He had brought with him a large sum of money in cash, how much the *Blade* was not informed. The Colonel was reputed a very rich man. Wholesale slaughter had been done for this fortune in gold and currency. There was not the slightest clue to the identity of the murderer; he had made a clean sweep, with none left alive to accuse him.

"But—" began Lucy, more puzzled than ever.

Her eyes, busied with the streaming headlines and big bold type at the top of the page had missed what Barry now pointed out. There were pictures of Colonel and Mrs. Hamilton, as of the other members of his household, the Colonel's aunt and two servants.

There was another picture. It was of a little girl five or six years old, the Colonel's daughter. At first it was thought that she too had been murdered. But her tiny body was never found.

Lucy gasped.

"Yes," said Barry. "Doesn't look much like you now, does it? But it's the same little girl that you were in these first pictures the Judge took. Going straight through the pack—well, you've got pretty good proof, proof enough for any jury on earth, that if you're Lucy Anybody, you're Lucy Hamilton and not Lucy Blue!"

It was hard reading that faded old newspaper by the light of a pine fire. Lucy, a tingle of excitement running through her rapidly coursing blood, looked up to exclaim:

"If we only had a lamp; even a candle! You've read all this? You know all about it?"

"Know it by heart, almost. The little girl—you,

of course—must have been carried off by the man or men who killed her parents."

"But why?" demanded Lucy.

"She was the Colonel's heiress; it was supposed that she would inherit when she was eighteen. It would seem that she was a very valuable piece of property!"

"You mean that my—that Judge Blue—"

"You're surely the girl in that paper, the little Hamilton girl, and Judge Blue kept taking those pictures of you, so at the proper time it could be proved. And you told me that night at Tylersville what you overheard at the stable, the Judge and Laredo talking—"

"And Laredo said he would marry me, but that he'd wait a few years, until I was eighteen or nineteen, I forget which—"

"And the Judge had this box, paper and pictures together. Then he lost it. That's where Laredo cut in on the deal, somehow stealing it from him. And the Judge was afraid of Laredo because of what he knew and could prove!"

"It's horrible!" She put her face in her hands, shuddering.

"Then," Barry went on, puzzled in his turn, "with Laredo fading out, while I'm hunting him from here to California and back again, Tom Haveril rides into the play! Next thing, Tom Haveril has this little box—and Tom Haveril marries you!"

"I am afraid!"

"Yes," said Barry sternly. "Just now I was ready to take you back to Tom Haveril, knowing that I'd made a mistake about him being Laredo. But how did it come that he had this box and the things in it? And just how are he and the Judge so thick? The Judge was afraid of him, knowing that what Laredo once had had gone into Tom Haveril's hands; then when he found out that the box had passed on to me, he was all for killing Tom Haveril. Am I going to take you back into that sort of mess? Damn it, Lucy, I won't do it!"

She looked at him strangely, afraid of him too, yet probing wistfully, hoping a little—no, not really afraid.

"Barry! Oh, *are* you the same Barry of that time at Tylersville? You were so true and honest then; I know it! The years have made you hard, haven't they? Have they made you into something not at all like Barry Haveril I knew so well, if for such a few hours, so long ago?"

"You should know that I'm honest and square with you, Lucy. Why, girl, you can tell! When a man is lying to you or telling you the truth—can't you *feel* it?"

"Can you, Barry?" A faint, infinitely sad smile that might have been nothing but a play of shadow touched her lips. "Tonight, when I came to where you were tied up, as I thought—I have

231

told you I meant to help you. Was I lying then?"

Barry stood looking at her a long while. "I've been thinking about that. You did come wearing my gun; outside of that I don't know how we could ever have got away, Sarboe and I. And I thought of something else. You knew, when I told you we were going where Sarboe was, that Tom Haveril's men would be there before us—"

"But—"

"Yes, I know. You couldn't tell me that, but you did do all that you could to keep me from going there. I remember, Lucy."

"And now you do know that I was telling you the truth?"

"Yes. You gave me every chance you could, Lucy." For an instant his eyes flashed up, then they darkened again as he muttered heavily: "I'm grateful to you, Lucy, but I'm almost sorry. You see, it just makes me love you all the more, and I guess it would be better for me if I could hate you instead. You're Tom Haveril's now—and Tom Haveril isn't Laredo—and I've no longer any excuse to go out and kill him—"

Lucy said: "Are you crazy, Barry Haveril? You know I'm married to Tom; no matter who he was, could you think I'd—I'd marry a man who killed him?"

"Of course I couldn't. I didn't ever think of it that way; I didn't get that far." He made a weary gesture of a hand across his eyes. In all his life there had been just two girls for him—and both were Lucy. And now, if anything in life was sure, it was that she was not for him at all.

"What are you going to do with me now, Barry?"

"I don't know what to do. We can't do anything tonight; it's too late and you're worn out. Get some sleep if you can. Maybe by morning things will be clearer."

But Lucy sat down on the floor, close to the fire, poring over the old newspaper. From time to time she would look at Barry, his head in his hands as he leaned over the table, profoundly thoughtful; or she would glance hastily at sleeping Sarboe, or at the man on the bunk when at times he muttered or groaned or turned restlessly. Always her eyes ran back to the old newspaper. For a time her emotions and thoughts alike were chaotic; it seemed an eternity since she had seen Judge Blue so treacherously kill a man, an eternity in which she had been whisked into marriage and away, then away again, Barry's captive.

Barry had said: "You don't love Tom Haveril. You married him just in a moment of horror, to escape Judge Blue." She looked at Barry again; she summoned up Tom Haveril in an imagination grown almost feverish; she made him stand right there at Barry's side. How much they were alike, those two dark, magnetic Haverils! She bit her lip; inwardly she cried defiantly; "I do love—"

Barry looked up and their eyes met.

"It's hell, that's all," he said heavily. "I love you so, Lucy—and I haven't any right."

Lucy put her head down hurriedly. She felt her face grow hot, as red as any rose. That angered her. Why should she redden like that now?

She plunged into her newspaper again, reading every line. Later she dozed, dreaming fantastic dreams, and started wide awake to find the fire still blazing, Barry still brooding at the table. She ran through the pictures of her, an unbroken chain from six in her life's clock to nineteen. Not Lucy Blue at all! That was freedom, the freedom Barry Haveril had promised her. "Get ready to be happy," he had said. None of the evil blood coursing through Parker Blue's veins rankled in hers. But she had loved him, and he had loved her; even when she feared him, she had loved him. He had been good— And was he the one who had killed her mother and father, and carried her off to hold all these years until he could make further gains through her when she, as Colonel Dave Hamilton's heiress, came into her heritage?

She was dozing again and it was almost dawn; Barry was just going to the door, meaning to saddle the horses, when they heard the cautious steps outside of someone coming guardedly to the cabin door.

XVI

Lucy looked at Barry, and Barry looked back at Lucy, and each knew what the other was thinking. Barry, already on his way to the door, kept on, pulling his gun up out of its holster. He said in a low voice to Lucy: "Don't worry. If it's Tom Haveril and the Judge, I'll do all I can to keep peace. I've been wrong about one of them; maybe about both? Anyhow, I'm not sure of anything much. Just sure I don't want to make any more trouble for you."

At the door he stood to one side, and asked curtly:

"Well? Who's out there?"

"That you, Sundown?" came an excited, high-pitched voice.

"It's good old Timberline!" Barry said to Lucy, and opened the door.

In came Timberline, a hat all in tatters pulled down lopsidedly on his head, his eyes red-rimmed and fiery, his shotgun gripped belligerently in both horny old hands.

"Shore, it's me," snorted the old fellow. "Who'd yuh s'pose it was? Lis'en here to me, Barry Sundown; all hell's busted loose an' she's a slidin' on greased skids down the fair-yuh-well to— Hello, Miss Lucy! So yuh're still with us, are yuh? Well, I reckon yuh better be trailin' yore luck, if any, with me an' Sundown than with them damn yeller pups, yore papa an' yore hubby. Say, who's that?" as Sarboe started up from his shadowy corner. Then Timber saw the still figure on the bunk and demanded, "An' who's that?"

"What's happened, Timber?" demanded Barry, getting the door shut.

"A plenty," said Timberline. "We're on the run, to save us our skelps, that's what. An' runnin' this general direction, me, I got the idee I might mebbe find you holin' up here. Better throw your laigs over yore saddles an' come ridin'. They're apt to ketch us up mos' any time, the yeller-bellied cusses."

"Who's 'Us' and who's 'They'?" demanded Barry. "You say, 'We're on the run.' Who? And what's after you?"

"Look at my hat," said Timber dolefully. He pulled it off, regarded it not so much in anger as in sorrow, and clapped it back on his head. "That was a damn good hat, Barry, an' out in Californy it was, I paid forty-six dollars for it, an' them coyotes shore shot hell out'n it tonight."

"As long as you didn't get hit—"

"Who said I didn't? Didn't yuh see me limpin' as I come in?"

"Can you make up your mind to tell us?"

"Yuh ask who's on the run; well, it's me an' your sister Lucy an' Ken March. Them two's

236

down in the pines, waitin' for me to look in here an' see if mebbe yuh did come this way. Ken March has got a bullet through one laig an' an ear mos'ly shot off. He's sorer'n a saddle boil. Who done it? Shucks, who would? It was Tom Haveril an' the ol' Judge an' a pack o' their varmints, stormin' in on us at camp, swearin' we was in on what yuh done tonight for Miss Lucy. But they knowed better, Barry. What they wanted was what they done. They druv us out an' they've jumped our claims, that's what. Juan, that owned this shotgun, he's daid now, so the gun's mine. She's loaded now, too. Coupla other fellers bit the dirt, as the feller says. We three got out, ridin' hell for breakfas', goin' some place. Any place but where we was; that's how we started. Then, what with Ken bein' hurt, yore sister thought of the old home yuh Haverils used to live in. So we're headed that way. An' yuh better sling along of us."

"Where is Lucy?" asked Lucy Blue hurriedly. "Near?"

Timberline jerked his thumb over his shoulder. "Right over yander, not more'n a coupla hundred yards." Of Barry he asked a second time of Sarboe and the form on the bunk, "Who's them fellers, Sundown?"

Barry said: "This is Sarboe. He's a friend of mine now, Timber—a friend, do you get me? And the other man—go take a good look at him."

Timberline, as full of a curiosity as any cat, limped over to the bunk. With a queer look stamped on his puckered face he turned to Barry.

"It ain't—it ain't Laredo, is it, Sundown?"

Barry nodded. Old Timber glared at him.

"Yuh shot him, an' yuh knowed well he was branded an' ear-marked for me. He was my game, whenever I could ketch up with him, an' now yuh stole him off'n me—an' I ask yuh, damn yuh, if that's any way for one pardner to treat another!"

"I didn't shoot him," said Barry, and explained.

"I'm going to your sister Lucy," said Lucy.

"Yes," said Barry. "That's good. You go to her. We'll be along."

She snatched the door open, but stopped to listen. Barry and Timberline regarded each other questioningly while Sarboe looked on. Barry said: "I've sworn to kill him. I never thought to find him like this." Timberline growled angrily. "He's a skunk an' ever was. I got a notion to go bash his brains out."

"Bash and be damned," snapped Barry.

Timberline glared at him. "How'n hell can I?" he asked petulantly. "He wouldn't even know who was a-bashin' him."

"What'll we do with him?" Barry asked.

"Leave him here; that's all we can do. An' we better step lively."

Barry could only reply, "Sure, that's right."

They began preparing hastily to go, Timberline insisting that they would be followed hot-haste by the ravaging crew worked up by the Judge and Tom Haveril.

"They'll find Laredo here," muttered Barry. "Then what'll happen, Timber, when those two, the Judge and Tom Haveril, find him lying there, neither alive or dead?"

"They'll blow his brains out, o' course," said Timber promptly.

"Of course. If we walk out and leave him like that— Well, we might as well screw up our nerve and cut his throat while he's unconscious, and be done with it."

"Damn," said Timberline violently. "Not as it wouldn't serve him right, the tomato-spillin' pup," he added hastily. "Only it goes kind ag'in the grain, Sundown. Don't it?"

Then Barry noticed Lucy, still standing at the door. "I thought you had gone," he said.

"I'm going now." She stepped outside; but instead of going, she stood by the cabin wall, waiting for them, listening to what they said.

"We kaint take him along with us," said Timberline. "Or kin we?"

"How'll we manage it?" asked Barry.

Then Lucy, marveling at men, ran off through the thin light of the new day, eagerly looking for Barry's sister. When she saw the three horses,

Lucy Blount holding Timberline's jaded animal, Lucy Blount saw her and instantly slid down from her saddle. The two girls ran into each other's arms, and certainly one of the Lucys, the one whose wedding night this was, was infinitely glad to have the other Lucy's arms tightening about her.

When Barry and Timberline joined them, they bore the unconscious Jesse Conroy—Laredo, damn him!—in their arms, wrapped in a blanket. Barry said:

"Hello, Lucy; hello, Ken. You folks ride along, and take Lucy with you. She'll be better off with you than anywhere else for a few days; until anyhow she knows which way to turn. It's about sixty miles on to Pa's place. I guess the house is still standing. Timber and I'll join you later. One or the other of us will ride in on you tomorrow. Nobody's apt to find you there. If you need anything, food or any kind of help, it's not very far to Tex Humphreys' horse ranch." Then he added solicitously, "Not bad hurt, are you, Ken?"

Ken March made light of his wounds, though Barry's sister exclaimed over them. But March raged about what had happened at the camp during Barry's absence. Those devils, Judge Blue and Tom Haveril and—

"Sh!" said Barry's sister hurriedly. "Don't, Ken."

"What are you going to do with your sick man?" Ken wanted to know.

"We're goin' to nurse him like a tender young shoot," muttered Timberline. "Barry knows a place where we can tote him; we'll feed him by han', an' keep his flame a-flickerin'. When he gits good an' lively ag'in, I'm goin' to blow his damn head off 'n his skunkery shoulders."

"You folks ride on," insisted Barry. "Timber and I, with Sarboe to lend a hand, will take care of this. Then one of us, maybe two, will join you. Ride happy, you three."

Lucy, his sister, ran to him and kissed him, clinging to him a moment, being bearishly caught in his arms. Lucy, Tom Haveril's wife, climbed into the saddle of her horse which the silent Sarboe brought to her; she sat as silent as Sarboe, looking at Barry.

"Let's get going," said Ken March. "We're not out of the woods yet, any of us."

The three rode off through the pines. Barry stood looking after them. Lucy, Tom Haveril's new wife, turned and looked back. He saw that she had the flat steel box clutched tight under one arm. He thought for a moment that she was about to say something to him. Lucy was thinking that Barry Haveril was about to call out something to her. Neither spoke. In a few moments the departing trio vanished among the pines.

"Now, which a-way?" asked Timberline irritably.

241

"You think that they'll be able to find my hide-out here," said Barry. "I don't. Just the same, we'll move off onto the mountainside a bit to a sheltered place where we can hole up. We can hide the horses in an aspen thicket I know about; we can keep an eye on the cabin all day. If they don't show up before dark, we'll move back into it."

So the three of them carried the half dead Laredo Kid the half mile to the place Barry had in mind, a bosky dell set like a green dimple on the shoulder of the mountain where it began sloping down into a wooded ravine.

"Snakes is hard to kill," observed Timberline after they had put their burden down.

Barry had noticed how the old fellow limped and he grew solicitous. Seeking Timberline's wound he came by the discovery that his old pardner had lost a boot heel; it had been shot neatly off his boot with no further damage done.

"You damned old four-flusher!" Barry called him.

Timberline looked hurt. "Me? Didn't I jus' tell yuh I'd been shot, Sundown? I didn't say where, did I? An' I've shore got a permanent limp, ain't I? Long as these boots las', anyhow."

All day they watched over Jesse Conroy who was obviously a very sick man, feverish and wasted and with fast seeping vitality. "He's a-dyin' on us, consarn the cuss," growled Timberline. All day, too, they kept an eye on the cabin, watchful for the coming of the Judge and Tom Haveril with such a crowd at their heels as Timberline was sure would be yelping along after them. And all day poor dumb Sarboe was in the throes of some agony all his own, bursting with the desire to speak, terribly tense as he strove to command his vocal cords. Timberline, looking at him, said: "Pore devil. Ain't it hell, Sundown? He's goin' to bust a blood vessel if he don't look out. What's he got on his mind anyhow? Somethin' about Laredo, ain't it?"

For Sarboe was forever going to stand and look at Jesse Conroy and coming back to Barry to look at him dumbly and pleading as a dog looks at its master.

"This boy's crazy to tell yuh somethin', Sundown," said Timber. "An', seein' how he can't talk—"

"He can talk," said Barry looking steadily at Sarboe.

"Then why'n hell don't he!" cried old Timber.

"Because—he can't!" said Barry.

Timberline gaped at him. "That don't make no sense an' yuh know it, Barry. Yuh say he can talk but he don't talk because he can't talk! Who's crazy, now, you or me?"

"It's funny," Barry conceded. "You see, Timber, I've been living off alone with Sarboe a long time, seven or eight weeks anyhow. And many's the night, especially when he's been fagged out or worried, that he jabbers all night in his sleep. Sleeping, he talks right out plain."

"Whyn't yuh wake him up?"

"When I do, he can't say a word." Sarboe, watching them and listening, was in his silent eloquence the embodiment of distress. "The harder he tries," said Barry, "the tighter he gets himself tied up. I believe that if he didn't much care whether he could talk or not, why then, he could talk his head off."

Timber scratched his head and puckered his mouth up; Barry, knowing him of old, stepped quickly aside and Timber's amber mist, projected aimlessly, merely stained the already russet brown pine needles underfoot. "Whyn't yuh teach him to spell, Barry, so's he could write it out?"

"I'm working on him," said Barry, and shook his head. "He'll learn, give him time."

"Start him off easy. Give him rat an' cat an' hat an'— Yuh know, Sundown. Yuh been to school, ain't yuh?"

"So you think he's dying on us, do you?" asked Barry, looking at Laredo.

"Yuh're a sort of a funny bird," said Timberline thoughtfully. "Savin' this skunk's life, when yuh been three year lookin' for him jus' to kill him."

"You can't kill a man in his shape—not like he is now."

"Why can't yuh?"

"Could *you?*"

"Me? Hell, no." And that was all that they said about that matter. Nor did they refer in any way to the Laredo Kid again until it was growing dark. They had done what they could for him and they had kept watch over the cabin. No one came near. In the first dusk Timberline observed in an offhand way, "He looks kind of skinny, Sundown. Like he hadn't been eatin' regular." Oh, Laredo? Well, he couldn't ask much at their hands. Still they made a little secret fire and put a pot on it, and it was old Timber who, picking over their scraps of food, made a watery soup. While Barry held the half conscious figure up in his arms, Timberline used their big iron spoon. Laredo came near choking to death but didn't. An hour later they carried him back to the cabin. As Timberline had remarked, "Snakes is hard to kill."

Half way through the next day Timberline admitted: "Well, I reckon yuh was right for once, Sundown; that skulduggery bunch o' hell-hounds lost our track." He ruminated, then added, grown suddenly waspish, "Yuh're takin' it layin' down, are yuh?"

Barry cocked up his eyebrows. "Taking what?"

"They've chased us out, kilt Juan, stole our

245

gold mine, an' yuh ain't said a word. How about it?"

"We'll straighten that out," returned Barry coolly. "They can't get away with a raw deal like that, Timber."

"Well, what's holdin' us?" snapped the old man.

"Just like you said, 'It's a funny thing.'" He looked over at wan but conscious Laredo on the bunk. "If you saw an animal out in the woods, dog or deer or cat, and it was in his shape, well, you'd either put it out of its misery or lend a hand. Happens we can't knock Laredo in the head, so we're simply tied up, old-timer, that's all."

But they decided while discussing so absurd a situation that there was no earthly need of three men sticking on here to feed a sick man soup and take care of his bandage. And they did want to know whether all was well with Ken March and the two Lucys.

"You ride along after them, Timber," said Barry. "I can tell you how to find Pa's place. They'll want to know we're all right too. You and Ken can talk things over. Then come back here in a few days and we'll get busy."

Timberline went willingly on his errand. Barry and Sarboe took turns in ministering to the wounded man and in providing provisions, hunting and fishing. At odd times they labored at spelling lessons over Barry's homemade table.

Weeks ago he had started the sort of instruction Timberline had suggested; Sarboe was both diligently and stupidly learning to write. Barry was perhaps not the best teacher in the world, but he was patient; he didn't clout Sarboe over the head for his stupidity the way Zachary Blount used to do with his "scholars." They made progress, but so does a snail.

The Laredo Kid, instead of dying, as he undoubtedly should, mended from the first day; the man's constitution was as tough as boot leather. In three days, having the lay of the land and feeling master of the situation, he spoke some part of his mind.

"Yuh been good to me, Cousin Barry," he jibed, with so much malice in his eyes that it must have been the overflow of the spleen within him. "Two times now, yuh've mothered me when I was all shot to hell. Shore yuh been good to me, Sundown—an' yuh been a damn fool always."

"As soon as you can hold a gun steady," said Barry angrily, "I'm going to hand you one—and kill you."

Laredo laughed at him. Two days later he appeared to have a relapse. It turned out to be just a bit of clever acting on his part. Sarboe was off stalking a deer; Laredo, gasping like a fish out of water, pretending that he was ready to give up the ghost, prevailed on Barry to rush off looking for Sarboe. "I got to tell him somethin' afore I die," said Laredo.

Barry was away an hour. When he came back he was wet with sweat and was breathing hard; he brought Sarboe back with him only to discover that the Kid had gone. Gone also were both saddle horses and the bulk of what little provisions the cabin afforded. Laredo, riding away, had neither gone empty handed nor left them a means of overhauling him.

If Sarboe could have spoken then! It would have been worth a man's while to listen to him, that's all.

Barry said, "He's like that, Sarboe, and it's time we knew it. It's just luck for us we didn't leave any guns in camp!" To himself he admitted, "I'm as slow learning Laredo as Sarboe's slow learning to read and write."

There was nothing to hold them here longer, unless it were the return of Timberline. But Timberline might be showing up either today or a week later, and they decided not to wait for him. Barry wrote in big letters on the top of his table with charcoal: "Gone on to see about Ken and Lucy and you." Then he and Sarboe shouldered their small packs and started on the long walk to Barry's old home.

On their way they were always on the lookout for Timberline coming back, though they knew there was not one chance in a hundred of seeing him in those forest ways even though he was returning. They slept out that first night, bedding down where they found a clear spot in the heart of a thicket. They slept the second night in a place Barry knew, where he used to hunt, a dry glade in a little crease in the mountains. The next day by mid forenoon they came within sight of the old home.

The old place tugged at Barry's heart as old home places must always do. It had been so long since he came this way! He knew every tree and rock, every knoll and dimple in the hills. Sharply clear as the day was, he saw the broken fences and the rock chimney and the spring house and all that through a mist. Yonder, under the tall pine boling slantingly up from a nest of boulders, he had fired his first shot. An old shotgun it was, with a poor old red-headed woodpecker for a high target; he'd knocked the bird but the gun had knocked little Barry clean over backward, sprawling, the mule-kicking old weapon flying out of his hands. And down there was the spring; a path used to lead to it; he and little Lucy would carry the big bucket between them, slopping the clear cold water over their bare legs. The cats, yellow and gray and tortoise-shell would follow them, often running ahead and crouching down in the grass, mimic small, tail-lashing panthers.

Suddenly Barry, leading the way, came to a dead halt.

"Somebody besides our crowd has moved in here, Sarboe," he said, and sounded angry, the old memories of a moment ago gone helter-skelter.

He pointed, indicating what he had seen. Under a tree, half hidden by a corner of the house was an old, travel-weary emigrant wagon. Some strange horses were in the clearing beyond.

"Little chance we'll find Ken and Timber and the two Lucys here," he added, "but come ahead; anyhow we'll get some word of them."

So they went on and a moment later Sarboe heard a strange sort of exclamation burst from the man again leading the way. Someone had come out onto the rickety old porch; it was a small, slender woman. She called out something and started down the steps as two men came out of the house behind her, one a tall rangy black-bearded man whose thick black hair was growing streakedly gray, one his duplicate save that he was years younger, with a youthful beard of the same black but with no streaks in it.

And then Sarboe was hard beset to keep up with Barry Haveril who went striding along to the house as though he could not get there fast enough. Next the two Lucys came running out of the house, with Ken March close behind.

The slender little woman who had been first to sight the oncomers started running along the path toward them, and Barry bore down on her faster and faster, presently sweeping her clear off the ground and hugging her, dropping everything to do so, while she hugged him as heartily if less crushingly. And then the two tall black-bearded men came and stood looking on and saying nothing until he set her down, when they both put out their hands.

"Home again!" cried Barry, his eyes wet and shining. "All of us!"

All of them except dead Robert who lay buried up in the hills toward Tex Humphreys' place, slaughtered by the Laredo Kid for the sake of a horse and saddle. Here was his father, Ben Haveril, who hadn't changed a bit except that he looked even gaunter than of old and there was that dusting of gray on him, and that he limped a little; and brother Lute, the same old Lute only grown up, like Barry; and their mother, always delicate looking and yet full of vitality under that pretty outward seeming of frailty, as pink-cheeked as ever. And of course Lucy, their own Lucy, was laughing and crying from sheer happiness, while the other Lucy, who used to be Lucy Blue, looked on smilingly—and then had to dash her own tears away.

They all sat on the porch, as close as they could together, with Sarboe sitting back against the wall to look at them and take it all in. There was so much to be said, such volleys of questions, most of which had to go without answers because there was really no time for answering with fresh questions being voiced with every breath drawn, that Lucy Blount began laughing again and Lucy Blue joined her, and then Lute broke out with a hearty, deep-toned laughter, and altogether they were as happy as most people ever get to be. Through it all Barry and his mother sat holding hands, and her quick nervous fingers never ceased touching the many little scars and scratches which the years had made. There was one scar at the base of his left thumb; she opened his palm and put her fingertip on it and said softly: "Remember, Baron?" He nodded, grinning back at her. "I was six years old, wasn't I, Ma? It was my birthday and my first knife, wasn't it? Robert and I—"

She got up hurriedly and went into the house, and he knew it was to throw herself down on her bed, her glad heart breaking because Robert wouldn't ever be with them again in this world. Barry's jaw set so that it went white where the hard muscles bulged.

When he thought to ask of Timberline it was just one of those scores of questions that didn't get answered, someone else's words cutting across his and being more insistent. Later he was to learn that Timberline had left two days ago, heading back to Barry and Sarboe. But this was not mentioned until they were having supper, when Timberline came riding back to them. He was calling out the news to them as he crawled out of the saddle.

"Anybody seen anything o' Sundown?" he clamored. "Anybody know where he is or what's happened to him?"

When it was Barry who answered heartily, "Why here I am, Timber," and led the way outside, the old miner drew a deep breath and expelled it with an eloquent "Whoof!"

"Glory be!" he said fervently. "Thought mebbe they'd got yuh this time, pardner."

"What's it all about, Timber?"

Timberline twisted his head about on his thin old neck to look back into the darkening pine forest lands as though he was half afraid of seeing some sort of catastrophe burst out of it and bear down on them.

"They got sight of me, the cusses, about fifteen-twenty miles back," he muttered. "But me, I was atop a ridge an' seen 'em first, an' I shore rid hell-for-leather, gittin' out o' sight. I don't reckon they've been able to foller me so quick, but they'll be comin', Sundown; you mark my words, they'll be a-comin'. An' soon."

Everybody started asking questions again. Timberline said: "I'm so damn dry; if somebody'll han' me a dipper o' that spring water, I'll tell yuh folks. An' while my drink's comin' I'll tell yuh the main part." His eyes, red-rimmed and bleak and wrathful, turned to Barry. "They've outlawed yuh, pardner, damn 'em; outlawed yuh for stealin' another man's wife. They've made it look like it was all lawful, goin' out an' gittin' the sheriff in on it, him an' a posse. An' Judge Blue an' Tom Haveril has both offered rewards for yore hide. Red Rock's buzzin' like a hornets' nest yuh throwed a rock in. They're out gunnin' for yuh, Sundown, an' all warranted to shoot on sight."

"Here's your water, Mr. Timberline," said Barry's mother quietly.

Barry looked at her. She was white to the lips with all the roses faded away from her cheeks. But as she handed Timberline his drink the brimming dipper slopped over never a single drop.

XVII

At the supper table, with very little eating going on, they looked at one another questioningly in the soft yellow light of their coal oil lamp. There were plans to be made and it was agreed they had best be made without delay. First, however, Timberline had to tell all that he knew and how he came to know it.

He had ridden back to Barry's cabin along the lower slopes, whereas Barry and Sarboe had kept higher up. It was just before he reached the cabin that he had the good fortune to encounter a man who had left Red Rock the day before, one Cliff Bendiger, an old prospector of Timberline's own breed and a friend. He had said, by way of greeting: "I hear young Barry Haveril's a pardner of yore'n. Well, if so, yuh better know now if yuh don't already, what the talk is." The two of them chinned for ten minutes, Timberline said; then he dug his heels in and scooted on to the cabin.

"I feared at first they'd got yuh, Sundown," he said, pawing away nervously at the stubble on his chin. "But then I said, Pshaw, Sundown's jus' walked out, over to jine up with us, mos' likely. 'Cause the door was shet proper, an' there wasn't any blood spilt, an' yuh'd even took yore bed rolls an' grub. So I guesses likely Laredo died on yuh, or yuh got impatient an' kilt the son-a-gun and buried him, so I struck back this way."

They speculated upon the riders he had seen some "fifteen-twenty mile from here." Ben Haveril, Barry's father, offered thoughtfully:

"If yuh saw them that close, well likely they're headed here. Where else?" And then he asked, while his heavy brows came down in a tangled black frown: "Yuh say they got the sheriff in this? That'd be Ed Brawley, from down Tylersville way."

"Yep," said old Timber. "Shore."

"He used to fit snug in Judge Blue's tail-pocket," said Ben Haveril. "Reckon he still does. He's a damn scoundrel—jus' like ol' Blue hisse'f. The two of them varmints—"

"Don't, Ben," said Barry's mother swiftly, and everyone, understanding, looked sideways at Lucy Blue. She turned red and stirred uneasily on her part of the long bench; then she said earnestly:

"You folks mustn't mind me. I already know about him, and—"

"Anyhow," put in Barry, his words clipping hers off like a pair of shears, "he's not her father. I'm pretty sure her father was a man named Hamilton, a Colonel Hamilton—"

"Not Dave Hamilton, down Laredo way!"

exclaimed his father. "Yuh don't mean Colonel Dave, do yuh, Barry?"

"He's the one, Pa. Didn't know him, did you?"

"Murdered, he was, him an' his wife an' others; all Laredo was up in arms about it. No, we didn't know the Hamiltons, but ever'body knowed of 'em. Must of been ten-fifteen year ago—"

"Twelve years," said Barry. "They had a little girl; that's Lucy here. Whoever did the robbing and murdering carried her off. You see, Pa, the Colonel must have left a pretty big property; it was in his will that Lucy was to inherit when she grew up. So she'd be worth holding, for a man to grab the stake by waiting that long."

Ben Haveril said emphatically, "The one man I know of to play a game like that is ol' Judge Blue."

Barry's mother interrupted them in that quiet way of hers. She never raised her voice; there was no need to. Every one of them always gave her his attention.

"Don't you think that we can talk about this later?" she asked gently. "If those men that Mr. Timberline saw are really coming here, Barry had better be somewhere else."

Timberline's mouth which had been hanging open while he listened to all this talk, now closed with a snap. He jerked erect where he sat and said vigorously:

"Yuh're the only one o' this crowd that's got

any sense, Mrs. Haveril—excep' me. Talkin' about a murder a dozen years ago ain't goin' to stop some more murderin' bein' done tonight. If a gang swoops in on us while Barry's here, we got to fight it out with 'em, ain't we? If Sundown'll do a quick sneak, let 'em come. Later on we'll figger how to play the right cards out'n the han' they're dealin' us."

"That's sense," nodded Ben Haveril. "Barry won't have to go fur, but he better step along. He c'n watch the house from the woods, come day, an' c'n come on back if the coast is clear. When I asked if it was Ed Brawley that they'd rung in on us, this is why: When yore mother an' Lute an' me come back here to the ol' place, Barry, we come through Tylers. What's more, I had a few words with Brawley; he knows we headed this way. An' he's shore to figger on it bein' anyhow likely yore droppin' in on us. So I reckon we c'n count on seein' him an' his houn' dawgs right soon, shore to if they're the ones Timberline seen."

"You had better go right away, Barry," said his mother. She got up and came to stand just behind him, her hands on his shoulders. He gave one of those dear hands a pat and a squeeze and stood up.

"Of course you're right," he said. He spoke quietly, like his mother, but there were smoldering angry fires in his eyes. "I don't want to run out on you folks, but it's clear as day that my staying

258

here now would only drag you all into it. Sure, I'll go. But there's something you're all forgetting—"

Lucy, the gray-eyed Lucy, Tom Haveril's bride, sprang to her feet. There were fires in her eyes too; she stood quiveringly tense. She could not wait for Barry to finish. She cried out passionately:

"What about me? What am I to do?"

"That's what I was thinking of," muttered Barry, "when I said there was something they were forgetting."

"Don't you see?" demanded the girl. "It isn't only Barry they want. They're after me, too!"

"But, dear—" Mrs. Haveril began, and stopped there. She was about to say, "One of the men will no doubt be your father." There was so much to think about, so much fresh news to assimilate, that she was on the verge of forgetting that this was not Lucy Blue at all, but Lucy Hamilton. She finished her thought though. She added, "But your husband will be one of them, or anyhow—"

Lucy's eyes were brighter than ever and her face was aflame again when she made her hurried rejoinder.

"I am not going back to—to anybody, until I know a lot of things! I—" She whirled to Barry. "Take me with you, Barry! I know that I can trust you; I'm not afraid of you! And I am afraid of—of them!"

Barry stood a moment frowning in sheer puzzlement. Hunted himself, had he any right to take her into danger with him? What could he do with her? Where could he take her? He said slowly, thinking aloud:

"She wouldn't be in any more danger with me, wherever we went, than she is here. If they find her, they'll grab her. Tom Haveril will find how to keep her. They've got it all planned out just how they're going to rob her."

"We wouldn't let 'em take her, Barry," said his father. "Not unless she wanted."

"But don't you see?" cried Lucy. "It would be the same as if Barry had stayed; they'd turn things upside down to get me—it's the Hamilton money they're after, I know it. Didn't they—didn't someone murder for a part of it long ago? And there'd be shooting and more killing. *I won't stay here!* I won't let them have me! I'm not just a rag doll for them to pull at. I'm going to run off by myself." And actually she did start to run out of the room.

Barry caught her by the arm. He didn't speak to her but to his brother.

"Get a couple of horses saddled up for us, will you, Lute? We'll be getting ready to go. We'll want the same horses we rode the night I carried her off from Tom Haveril's ranch; they won't find anything then to show we've ever been here. Sarboe, will you lend Lute a hand?"

260

The two hurried out. Ben Haveril went to the chimney for his old deer rifle.

"Me, I'll step along outside too," he said, and turned to shake hands with Barry. "Ride lucky, Barry. It won't be long. Meantime I'm out where I c'n do a mite o' watchin' an' listenin'. Jus' in case, yuh know," he concluded, and went out.

"Where will you go, Baron?" Mrs. Haveril asked, her lips betraying her only with the faintest quiver.

He hugged her and laid his cheek against her hair. "Not far, Ma, and we'll be all right. Even if I did know, better not to tell you; if they do come and start asking questions— Well, you can tell 'em you haven't the faintest notion where we are. Now, let's get some blankets rolled, and a speck of something to eat."

Timberline got to his feet and stood teetering nervously.

"Look ye, Sundown," he spoke up, and showed his teeth like an old wolf, "yuh take damn' good care o' yuhse'f, but yuh don't need to go fur. Meantime we'll do some figgerin'. An'— Say! What happened to Laredo? Yuh never told me. Died, did the son-a-gun? Yuh didn't let him crawl out on us, did yuh, Sundown?"

Barry said: "Never mind him now, Timber. Yes, he got away."

"Your Ma an' Pa knows something about him, Barry; that is if yuh're shore he's Jesse Conroy

261

too. Mebbe they ain't got aroun' to tellin' yuh about it, but—"

"I can tell him later," cut in Lucy Hamilton hurriedly. "They told me. Come, let's hurry— let's run!"

"What's all this?" he demanded, mystified.

But his mother came to him with the pack of provisions she had prepared and said in her quietly emphatic way: "Never mind now, Baron. As Lucy says, she can tell you." She pulled his head down to kiss him and whispered in his ear, "Be good to her, Baron. Oh, mighty good."

The wanly lighted windows behind them were blotted out in the dark. The black limbs of trees like monstrous arms spread above them; stars glinted through only to make the blackness of the night seem blacker. Their horses' hoofs made little sound upon the thick mat of dead pine needles; saddle leather creaked, bridle chains jingled softly and there was the hushed whispering of the pinetops. So it was through a starlit world of dark and silence that the two, side by side, drifted away from their own kind into the heart of the wilderness.

A sigh escaped the girl. That was when, after a few minutes of riding, she experienced a sensation of relief, of escape. At the same instant Barry spoke.

Barry said, "You know I love you, Lucy."

And Lucy, her voice hushed like the breath of night air through the pines, answered him with the question, "Do you, Barry?"

"And you, Lucy—down in your heart—"

"Don't, Barry!" For he had reined in close to her and his hand had found hers upon her bridle reins. "You mustn't, Barry."

So he freed her, and stared straight ahead as they rode on.

Presently she said: "Barry, life is terrible, isn't it? It isn't fair! It doesn't give us a chance. If one only knew—"

"Why didn't I take you away with me that time from Tylersville?" he exclaimed bitterly.

She didn't answer, but in her heart she whispered despairingly, "Oh, why didn't you, Barry?"

"Tonight I'm going to take you to Tex Humphreys' ranch," said Barry. "It's not far; we'll be there in an hour or an hour and a half—"

"Sh!" whispered Lucy, and reached out to catch his sleeve. "I hear someone coming!"

He, too, heard horses' hoofs on a bit of rocky trail in the distance, and a moment later there were faint, faraway voices.

"Let's hurry!" said Lucy. "Let's ride into that darker place, down there, where all the aspens are. They won't find us, will they, Barry?"

They had scarcely drawn aside from the trail when a dozen men went riding by where Barry and Lucy watched and listened, as still as the mountains about them, far stiller than the quivering aspens down in the little whispering glen in which Robert Haveril took his long last rest under a heap of stones. Two of those men were Judge Blue and Tom Haveril, for they heard their voices. Barry, since a man must always hurt himself and her whom he loves most, could not help saying: "There's your chance, Lucy. It's your husband."

And all she said, fighting back the tears, was, "Don't, Barry."

The riders passed on; the wilderness drank them up. Barry and Lucy struck into the dim trail leading to Tex Humphreys' horse ranch, a trail far dimmer than in the old days when Robert used to travel it to his trysts with the shy half-Indian maid, Molly. When they drew near Tex Humphreys' cabin in his clearing among the pines, Barry said, "Wait here a minute; I'll go ahead and make sure it's all right," and swung down and left her holding his horse.

The house was dark, but then it was high time folks were abed. Barry walked softly, his carbine cradled in the crook of his left arm, his right hand resting lightly upon the worn, red grip of the old gun he had had so long ago from the Laredo Kid.

A slim little figure started up before him, materializing out of the blackest of the shadows.

"Jesse! So you did come back to me!" said a soft voice murmurously.

"Molly!" exclaimed Barry. "It's you, isn't it, Molly?"

She drew back, poised for flight. "You— Who are you?" She sounded frightened.

"I am Barry. Don't you remember Barry Haveril, Robert's brother?"

"Oh!" She gasped out the one syllable and drew still farther back from him.

"You thought I was Jesse," he said. "What Jesse? Who is the Jesse you looked for?"

"No one," said Molly, and would have slipped away but that he caught her by the arm.

"Yes," said Barry insistently. "You were waiting out here for Jesse Conroy, weren't you?"

"You let me go," the Indian girl commanded in a small, hushed storm of rage. "You let me go."

Barry still held her as he said sternly: "You remember Robert, don't you, Molly? You remember the day someone killed him, and we found him lying down yonder in the cañon?"

Molly was trying to bite his hand but suddenly froze still. Faint as was the starlight he could see the glimmer of the whites of her startled eyes.

"Don't you talk like that! He—he is a ghost that walks at night—" She broke off shivering.

"It's Jesse Conroy, isn't it?" Barry persisted,

still gripping her arm. "You're waiting here for him. And he is the man who murdered Robert! You are taking for a lover the man who murdered Robert who loved you."

She didn't say anything then; she no longer tried to break away, but he felt her physical rigidity and, after it, her sudden breaking down. Even then, though she was weeping, he heard never a sob from her.

"You did love Robert, didn't you, Molly?" he said gently.

She nodded miserably. She said faintly: "Robert, gone now. His ghost walks at night. Every night it comes and, over the fence, talks with me. All the time, Barry, a fence is there between."

"And then Jesse Conroy came!"

"I was so sad," she said. "And Jesse— He looked like Robert, just a little. And—and—"

"And so you loved him, too, Molly?"

She grew fierce, stamping passionately. "No! You tell me he killed Robert? That is true! I know. One time Jesse asks me about Robert— and when I cry he laughs. And he says something then I can't understand until now! He says, 'If I hadn't come, your Robert wouldn't be gone, huh?' And he laughs some more, like a bad joke."

"Damn him," muttered Barry.

"Let me go," said Molly, and he freed her. A

moment she stood still, and he could feel those big dark eyes of hers fixed tragically upon him. Then she sped away, running off into the forest, just as she had fled those three years and more ago from the presence of her dead lover, seeking now as then whatever solace the solitudes had for her wild soul.

Barry went on slowly toward the dark cabin. When he rapped lightly there was no answer. He knocked louder and then tried the latch. The door opened and he called, "Tex! Oh, Tex!" The silence, when his voice died away, remained unbroken.

He stepped into the house and in the dark found a remembered way to the fireplace, struck a light and ignited a small fire from scraps of bark and splintered wood scattered about the hearth. Carrying a blazing pine knot for a torch he passed through the four small rooms. The place looked long deserted; save for a few bits of food on a kitchen table and a bed of sorts in a corner, there was no sign of recent occupancy.

"Molly slept there," he muttered. "But where's Tex? Where are the rest of them?"

The empty house afforded no answer. Puzzled, he went back for Lucy.

XVIII

The fire on Tex Humphreys' long cold hearth, built up afresh by Barry, blazed cheerily. Lucy crouched close to it, warming her hands, toasting a slim body that was cold not so much with the sharp mountain night air as with apprehension, while Barry stood, a somber figure, across the hearth and stared down at her. Doors were fastened, board shutters closed at all the small square windows.

"That girl?" said Lucy without looking up. "I saw her run off into the forest like a mad thing. Who was she, Barry?"

"Poor little Indian Molly." He told her of Molly, of Robert, of Laredo who had murdered Robert, then had come back after the wound in the half-wild girl's bosom had scarred over and had made her love him.

"Men are such beasts," said Lucy.

"Yes."

She looked up at him then. "But—but not you, Barry!"

She drew even closer to the fireplace, looking very tiny as he towered so high above her; there were high heels on his boots and his shadow, which she saw out of the corners of her eyes, was like a giant's. After a long while she said, ever so softly.

"You are the best, the finest man I ever knew, Barry."

"Lucy!"

"Don't!" she cried warningly. "Stay where you are, Barry. Don't come any closer to me."

He demanded, sounding stern, not at all lover-like, "Do you love me, Lucy?"

"I—I think I do, Barry. Oh, I shouldn't tell you that, should I? I think I have always loved you, since the very first day. But you stay where you are, on your side of the fireplace!"

But he couldn't stand still; he began moving up and down, taking the small room in three or four strides, striding back. A queer pain came into her heart, throbbing so wildly under the soft whiteness of her breast, seeming to her about to burst; she had never seen his face look so bleak. Largely to break the silence which had fallen upon them she asked:

"Where did Molly go? Do her folks live somewhere near?"

"That's what I don't know; I didn't have sense enough to ask. I was thinking about something else."

"She thought you were Jesse Conroy—the Laredo Kid? She was expecting him here?"

"He'd keep a girl waiting and come or not as suited him," said Barry. "No use speculating on him. The important thing right now is that you've got to have some sleep. Where'll I put your bed, Lucy? In this room, where the fire is?"

She rose slowly. "In the corner, there. And your bed in that other corner. I—I am afraid, Barry."

She was helping him with the blankets when there came a soft scratching sound at a window which made them start erect.

"It's all right," said Barry, but he did not raise his voice above a whisper, and Lucy saw how swiftly and instinctively his hand dropped what it was doing and ran with quicksilver fluidity to his old worn red gun. "Anyone who knocks like that—"

The sound at the window came again. Barry spoke up, saying curtly, "Well? Who's there? What do you want?"

It was Molly. She said: "I want to talk with her, Barry. The girl. You, Girl, come out here."

"She frightens me," whispered Lucy. "What does she want, Barry?"

Barry called to Molly, "You come in here, Molly."

"No! I will never go in that damn' house again!"

"I'm going!" said Lucy, drawn by Molly's voice.

Barry went with her to the door, lifting down the bar. At the last minute he slipped his belt gun into her hand. "You'll be all right with Molly," he assured her. "There's no harm in her.

270

But take this; you'll feel safer. And don't go ten steps from the door. Call, and I'll come running."

Opening the door, he saw Molly's tragic eyes, enormous and glittering in the uncertain light from his pine fire. The two girls stood a moment looking at each other, then as Molly beckoned insistently, Lucy stepped after her, out of the light, into the dark.

Barry returned to his task of preparing beds for the night on Tex Humphreys' sitting room floor. Outside he heard the girls talking, Molly urgent, whispering sibilantly, Lucy asking swift, breathless questions. They seemed to draw a little farther way; either that, or in his preoccupation he no longer listened to their hushed voices.

His own bed was ready in no time at all; all his life he had been used to throwing a blanket down, when he had a blanket, and rolling into it and going to sleep. To make a cozy nest for Lucy was an altogether different matter, the floor boards were so hard, the blankets so thin and inadequate.

He was just straightening up when he heard a voice speaking drawingly close behind him. Someone had stepped quietly into the room through the door he had left open for Lucy. He was sure it was Laredo come late to a tryst with Molly.

"You damn woman-stealer!" said the voice. Barry pivoted to face Tom Haveril. "I'm going to kill you this time, Sundown Haveril, just as sure as you're a foot high."

Barry did not for a second expect anything but sudden death. He had given Lucy his belt gun; his carbine stood tantalizingly just out of reach against the wall, as useless as a broom stick.

"Kill and be damned to you," he said, and sounded merely disgusted. It was disgusting, come to think of it; downright disgusting. A man could only wish to have it over with. You played your hand; you lost; let the devil sweep your discard down to hell along with the rest of the deadwood. So he said, "Shoot and be damned to you, and let's get it over."

"So you're going to face it like a little man, taking it standing up, are you?" jeered Tom Haveril. "You can't run away and you can't grab a gun, so like any cornered coyote you'll look it in the face, will you? All right, you — — — —! Only I'll tell you before you go climbing up them golden stairs after your wings and a harp—"

Barry wasn't listening. The greatest rage of Barry's entire life flamed up within him then, but it was perforce a hopeless, futile rage that died down in a sort of ash heap of despair. Yet somehow he must warn Lucy, to prevent her from falling into this man's hands.

There had been a blank; he had missed what Tom Haveril was saying.

"What's that?" he demanded. "What did you say?"

Tom Haveril laughed at him, thinking him so gripped by terror as to have no power of attending to what was being said. So now he spoke with slow, emphatic deliberation.

"You yellow dog," he said, "you're scared; that's what's the matter with you. Well, you better be, and I'm damn glad to watch you go out like this, with your tail between your legs. I always knew you for a four-flusher and a cheat and a coward."

"So you're going to murder me, are you? No killing for you in fair fight—"

"Shut up! Where's Lucy?"

"She isn't here," said Barry. He was thinking: "One lunge, throwing myself sidewise and down, will bring me to my carbine. By then I'll have two or three of his bullets in me, but maybe I'll still be alive. It's my only chance." Still looking Tom Haveril in the eye, he added, "You can see for yourself she isn't here."

"And she's not far!" Tom Haveril snapped angrily. "You and her, you two — — —! If you'll die any happier, I'll tell you that I wouldn't dirty my hands touching her after you've had her—"

"You fool! Lucy and I—"

"Two little saints, huh?" Tom Haveril mocked him. "Well, as my wife she won't last long, but as

Colonel Hamilton's heiress, that's different! Oh, you know all about it too, don't you—you damn thief who'd steal a man's papers and his wife and anything else. You— Get ready to take it, Sundown. You're a dead man in two ticks. I'm sick of jawing with you."

Barry's whole body, every muscle coordinating with his brain, was as tense as a taut violin string, ready for that last desperate lunge. Just then he heard a quiet footfall and Lucy's voice at the same instant; he even caught sight of her, vague in the dark just outside the door.

"Tom!" cried Lucy. "Don't! I—I'll kill you, so help me God—"

Tom Haveril whirled. Barry made his dive for his carbine. A shot rang out—another shot. The heavy lead from Tom Haveril's weapon gouged splinters from the floor an inch from Barry's prone body. Tom Haveril himself took the other bullet, high up in the chest. He reeled backward, struck against the wall near the door, made a staggering step forward, fumbling with his gun. He couldn't find the strength to squeeze the trigger. As the weapon slipped out of his hands he sagged at the knees, his mouth open, his eyes staring horribly at Lucy. He tried to speak but only blood bubbles came up in a pink froth to his lips as he crashed to the floor.

Lucy came running in, Barry's red gun smoking in her hand, her face as white as paper, and dropped down on her knees beside the body of her husband. A thin scream of horror burst from her.

"I have killed him! Oh, God forgive me—I have killed him!"

"You have saved me from being murdered," said Barry. He scrambled up and hurried to her, but by the time he reached her she had slumped down and lay on the floor, her face in her arms, her body shaking with a storm of sobbing. He extended a hand toward her, then instead caught Tom Haveril by the shoulders and turned him over.

"He isn't dead," he said. "Maybe we can pull him through."

He had not the slightest hope of saving Tom Haveril's life, but for Lucy's sake he had to say that. He was glad that he did. She sprang up and came to hover over the already unconscious man.

"We've got to save him, Barry. We've got to! Oh, if you love me—"

The next instant she was sobbing wildly in Barry's arms.

XIX

"He is dying!" moaned Lucy. "He is dead. Oh, my God, I have killed him!"

Barry, holding her crushingly tight, tried with all his might not to keep on thinking: "She killed him to save me. She never loved him. She loves me and always did. So she killed him."

Throttling such thoughts as best he could, stifling a savage gladness that was like a red flower in this moment of death—for he knew that Tom Haveril would never live the night out and would in all likelihood be a dead man in a scant handful of minutes—he strove to comfort her in the only possible way, assuring her that Tom Haveril was not yet dead and that somehow they would pull him through.

He said, to get her out of the room, to give her something to do: "Run into the kitchen. Get a fire started; we'll want some hot water." She flew upon his bidding, came running back for a burning brand from the fireplace and ran out again. He carried Tom Haveril over to his own bed in a corner. Stooping close he looked at the gaping wound below the base of the brawny throat. Tom Haveril stared at him glassily, quivered from head to foot—and was dead.

An agonized sweat broke out on Barry Haveril's

forehead. This, he thought, was going to kill Lucy or drive her mad. He looked at the blood on the floor, glinting with the lively light of the dancing fire on the hearth; he saw his gun where Lucy had dropped it. Hastily he picked it up, shoving it out of sight in his holster.

He heard her at the stove, making a fire, running for water. He wondered what he was going to find to say to her. "Tom Haveril is dead, dear. You had every right to kill him; he was going to murder me. You saved my life when you took his. God will not set the deed down against you. But—he's dead."

She called to him, panic-stricken. "I'm hurrying, Barry!" And he called back heartily: "You don't have to hurry so, Lucy. It's going to be all right."

He couldn't help that. Strong as he was, he was all running water and melting wax when he thought of her utter misery. He said to himself, "Dammit there must be some way. Why, I could put a bullet into his brain now—swear that I killed him, just because I hated him so!"

Dead Tom Haveril stared at him. Slowly, horror crawling up and down his backbone, Barry dragged his old gun from its place. "I can say that he was only fooling; that all of a sudden he grabbed his gun and started to let me have it. I mustn't shoot him through the head; through the neck, that's it, right close to where she shot him. Then nobody would ever know—"

It should be a simple thing, with the cogent reason he had, to shoot a man already dead, yet his hands went cold as he tightened his grip on the gun. One shot, and for all time Lucy was going to be free from the horror which otherwise would start her into wakefulness, bathed in a cold sweat like Barry now; and that one shot, he knew full well, would be like a slash of a knife cutting any bond between his life and her life. It was going to be he who killed Tom Haveril, her husband—and though he and Lucy might eat their hearts out, it would be all in hopelessness. He raised his gun—

"Barry!" screamed Lucy in the kitchen doorway. *"What are you doing?"*

His face flushed red, burning hot; his glance, usually so fearlessly steady, fell from hers; as his hands fumbled awkwardly with the gun in his hands he muttered stammeringly:

"Nothing, Lucy. I was just looking at my gun —I'd picked it up." He began turning the cylinder, turning it slowly with his eyes on it simply because he couldn't somehow meet her frightened look.

She came tiptoe into the room. She was no longer looking at him but at the quiet form on the blankets, the dead, white face seeming weirdly alive with the flicker of firelight and shadow.

"He—he's dead!" she gasped. She cowered down where she stood, her face in her hands.

"Dead! And I—I was heating the water—I killed him and—"

Barry thought miserably, "Why didn't I pull the trigger? I could have done it before she knew." He did not lift his eyes to her; they remained brooding upon the gun. He kept turning the cylinder slowly.

It was a six-shooter. He counted the shells, through force of habit. There were the full six of course; he looked for the exploded one. It eluded him. He turned the cylinder again—

"Lucy!" he shouted, and she jumped to her feet as though it had been his hands upon her instead of the sound of his excited voice bringing her up. "Lucy! You didn't kill him! You couldn't! There's not an empty shell in the gun! You didn't shoot at all!"

"Barry!" Then her face, for a joyous instant so bright, clouded instantly. "You are not telling me the truth, Barry. You want to save me and so you have put in a fresh cartridge."

"I swear to you, Lucy! Say, this is funny. I thought you shot him; you thought so; he thought so. But you didn't fire a shot out of this gun! We were all keyed up—there was the sound of his shot, and of another shot from where you stood—Molly! It was Molly! Was Molly with you, Lucy?"

Again a flood of light flashed across Lucy's face. "She was just behind me, Barry! When we first heard Tom with you she said, 'It's Jesse.' We started to find out. I didn't know that she had a pistol—I don't know even now. But we both thought for a minute that it was the Laredo Kid. She was expecting him, wasn't she? And just as I called to Tom, and he whirled about— the shot was fired then and I was just ready to shoot, to save your life, Barry, and in the shock of the thing I did think that I had shot. Oh, Barry, do you think—"

"I know it!" cried Barry joyously, and for the moment was altogether oblivious of dead Tom Haveril lying there in the corner. "Molly thought he was Laredo, and killed him!"

"If I could only be sure—"

"I am sure! Wait!" He dashed outside and began calling at the top of his voice, "Molly! Molly, where are you? Can you hear me, Molly? If you'll come here just a minute—"

From out of the dark almost at his side Molly stepped silently up to him.

"I know," she said quietly. "Me, I run, Barry, an' I come back, an' I listen. I see that man; he is jus' like Jesse Conroy. I see him with gun, an' he is goin' kill you. But I kill him for other thing, Barry. Long time, he kill Robert, like you tell me. Then he come back; he laughs; he makes me forget Robert. Now I have baby, Barry; I hope baby dies. So I kill this man, that in the bad light is like Jesse and has same voice—"

"Let me see your gun," he commanded.

She shrugged and handed it to him, drawing it from the bosom of her dress. He stepped toward the lighted room with it and met Lucy in the doorway. Together the two discovered the one exploded shell.

Suddenly, with no hand lifted to stay her, the half-Indian girl melted away into the night. But before she went, Barry asked about Tex and the rest. "Gone, far away, long time," said Molly. "Me, I go, I come back; that is because Jesse Conroy wanted me. Now? Goo' night, Barry and Lucy." The wilderness swallowed her.

"I am so glad, so grateful to God!" cried Lucy. "And so ashamed to be glad at a time like this!"

"God wants you to be glad, dear," he said very gently. "He made it happen like this."

"Everyone will always think—"

He interrupted, wishing to shunt her thoughts aside, also seeking information. "What was it Molly wanted with you?" he asked.

"She wanted to ask about Jesse Conroy, and to warn us to watch out for him, since he might come here any time. And she was telling me something about—about Tom Haveril—"

"She knew him too?" he asked swiftly.

Lucy shook her head. "She had never seen him, but Jesse Conroy had told her boastingly of a man he called Cousin Tom that he was working a big scheme with, and I knew he meant Tom Haveril."

"How did you know?"

"Your father told me; he knew Jesse Conroy's father, Philip Conroy. He said that Philip's son Jesse, from the time he was big enough to load and fire a gun, was the worst of a bad lot. He ran away from home with a wild cousin of his, named Tom Haveril. And your father said that, though Jesse Conroy came to be called the Laredo Kid, half the things laid to his door were done by—by Tom Haveril."

"That tells us how Tom Haveril came by the flat steel box and your pictures," mused Barry. "Jesse stole them from the Judge, Tom Haveril stole them from Jesse." Puzzled, he added, "It's funny my folks never mentioned either of them."

"Your father might have told you; your mother is very proud, Barry, and it shamed her that anyone related to the Haverils should turn out like that. But, Barry— We don't have to stay here now, do we?"

"No, we don't have to stay here any longer," he assured her. "We know that the posse we saw tonight were headed where my folks are; long before now they've got there, have found you and I had given them the slip. They wouldn't stay there all night; they'd keep on looking for us."

"Barry! Oh, let's hurry."

"Yes, we'll hurry."

Lucy started instantly to the door; Barry stepped across the room to where Tom Haveril's body lay. He was drawing a blanket over the upturned face when he noted the corner of a wallet sticking out of the dead man's leather coat. He spoke over his shoulder to Lucy:

"There's a wallet in his pocket. Maybe—"

"My marriage certificate!" exclaimed Lucy. "I gave it to him to carry for me until— He put it in his wallet. Will you get it for me, Barry?"

Barry opened the wallet; he found a folded paper which he opened to make sure it was what Lucy wanted. At first glance he saw it was not, for it was discolored with years, breaking along its folds. He made out that it was a letter written to Philip Conroy, Esq., Laredo, Texas. It was signed, David Hamilton. Enclosed was a second brief note, also years old, addressed to Col. Dave Hamilton, Laredo, Texas. And this one was signed Parker Blue.

He and Lucy, going close to the fireplace, read the two letters together and at the end both exclaimed, voicing the same thought almost in the same words:

"This was the hold Jesse Conroy had over Judge Blue!"

"Enough to hang him," muttered Barry. "Somehow Tom Haveril got it from Jesse, along with the iron box, I reckon. Jesse was just waiting until the time was ripe, when you came of age and into the Hamilton money. But I'll bet he had been shaking the Judge down for years."

The first of the two notes read:

Philip Conroy, Esq.,
Laredo Flats.

Dear Philip: I have just received this curt communication from Parker Blue, of whom I spoke to you a few days ago. It would seem that all is ripe to go ahead. I have the money at hand, ready when he comes. You will note that he is to come next Monday; also that he wants the matter kept sub rosa. So I suppose you had better postpone your visit to us. I'll write you about it as soon as it is settled.

With our sincerest regards to you and your dear ones,

Y'r. Most Obd't. Servant,
David Hamilton.

The enclosure read:

Dear Col. Hamilton:

I'm coming Monday. Be sure to have the Ten Thousand Dollars in Cash. We will make a Hundred Thousand out of it sure. But keep it all secret. I will tell you why. I am counting on finding you alone Monday. This is

Important, Colonel. I am sending this over by one of the boys. He don't know what is in it.

Yours truly,
Parker Blue.

"And then," growled Barry angrily, "he went over and murdered everybody in the house except you, grabbed the ten thousand and, maybe in a flash of inspiration, carried you off!"

"But these letters! How on earth did they happen to last so long?"

"Kept by Philip Conroy's son—my Cousin Jesse!"

"But how did he—"

"We'll never know. He'll never tell. Anyhow Jesse got the letters. That ten thousand dollars stuck in his mind! Come, Lucy; we are not hurrying after all."

He covered dead Tom Hamilton, gathered up the blankets meant for Lucy's bed, and they hurried out, drawing the door tight after them. Before another word was spoken they had gone to the tethered horses, had saddled and were ready again to ride.

"We may meet those coming back this way," said Lucy.

"It's possible, since Tom Haveril may have told them he was coming here. He could have known from Cousin Jesse, you know, about the Humphreys and that I knew them. But we'll ride slowly; we'll go in a little longer way; we'll keep such a sharp lookout that we'll see them or hear them before they even get a notion we're anywhere near."

But they heard no sounds as they rode along saving those quiet noises that belonged to the wilderness night, nor did they catch a gleam of any fire until they were almost at journey's end. Lucy saw it first, just a bright glint through the pines.

"That's not a light in the house," said Barry, puzzled, as they pulled their horses down. "It's a fire out in the pasture; maybe it is a campfire. You wait here a minute, Lucy; I'll go ahead on foot."

"Oh, be careful, Barry!"

The pasture was a clearing surrounded by a dense growth of timber, and Barry made his silent way forward with scant misgivings of being seen or overheard. The fire was burning brightly, fed on a small heap of dead wood near an old land-mark tree, one he remembered well from his boyhood days of tree climbing. It was an august old fellow, gnarled and twisted by a hundred winters; there was one broad horizontal branch on which he used to inch along until almost at the end.

Barry, peering around a leafy buck-eye, saw that there were three men under the old tree, and that two of them were busily occupied hanging the third!

XX

The man with the noose about his neck was being drawn slowly upward by the simple expedient of his companions laying their hands to the rope that had already been thrown over the horizontal limb. Barry, arrived in the very nick of time either to watch an execution or to stop it, experienced a shock of surprise when he saw clearly the two men pulling on the rope. Though one was an utter stranger to him, an old, bald-headed man with a long white beard, the other was Timberline.

As yet their victim's feet were scarcely off the ground; his toes could still touch, for Barry saw a little puff of dust rise ghostily in the firelight as he struggled frantically. Timberline's cackling voice broke out, high pitched and quavering, and Barry wondered more than ever.

"Yuh don't die quick an' git it over neither, yuh low-down thievin', cheatin', lyin', crawlin' son of a t'rantler!" he announced scathingly. "Yuh fell inter the right hands, yuh skunkery kiote. Me an' ol' Cliff Bendiger here has got Injun blood in us, an' yuh're goin' ter know it afore yuh slow choke to death. Torturin' is too good for yore kind, so we're givin' yuh the best we got. Ain't we, Cliff?"

"That's right, Timber," agreed Cliff Bendiger, and added: "He's restin' too much weight on his toes. Heave the varmint up a mite higher. He won't even strangle slow this way."

The two old men pulled on their rope and their prisoner swung about so that Barry could see his congested face and his wildly glaring eyes. It was Sarboe!

"Stop it!" Barry shouted then, and ran forward.

With a snort of disgust Timberline let go the rope; his assistant did the same, and Sarboe, firmly planted again on solid earth, teetered a moment, caught his balance and turned eloquent, bulging eyes on his rescuer.

"Damn you, Timber!" Barry raged as he jerked the rope from Sarboe's neck. "What in hell are you up to? Have you gone crazy?"

"Nope," said Timber. "Yuh see, Sundown—"

Barry was due to be startled once more. Sarboe had caught his breath and now burst out into such a tirade of curses and accusations and dire threats against Timberline and Cliff Bendiger that his stream of invective was like a torrent from a dam breaking. The long silent Sarboe had at last found his tongue, and with a vengeance. The words he used were never in any Sunday School's bright lexicon. He called Timberline all the names that no gentleman is expected to accept, even though the speaker smiles while he is about it.

The odd result was that Timberline smiled as complacently as a fond mother admiring her first born, jerking his thumb toward the storming Sarboe, while remarking to Barry:

"That's why we done it, Sundown! Yuh see, we figgered out, me an' ol' Cliff here, we could make him talk. Well, we done it! Now I reckon he kin tell us all he knows!"

"You mean," demanded Barry, "that he has just been pretending all this time that he couldn't talk?"

"Hell, no," said Timber, and spat sizzlingly into the fire. "At firs' I kinda thought so; but no, he wanted to talk an' couldn't. Yuh tol' me yuhse'f, Sundown, as how he could talk all right in his sleep. Well, Cliff here dropped in on us tonight. He's an ol' trail mate o' mine, Sundown. Shake hands: Mr. Cliff Bendiger, Mr. Barry Haveril, known to some as Sundown."

Barry felt his hand gripped by a leathery old claw as he received the polite assurance, "Glad ter meet yuh, Sundown." For his own part he was rather remiss in the conventional niceties. He couldn't get out of his mind the picture of poor Sarboe a second time experiencing the horror of hanging. He asked sharply:

"What in hell's name are you driving at, Timber? I think you *are* crazy!"

"Nary, Sundown," said the placid Timberline.

"It's like I was a-tellin' yuh. Me an' Cliff got ter chinnin' like ol' cronies does. I tolt him about Sarboe here, how he could talk, like you said, only he couldn't. An' I got me a grand idee. I says to Cliff, 'Hell, Cliff, he can't talk because he got it scairt clean out o' him by a hangin'! That's what Sundown tolt me. He c'n talk, only he kinder thinks he cain't. I'll betcher if he was to git hung ag'in, it would scare it back inter him! What say?' I asks Cliff. An' Cliff says, 'Hell, it cain't do no harm to try.' So we was a-tryin', Sundown." He turned gentle eyes, yet eyes full of pride, on Sarboe. "Yuh c'n talk fine now, cain't yuh, Sarboe? Cuss some more."

Sarboe started in again, naming Timberline all the unforgivable names he had overlooked. And Timberline, as was plain to see, not only forgave but glowed!

"Yuh see, Sundown? Now ask him what he's been bustin' to tell yuh ever since that night Tom Haveril strung him up, an' he'll spill it. Won't yuh, Sarboe, ol' comrade?"

Barry began to laugh. Timberline of a sudden saw humor where until now he had seen only a job of work to be tackled earnestly, and started laughing too. Cliff Bendiger's old face, what was to be seen of it through his white whiskers, crinkled genially. In the end even Sarboe, though there was no room for laughter within him, softened of mood.

"Swear to Gawd that's the truth, Timber?" he asked gruffly.

"Shore, man! That's why we made out like bein' Injuns, killin' yuh slow by torture. We didn't hurt yuh none, we didn't scercely choke yuh a-tall—"

"Like hell yuh didn't," growled Sarboe.

"Well ain't yuh glad an' thankful to me 'n' Cliff here? Yuh c'n talk now, cain't yuh?"

Barry, still laughing, said, "Wait here a minute," and hurried back to Lucy. A few minutes later all of them were in the house, where no one had thought of going to bed, gathered in a general conference. Barry's mother, with both anxiety and gladness in her eyes, had hastened to meet him, but had seen something written upon Lucy Hamilton's white face that carried her straight on to the girl, to take her into mothering arms. The other Lucy, Barry's sister, came hurrying and for a little while the three women were apart from the others, while the profoundly shocked Lucy Hamilton told of the night's tragedy and her own sudden widowhood.

"It was God's will, dear, working in devious ways," said Barry's mother. "He would never let a lamb like you fall to the lot of those wolves."

"He—Tom Haveril—he is dead now," whispered the trembling girl.

Barry's mother could be stern as well as gentle.

291

She said firmly: "He deserved to die. You would be a hypocrite to seem sorry. Just you get down on your knees and thank God for His mercy and justice."

When they returned to the sitting room Sarboe, half the time fingering his throat, was talking eagerly. He came to a stuttering pause, looked strangely at Lucy Hamilton, and said hurriedly, as though to get it done with:

"When me an' Pennel an' Longo tried to grab her that time on the trail, an' Sundown busted up our play, well, we wasn't doin' that for Tom Haveril, though we was on his pay roll. It was Jesse Conroy hired us, offerin' a lot o' money an' payin' part down. He wanted her, an' he wanted her bad. Mos' of all, he wanted to keep Tom from gettin' her. Yuh see, folks, Jesse was on the jump right then, havin' got in trouble same as usual, an' he feared Tom would marry her. Yuh see, Jesse an' Tom was as thick as thieves for a long while; me, I'd worked with both of 'em, an' I knowed a lot about 'em." He shifted uneasily. "Yuh see, folks, times I worked in with Tom, times I worked in with Jesse—"

"Yuh cheated both the skunks!" cried old Timber approvingly. "Good boy, Sarboe, says I!"

"You—you knew a lot about Tom Haveril?" put in Tom Haveril's young widow.

"So much, Miss," muttered Sarboe, "that he was the mos' anxious of 'em all that night to see me hung afore I could talk! He hit me in the mouth—"

"Let's get on with this, Sarboe," said Barry curtly. "What else?"

"A-plenty," said Sarboe. "Some of it I'll get out tonight, I reckon; mos' likely more of it'll be pourin' out'n me's long as I live. I knowed this much: Them two is a match-team for gen'ral cussedness. I've knowed bad men, but none worse'n them two—onless yuh count the Judge. Them three, Jesse an' Tom an' ol' Judge Blue! An' both Jesse an' Tom somehow had the ol' Judge over a barrel; he was scared o' what they might do, or what they might tell on him, I reckon; an' for years they bled him o' money, an' he was a hard-bleeder, too! Yuh've all heard o' the Laredo Kid? Well, I used to think it was Jesse Conroy; I got to thinkin' later it was Tom; an' later on, I got to wonderin' if both of 'em wasn't him! Times, Laredo worked masked, didn't he? Well?" He shrugged. "I ain't shore about that."

"What else?" asked Barry.

"This: Many a time the Judge would 'a' kilt either or both of 'em, only he was scared to! They had the deadwood on him, somethin' wrote down on paper, an' he was scared, if he kilt 'em, them papers was where they'd turn up in the wrong hands. More, the two boys wanted to kill Sundown here, an' the Judge, he talked 'em out of it. Says he, 'Barry Haveril's stumbled on such gold I never seen, playin' in beginner's luck. Wait until we get his gold, then kill an' be damned.' "

"That's true enough," Barry nodded. "I reckon everything Sarboe has told us is the truth."

"I was sorry I couldn't talk sooner," said Sarboe. "I'd mebbe have saved Miss Lucy marryin' Tom Haveril. I—I never had anything ag'in her." He dropped his eyes, got both hands down in his lap and began pulling at his fingers. "When I tried to grab her that day— Shucks, it was jus' in the day's work. There wasn't nothin' personal."

Timberline chuckled and clapped Sarboe friendliwise on the shoulder. "Ain't yuh glad, Sarby, I learned yuh how to talk ag'in?"

Barry's mother spoke up to say quietly: "Tom Haveril is dead now. Has Barry told you?"

They discussed briefly what effect the taking off of Tom Haveril might have upon the strategy of their persecutors. There remained the Judge, Laredo and Sheriff Ed Brawley, all planning murder in the name of summary justice.

Ken March offered thoughtfully: "There's a lot of square, fair-minded men in and about Red Rock. They've heard only one side of the story. The thing to do is get the truth over to them."

"Me, I was thinkin' o' that," piped up Timberline. "Cliff Bendiger here tells me as how there's two kinds o' talk in Red Rock. Some's fer shootin' Sundown on sight; some says, 'Aw, hell, give him a chance to say his speech firs'.' S'pose me'n Cliff has another snack right now to stay our stummicks, then rides back to Red Rock an' starts preachin' the gospel? Anyhow, we'd ought to sorta split their crowd in two."

Ben Haveril nodded and said emphatically, "An' Sheriff Brawley c'n be talked to. Happens I know! For six-seven years the Judge has had him like that." He indicated what he meant by flattening his thumb on the table. "Let Brawley know what the Judge has been up to, that it was him that kilt the Hamiltons an' carried off Miss Lucy here— Hell's bells! Brawley'd turn aroun' an' snap the Judge up like a houn' dawg swallerin' a greased potater."

"What'll we do then, Pa?" asked Barry.

"Do!" thundered Ben and got to his feet as lithely as a mountain cat. "We'll send Timber an' Cliff along, like Timber says; they're too old to do any worthwhile fightin' anyhow." Timberline snarled at him, but Ben went on unheeding. "Meantime us boys head straight back to yore mine. We'll take them polecats by surprise, an' we'll dig in solid after bootin' 'em clear off the ranch. It's by rights yore mine, they tell me, son, an' yuh got a right to it."

Barry, too, got to his feet.

"There are five of us, not counting Timber and Cliff," he said. "Let's get going, boys."

"There *are* only five of you, Baron," his mother reminded him, "and many more of them." Barry hugged her, and she, half smothered by his bear-like embrace, added: "Have you plenty of ammunition, Baron? In the cupboard I found a rifle that used to belong to Robert, and his cartridge belt."

"Let me have that snack to eat in the saddle," barked Timber. He looked wistfully at Barry's mother. "Yuh ain't got a can o' tomatoes yuh could spare, have yuh now, Mrs. Lucinda?"

"Why, Mr. Timberline, I just have! And you shall have it."

"And now," said Timber, when he pocketed the tin, "let's light out."

They lit out, the seven men, assured that no danger threatened their women folk left behind. One of those women folk merely said in her gentle voice: "God is with you. I shan't worry," and went to work cleaning up the littered table. Two of them, two Lucys, went out on the porch and even down the steps and into the yard.

A blue-eyed Lucy clung to Ken March, murmuring, "Oh, Ken! Ken! If—"

"It's going to be all right, darling," Ken told her.

A gray-eyed Lucy, so recently and recklessly wedded, so violently widowed, at last allowed herself to speak words she felt she should not voice—not until some later day. But would that day ever come?

"I do love you so, Barry! I have loved you with all my foolish heart since that day in Tylersville. And Barry, if you didn't come riding back to me— Kiss me, Barry."

Never before had they kissed. He drew her into his arms, he lifted her off her little feet, he almost crushed her.

"Hi!" yipped Timberline. "Are we ridin' or ain't we?"

So they rode, the seven of them. And Timberline and old white-bearded, shinily bald-headed Cliff Bendiger spurred to their fore, to lead the way, to show 'em that nuther of 'em was too old, by gosh, fer anything they could give a name to. To put the expedition on the proper basis, Timber struck up a song.

"Little ol' Liza Jane, Jane!
Oh, little ol' Liza Jane!
Oh, little ol' Liza Jane, *my Lord!*
Oh, little ol' Liza Jane!"

The whole seven put their hearts as well as their voices into that song, and their hushed women folk heard them ride over the ridge, singing.

With between sixty and seventy miles to go,

they couldn't take it all at one bite, despite their lusty appetites for decisive action. Their horses began to lag, the riders themselves yawned and dozed in their saddles. They bivouacked in a glen to which Barry led them, and started on again in the first glint of dawn. They came in the brightly sunlit morning to a parting of the trails. Timber and Cliff Bendiger headed straight for Red Rock on their errand, while the others turned off toward Barry's old cabin and the mine higher up and beyond.

Barry and his father rode side by side, with Barry's brother Lute just behind. Ben Haveril said, and was a bit shy about it: "We ain't seen much of each other these las' few years, huh, Barry? I'd sort of like to have a good long talk with yuh some day."

"Me, too, Pa," said Barry, and added: "I was headed to see you and mother about three years ago, when I first went down to Tylersville. You left in a hurry; that was when Judge Blue, too, pulled up his stakes all of a sudden."

Ben Haveril nodded. "The Judge sent us off on a wild goose chase; I reckon he wanted to keep you an' yore gold mine shet away from us knowin'. He sent me out to take a job on a new ranch more'n a hundred miles off; when we got there, there wasn't any job. We jus' nacherally kep' on headin' West. And the Judge hisse'f jumped out the same time; I've thought later somebody throwed some sort of scare into him, Laredo mebbe, mebbe young Tom Haveril who come along about that time, mebbe a young dep'ty sheriff from down Laredo way that was pokin' aroun' Tylers askin' all sorts o' questions."

Ken March and Sarboe, riding ahead, stopped when half way up a timbered ridge, looking back and waiting for them. Barry explained.

"We're almost there. The camp where the mine is is just over the ridge, on a sort of shelf in the ravine."

"We better light down an' leave our horses in the pines," said Ben.

They topped the ridge on foot, moving stealthily, bent on getting the lay of the land before they showed their hand. Ken March from a point of vantage whence he could look down a long vista through the pines into the heart of the camp, beckoned Barry to him.

"It's going to be as simple as walking downhill," he said. "Looks almost too good to be true, don't it, Sundown?"

Barry saw what he meant.

Down in the bed of the ravine were a score of men who had been stationed here by the Judge and Tom Haveril "to guard the property until the rights of the matter were settled." At the moment their "guarding" the property consisted in looting it. They had gone gold-crazy. They labored like demons, reeking with sweat, and they slaked their thirst not with the pure mountain water as often as from a stout oak barrel standing under a tree, a gift of Judge Blue's. Pans flashed as some washed sand and gravel; others hunted feverishly for the potholes which they expected to fill their pockets with a few scooped-up handfuls of pure virgin ore.

The gold seekers were unencumbered by any weapons which might interfere with the free swing of their arms. Whereas they wore for the most part holstered guns, their rifles leaned idly against tree trunks and boulders, forgotten.

"We can be on top of them before they know it," said Ken.

"Come ahead, boys," said Barry, and led the way.

They went swiftly but without revealing themselves. Five minutes later a score of astonished gold thieves found themselves staring into the muzzles of five rifles.

"Take it easy, down there," Barry sang out. "We can blow you all to hell before you know what it's all about."

They gaped and rubbed wet hands on their overalls and chaparejos, and never a man of them said a word meant for Barry's ears.

"Some of you know me and some of you don't," said Barry. "I'm Barry Haveril, and these are my diggings. You've been put here by Judge

Blue and Tom Haveril. Well, Tom Haveril's dead, with a bullet through his gullet, and the Judge is as good as hanging from a tree for murder done a dozen years ago. If you boys want to stick with those two, go for your guns!"

"Wh-what's that?" a man called back.

"I'll prove what I'm saying," returned Barry swiftly. "One of you can come up here and look at some papers I've got in my pocket. They'll show you how the Judge is out on a limb that's already broken off. As for Tom Haveril being dead, well you'll have to take my word for it—and I'll shoot daylight through the first man that calls me a liar!"

"Papers?" said the men among themselves. Someone called out, "You go see, Bendigo; you can read like a lawyer."

Bendigo, one of the Judge's men, long and lank and with a high, bald forehead, stepped forward gingerly, and began climbing up out of the creek bottom. As he came Barry finished what he had\ to say:

"You're a flock of damned thieves, but I've got too much on my hands right now to bother with the loss of a few hundred or thousand dollars. You can keep what you've got, and be damned to you. But you're on your way out of here in ten minutes, or you can start dodging lead."

"Show Bendigo them papers!" a man called back.

Bendigo read and Barry explained. Bendigo scratched his head and said, "It looks like to me—"

Barry called out the full explanation to the men down below. He ended by saying:

"You fellows that worked for Tom Haveril, you know I'm telling you the truth. Sarboe has told us what he knows, and it's plenty! You're all ripe for hanging to the first tree. The Laredo Kid is still riding free, sticking close to the Judge because either one of 'em can hang the other, and they're afraid to separate! Want to stick along with them? Then fill your hands! Come a-shooting, or get to hell out of here!"

"That's teachin' 'em their ABC's, I reckon," said Ben Haveril.

There are in this world certain honest sounds, as for example the ring of the blacksmith's hammer on his anvil. Just so did Barry's voice ring out, and never a single man within hearing for a moment doubted a word he said.

They were ready to throw their hands up and go like so many rats scurrying ashore from a sinking ship. Just then, however, something happened to delay them. Two men came roaring into camp, headed from down-cañon, lashing their jaded, sweat-lathered horses. They were the sheriff Ed Brawley, his face sick-white, his shoulder red, blood dripping from his fingertips, and the old man, Cliff Bendiger. The Sheriff slipped out of his saddle and lay on his back, at the end of his tether. Old Cliff Bendiger, holding on to his saddle horn, swaying from side to side as though about to fall, shouted in a quavering voice as thin yet far-carrying as the high notes of a bugle:

"The Judge an' the Kid—they've hightailed fur parts unknown. Got clean away—damn 'em!— Brawley was goin' ter arrest 'em. An' pore ol' Timber—"

He collapsed and slid to the ground, both thin old hands clutching his side. Barry ran to him and heard his last words. Cliff Bendiger tried to grin as he voiced what later became his epitaph:

"Too ol' to fight?— Hell!"

"I wisht I hadn't said it now, Cliff," muttered Ben Haveril. But he spoke just too late; so many times wishes like that seem to come when the proper wishing-time has passed.

Barry went to where Brawley lay. The Sheriff muttered weakly:

"It was the Kid. Damn it, I didn't know who he was! The Judge says, 'Meet a friend of mine, Jesse Conroy, a cowboy workin' for me.' If I'd only knowed! He shot fas', after Timber done his talkin'; shot an' rode away on his spurs, laughin' his damn' head off!"

"And Timberline?" asked Barry anxiously.

"Shot him, too," muttered Brawley. "Don't

know how bad hurt Timber was, pretty bad, I'd say, from the way he flopped off'n his horse. But he clumb up ag'in. As the Kid an' the Judge rode off, hell-for-leather, we seen ol' Timber climbin' in the saddle ag'in, yellin' cusswords an' ridin' after 'em."

"But why—"

Brawley said, still more faintly:

"Reckon he was sorry he spilled the beans. You see, he let out where your women folk was. An' he knowed that them two, the Kid anyhow, was headed straight to get his hands on them females, figgerin' that if he could get clean away an' take Lucy Blue along with him, he'd still have things by the tail an'—"

"Good God!" gasped Barry, and for one paralyzed instant felt as though the blood in his veins had frozen. Then he ran for a horse.

XXI

It was in a never-to-be-forgotten early dusk that Judge Blue and the Laredo Kid rode into the yard of the old Ben Haveril home.

The Laredo Kid, on an exhausted horse, rode jauntily. His broad hat was cocked back at an angle and he jingled his spurs, while the devil looked out of his eyes. The Judge was ponderous in the saddle; he sagged and scowled and looked to be a good ten years older than Judge Blue of last week.

Barry's mother and the two Lucys ran to the door, all eagerness. Already the Laredo Kid was standing on the porch, his hard brown hands on his narrow hips. From the first he jeered and mocked them. It is to be doubted that any man had ever seen him in a more evil mood.

The Judge was worn out in body and mind; like an old man he wanted things to go smoothly. He called over the Kid's shoulder with an affectation of heartiness:

"Hello, Lucy, my darling. Howdy, Mrs. Haveril. Howdy, Miss Lucy."

As the three women flinched back the Laredo Kid laughed and leaned indolently forward, one hand against the door jamb, making sure that they did not slam the door in his face.

"Make a move that ain't damn' hospitable-like," grinned the Kid, "an' I'll slap yore scared faces off 'n yuh."

Barry's mother stood in the doorway; at a commanding glance from her the two girls retreated into the house and stood looking fearfully over her shoulders. She said in that low, quiet voice of hers:

"What do you want here?"

"A plenty," said the Kid. "An' I want it now, bein' as I'm in a hell of a hurry. Yuh kin start in feedin' me; I'm as hungry as a she-wolf with a litter o' suckin' pups."

"Go into the other room, girls," said Mrs. Haveril. "I'll attend to this *gentleman*." To save her life she couldn't have helped stressing that last word.

"No they don't!" the Kid commanded sharply. "I want the three o' yuh where I kin watch ever' breath yuh draw. We'll all go together inter the kitchen." Over his shoulder he called curtly: "Come ahead, Judge. Light down an' step up. It's free grub."

"Look here, Jesse," said the Judge smoothly, "there's no use—"

"Shut yore mouth an' come ahead," snapped Laredo.

The Judge was not too tired, not too beaten down to resent that.

"Look here, you," he said sharply.

"Oh, go to hell," retorted Laredo, and went on into the house.

When the Judge found his way into the kitchen, the Kid, watched by three frightened, fascinated women, was eating like an ogre, stuffing down half a meat pie. Grease glistened on his face and hands. He wiped his mouth carelessly on his sleeve.

"Gi' me some water," he grunted. Handed a dipper, he drank thirstily, slopping the water out, letting it run down from his mouth corners, while his eyes roved from face to face.

"I'm gittin' out'n here an' I'm goin' fas', but I ain't goin' alone," he said, and flung his dipper into a corner. His eyes pounced upon Lucy Hamilton's. "Yuh're comin' with me."

There was murder in his eyes then and she saw it, stark and brutal and merciless; and utter terror gripped her. The Kid, desperate and enraged, staying a moment in his full flight only that he might not go empty handed, made no slightest effort to wear any flimsy mask of pretence. He was a killer an' they better know it! His nature and his career had made of him a purely destructive force; he had never built up anything in his life, he had always torn down, beginning as a boy when he had shot a stranger in the back with his old squirrel rifle, simply because young Laredo coveted the other's rifle and ornate gun belt and over-large Mexican hat.

He said again to the terrified girl, "Yuh comin' with me."

"No!" she cried. "I—"

That quiet little woman, Barry's mother, became like a she-wolf protecting her cubs. Incredibly swift, she leaped for the old rifle standing against the wall, dead Robert's gun where she had placed it when thinking that Barry might want it. Her eyes were as savage then as the Laredo Kid's, her determination as ruthless.

The Kid's gun came up out of its holster in a gesture too quick for the eye to follow; it was almost as though the weapon of its own volition jumped upward to meet his hand half way. His hand was greasy, but that did not matter; actually his gun seemed the better able to flip into the desired position. He touched the trigger gently, that devil's grin still on his face; there was the roar of explosion, the flash of orange fire, and the rifle clattered to the floor.

He had very adroitly shot the woman through the right forearm. He laughed as she stood there, her face white, blood splashing to the floor from her fingers, her eyes like a wild thing's. Laughing, he said, "That's jus' to show yuh how good I kin shoot! Pretty slick shot, huh, for a quick one?" He stooped for the rifle and flung it out through the open door. "Now let's get goin'!"

The Judge burst out explosively, though he made no gesture toward his own gun:

"Look here, Laredo! This sort of thing—"

Laredo whirled and all without warning fired a second shot, and the Judge clutched his abdomen with both hands and sank down, sitting a moment with his back against the wall, then doubling over and lying on his side, his hands bright red now, his expression one of utter bewilderment. A man knows when he has taken his death wound, only —only, it oughtn't to come like that—without an inkling—

"I been wantin' to kill yuh for a long time, an' yuh oughter knowed it," said Laredo. "Now yuh ain't no more use to me, an' I'm goin' to need yore horse. Tell 'em down in Hell not to wait for me, Judge. I got me consider'ble more hell to raise up here afore I see yuh ag'in."

The Judge's gun was still in its holster; he had no strength to drag it forth. He had lurched toward Barry's sister. Instinctively she made a swift movement toward it.

Why Laredo did not shoot her is not to be known. Perhaps he had a thought to saving ammunition; perhaps the easiest thing was what he did. As she stooped, he struck her brutally with the barrel of the gun in his hand, and little blue-eyed Lucy dropped, mercifully unconscious, across the Judge's legs.

"Comin' along peaceful-like now?" asked the Kid of the other Lucy, standing and grinning at her, spinning his gun about upon a forefinger through its trigger guard. "Say yes in a hurry, an' I won't hurt no more o' yore frien's. Hang back like a balky mule an' I'll pop another bullet through ol' lady Haveril."

Lucy tried to answer and could not speak. His lips twitched as he watched her.

"Aw, I won't hurt yuh none," he said. He squatted by the Judge who was still staring at him with that awful look in his eyes; he wanted the Judge's gun and also a wallet and a small heavy purse which his agile fingers knew just where to find. Standing up again, as graceful and lithe as a big cat, he turned again to Lucy Hamilton.

"Yuh're my ace in the hole, that's what," he said. "Yuh're goin' to be worth money to me. Now, are yuh comin'?" He flipped his gun over and drew a fine bead on a spot between Mrs. Haveril's eyes.

Lucy's voice came to her then in a thin scream. With the Judge dying on the floor, with Barry's sister lying unconscious, a smear of blood spreading on her face, with Mrs. Haveril looking like a dead woman standing erect, she knew that the Kid would welcome another killing, just to show off before her and to convince her that he was a man of his word, and not squeamish about things.

"Yes, yes! I'm coming!" she gasped. "Oh, God help me—"

"No!" said Mrs. Haveril. "No, dear. I'd rather have him kill me."

Laredo caught the girl by the arm and jerked her to him.

"We're in a hurry from now on. We've wasted enough time."

It was all like some horrible, impossible nightmare. They were mounted, she in the Judge's saddle. The Laredo Kid jerked her horse's reins over its head, raked his own weary beast savagely with his spurs, and they were off at a gallop.

She clung to the horn of the saddle and turned for a last look back. Mrs. Haveril, one arm dangling, had run outside and had retrieved the rifle which Laredo had thrown into the yard. She tried to get it up to her shoulder with one hand, but could not steady it. She ran to a post where a hitching rack had once been, and used that for a rest. Even so she was hardly able to get the heavy weapon into place.

Laredo, too, turned and looked back.

"She's askin' for it," he grunted and jerked out his newly holstered gun.

"Don't!" screamed Lucy, and tried to come abreast of him to strike his arm down. "For God's sake—"

He only laughed at her as he fired; this time he shot to kill. There was the crack of the rifle; Lucy heard the angry hiss not a yard from her own head; she heard the explosion of the gun in Laredo's hand and saw Mrs. Haveril fall.

"Gawd, He's takin' Him a vacation t'day," he chuckled.

Those last shots were heard from afar, dully muffled sounds, by Barry Haveril riding hard to come up with Laredo. From the string of saddle animals at the camp on Sundown Creek he had taken the best two, leading one so that every few miles he might change for the sake of greater sped. Now, as he burst into the clearing about the house, he was just too late to see the Laredo Kid and Lucy, vanishing among the pines.

He began shouting as he rode into the yard. Ice went to his heart at the ominous hush which was his only answer. He ran into the house, still calling, only to grow momentarily rigid, filled with horror. The Judge was dead. His sister Lucy he thought dead, too; she lay on the floor, still unconscious, her face covered with blood.

He dashed through the house, seeking. Where was his mother? Where was Lucy Hamilton?

The first moving thing he saw was his mother, weakly trying to rise from where she lay out in the yard.

"I'm all right, Baron," she whispered. Then he saw her broken, bloody arm and saw too that she had been shot through the shoulder. As he drew her into his arms he heard her, still whispering, say as steadily as she could: "He—

he's taken your Lucy away with him, Baron."

"Laredo? When? Where, Mother?"

She tried to point but could only nod feebly to indicate the direction.

"Only a minute ago. Go, Baron. Kill him, Baron. He—he is not a man—just a murder machine. God wants you to kill him, I think, my son—to put him out of his misery—"

Barry put her down gently where she was.

"I'll be right back, Mama," he said softly, "with Lucy. Just a minute, Mama."

His horse was fresher than the two with which Laredo was trying to escape, and Barry overhauled them before they had gone a mile. Laredo heard and saw who followed; cat-quick he was down out of the saddle, dragging Lucy along with him. As his cousin Tom Haveril had done in like circumstance, so now did the Laredo Kid do, holding the half fainting Lucy before him with one arm, his other hand on his gun.

"I see yuh're bringin' me back my ol' red gun, Cousin Barry," he mocked, but Lucy saw that for all his jeering there was a look of fear on his face. She turned toward Barry who had also dismounted, and did not wonder that the killer was afraid. Barry's face frightened even her.

Barry came forward, walking slowly, the old red gun in his hand. Laredo shouted, "That's close enough, Sundown! One more step an'—"

"I'm going to kill you, Laredo," said Barry and came on. Laredo yelled back at him, "Yuh fool, yuh'll kill her!"

"Barry!" screamed Lucy. "Barry, save me! I don't care if I am killed! I'd rather be dead—"

She tried to break away, but could not; no such strength resided on her whole body then as in one of the killer's arms. He crouched a little, hiding himself all that he could behind her.

Barry thought as Lucy was thinking: She'd better be dead than carried off by Jesse Conroy. He could see little of Laredo—one high shoulder and his eyes and the top of his head over Lucy's. He came on slowly, watchfully, watching those hard bright eyes of the killer. And Barry was praying softly within his soul then, his lips moving to the silent words: "God, let me save her. God, send this bullet true." He knew he had to take the chance.

It wanted something next door to a miracle to speed that bullet by the girl without harming her and to bury it in Laredo's lean body. The miracle was not forthcoming. Barry's bullet hit Lucy. But it hit Laredo too. It struck her in the tip of the shoulder and went clean through and drilled through Laredo's shoulder an inch or so lower than Lucy's. The impact of the screaming lead was fearful. Lucy simply sagged and slumped down, a dead weight which Laredo was unable to support.

He dropped to his knees, caught her inert body up and held it as best he could between him and Barry, while he steadied his gun arm. He and Barry fired at the same instant, both with deadly accuracy. Barry reeled backward, then fell sprawling, a bullet through his side, as the Laredo Kid dropped down behind Lucy, shot through the chest.

Laredo lifted himself a fraction of a second first, but his arm was heavy and as he threw his gun forward Barry was already firing again. A long red furrow sprang into being on the Kid's cheek; the blood streamed down his face as he fell backward. Yet, dropping back, he loosed another bullet with that almost uncanny certainty of his.

Barry, twice hard hit, lay for a moment unable to stir, his brain swimming dizzily, his hand going lax on his gun. Yet he managed to keep a grip on himself; he knew that he was either fainting or dying, and that Laredo was still alive and had Lucy at his mercy.

He shook his head; his teeth set hard; with a supreme effort he sat up. He saw Laredo sitting up as awkwardly as himself. The gun in Barry's weakening fingers was heavy, and his hand, grown numb and weak, was about to fail him altogether. Only with the greatest difficulty, exerting his will to the uttermost, did he lift his gun.

He heard Laredo speak as across some tremendous, storm-filled distance.

"I'm done for," was what he was saying, "but I'm takin' Lucy with me."

As the Kid spoke, he managed to shove the muzzle of his gun against her head. Barry fired without conscious aim. The bullet broke Laredo's gun arm before he could pull trigger. The second bullet, as the Kid, swaying horribly, picked up his failed weapon with his left hand, thudded into his body. He fell over backward.

Barry got to his feet, took two or three uncertain steps toward Lucy and pitched forward on his face.

When he regained consciousness he was in bed, and there were many anxious faces turned toward him, his father's, Lute's, Ken March's— yes, and here was his sister Lucy, alive, and there on another cot lay his mother, white but serene. And his own Lucy, too—

Why, there even was old Timberline!

Barry's first coherent words were, "But Timber! I thought he'd shot you—"

"Hell, no," said Timberline. "Yuh see, I seen murder in his eye, Sundown, an' I flopped out 'n my saddle *jist* afore he shot. All he done was shoot me in my tomato can! Th' one yore ma give me, remember? Warn't he hell shootin' tomato cans? Even at that he didn't spill it all; me I saved it up. An' jus' now—"

"Is Lucy all right?" asked Barry, as though he wouldn't trust his eyes and wouldn't trust her to tell him.

"Hell, yes," said Timber. "An' now yuh lis'en, Sundown. I'm tellin' yuh about Laredo, ain't I? Well, pardner, mebbe yuh kilt the son-a-gun, an' mebbe me, I c'n take a mite o' credit for cuttin' off his capers. Anyhow, I gets here jus' after the fireworks is over, an' there lays Laredo lookin' up at me like a sick dawg, an' hc says, says he: 'Dammit, Timber, cain't yuh see I'm a-dyin'? Gi' me my las' big shot o' licker to ride out on.' An me, I says, 'Thirsty, Kid? Well, I been thirsty too, an' know how it feels. No hard feelin's, Kid. Take a shot o' this,' says I. An, I hands him what's lef' of my tomato juice!"

"You old scoundrel," murmured Barry.

Timber's face was wreathed in a beautiful smile.

"Sundown," he said gently, "at them words o' mine the Laredo Kid simply jist busted him a blood vessel."

Time ran quietly on.

Barry and Lucy stood high up on one of the bold rugged old mountains that Barry loved. Lucy was always to be first in his heart, standing shiningly high like a star, but those old mountains must ever be a close second.

They looked where the red sun in a troubled sea of glory, golden in broad ragged bands with splashes of red everywhere, went down. In the sunset was promise of gallant loves and bright danger and life expanding, large and beautiful, like the unfettered, unlimited wildernesses reaching out into the farther West. Barry's eyes, tender from being so recently lifted from Lucy's, turned to those far, bright distances.

And Lucy, snuggling closer, understood and nodded.